SETTING OFF SPARKS

JENNIFER BERNARD

Publisher's Note: This is a work of fiction. Names, characters, places, and incidents are a product of the author's imagination. Locales and public names are sometimes used for atmospheric purposes. Any resemblance to actual people, living or dead, or to businesses, companies, events, institutions, or locales is completely coincidental.

Book Layout ©2017 BookDesignTemplates.com

Setting Off Sparks/ Jennifer Bernard -- 1st ed.
ISBN 978-1-945944-21-5

CHAPTER ONE

Big Canyon, sixteen months ago

Finn Abrams had aced every training drill, certification test and physical challenge on the way to becoming a wildfire hotshot. He could do forty-two sit-ups in under a minute, followed by thirty push-ups and a five-mile run up a mountain wearing a forty-five-pound pack. He'd made top marks in every fire science course, and his crew captain called him the best rookie he'd ever hired.

But right now, staring down the massive flaming beast known as the Big Canyon Wildfire, he realized nothing could prepare you for this. Not even a whole summer of fighting fires, of proving himself in the hundred-degree heat, cutting line with guys who'd been doing this for years. This fire was so ferocious, so unpredictable. It had just changed course again and was now headed right toward the twenty members of the Fighting Scorpions Hotshots. Acrid whirlwinds of smoke blasted the crew and the roar of the fire-generated wind deafened them. Finn nearly choked on the hot stench of burning leaves and tree trunks. To one side of their location, the bare rock wall of a canyon loomed like an oasis in a world gone mad.

He barely heard Sean Marcus when he shouted the command to the crew. "We'll deploy here."

Oh fuck. Deploy. That meant the crew members would shake out their emergency shelters and hunker down as the flames ran over the top of them. A burnover, the hotshots called it. The worst possible scenario. They'd have to trust their lives to a thin layer of aluminum fabric. It was their only chance for survival.

It was a good call, and Finn knew it. He'd trained for this. He knew the drill. He wanted to follow the order to deploy his shelter. His life depended on it.

But he couldn't move. Couldn't make himself move.

Josh Marshall whipped out his shelter and dropped to the ground. Rollo Wareham did the same, barely managing to squeeze his big body under the edges of his tent.

Do it, asshole. Do it.

But he couldn't. Because all of a sudden, he was somewhere else.

He was a boy trapped inside a world on fire. His parents were downstairs. They'd come back earlier, drunk and laughing from the bar where his father worked. He was hiding from the fire inside his toy chest—an old steamer trunk. He kept screaming for his parents but no one came.

With shaking hands, he opened the trunk lid just a crack. Orange flames filled the entire doorway like monsters. That was his death out there. He knew it. The fire was coming for him and he was trapped in this tiny space, alone and about to burn to death.

Sean shouted something and ran toward him. The world came back in a hot rush. Big Canyon. Wildfire. Deploy. NO.

He yelled something to Sean, words of pure panic—he didn't even know what they were. He spun away and ran from the wildfire. He heard more shouting behind him, but then the roar of the flames overtook the sound.

Finn ran the way he'd wanted to back then, when his toy chest was his shelter. He ran until he came to his senses, until his lungs ached for oxygen. He bent over, heaving, shaking. Behind him, a wall of flames separated him from his crew. Smoke unfurled toward him. What had he done?

Oh God. Please let the guys survive.

He had no idea how long he'd been running, or which direction. He also had no idea what to do next. So he veered toward the next downslope. Maybe he could find a cave or a deep ravine the flames wouldn't reach.

Heat fanned his back. He fought with his panic. Think, Finn, think.

The wildfire was coming. He was going to die. Deploy that damn shelter.

And then he saw a flash of cool gray off to the side. He blinked—was it smoke? Rock? Something that could help him? Tears streamed from his stinging eyes and he stumbled onto his hands and knees.

Get up, get up.

He pitched forward, half-tumbling, half-scrambling to his feet. The gray expanded to include some deep brown and even black. It was a stream bed. A dry one with an exposed gravel bottom.

He ran for it with everything he had. He dove into its exact center, where several feet separated him from the fire devouring the forest on either side of him. He plastered himself face down against the gravel to stay as low as possible.

Again that same vision came back to him. The steamer trunk. The terror.

He was five years old. His name was Elias, not Finn. And he was going to die.

Something whacked him in the face. A flaming log had flown through the air and struck him on the head. He batted it away as pain erupted across the left side of his face. He rolled to the side but not quickly enough, and the wind blew the burning wood against him and all of a sudden his entire side was on fire, despite his fire-resistant Nomex pants and shirt.

He rolled over to suffocate the flames, even though the agony made him scream.

Everything went dark.

When he came to, the entire landscape around him was a blackened, smoldering wasteland. But he was alive.

Over the next few hours, he hiked across the black toward the nearest checkpoint. Each step sent pain shooting through him. His clothes were rags, his face and body burned and throbbed.

And the entire time, he kept asking himself one thing. Where the fuck had that memory come from?

As far as he knew, he'd never been trapped in a fire. His name wasn't Elias. His father didn't work at a bar, he ran a movie studio and dated one actress after another. He hadn't hidden in a toy chest. He'd never owned a toy chest.

Or had he?

CHAPTER TWO

Lisa Peretti had stopped believing in fairy tales somewhere between her mother's third divorce and her first year of nursing school. But right now, pushing Molly McGraw's wheelchair down the sidewalks of Jupiter Point, she wondered if she'd missed something. The town had storybook charm oozing out of every cedar shingle and wrought-iron lamppost. It was enough to make even a jaded big city ER nurse like herself give a sentimental sigh.

Of course, it was all designed to inspire that reaction. Jupiter Point knew how to draw in the honeymooners and the tourists, not to mention the stargazers. Like naming every business with a "star" theme. Come *on*. Moon Glow Spa and Hair Salon. Really?

"Give me a Supercuts any day," Lisa told Mrs. McGraw as they approached the salon, whose glass storefront was decorated—adorably—with beaming golden moons. "Haircuts are one thing, but I flat-out refuse to glow."

Molly tilted her head back and laughed up at her, her lined face haloed by a white fluff of hair. Molly was, in fact, glowing. She had a perfect right to do so. She didn't leave the house much anymore, with her advanced Parkinson's. But with her daughter Evie getting married, and the whole family busy, they'd hired Lisa as a temporary caregiver. And Lisa's first mission had been to get her out of the house more.

"But you, my dear, are another matter." She smiled affectionately at the older woman. "You're going to be glowing so much we'll have to wear sunglasses to the wedding."

"Be c-careful," said Molly. "That smile glows."

In the two weeks that Lisa had been working for Molly, they'd developed a teasing kind of banter they both savored. "You know me, I'm a hardhearted cynic. We don't weep and we don't glow."

"But you smile. That's a s-start."

They reached the entrance. Lisa stepped around Molly's wheelchair to open the door to the salon, only to find it already swinging wide. An older woman with foil in her hair held it open for them with a beaming smile.

"Molly McGraw, what a treat to see you here."

A chorus of agreement and greetings came from the other ladies in the stylists' chairs and under the hair dryers. The flowery scent of shampoo and overheated hair products made Lisa's nose prickle.

A young woman with a pink bob wiped her hands on her smock and hurried toward them. She bent down to kiss Molly on the cheek. "You didn't have to come all the way here. You know I'm happy to come to your house."

"I know. But Lisa here is g-getting me on the move. I have to do what she says because she's my f-favorite nurse. B-beautiful and kindhearted, although she tries to hide it."

Lisa felt a blush sneak across her face. She hated her tendency to blush because it went counter to her badass, never-miss-a-beat crisis-manager reputation. "Where would you like us?" she asked the stylist.

"Call me Annie, and you can bring her right over here."

Lisa pushed the wheelchair over to the spot Annie indicated, set the locks, then pulled a covered plastic cup with a straw from her tote bag. She gave Molly a sip, then made way for Annie, who offered her a warm smile.

"You can help yourself to water, or something from the Keurig." She waved a hand at the cozy seating area just inside the bay window up front. "We have a pile of old magazines or you can just enjoy some good old-fashioned gossip."

"We already covered all the big news in town, thanks to me." The woman with the foil, who Lisa now recognized as Mrs. Murphy from the Third Book from the Sun bookstore, settled back under a dryer. "Now we want to hear about you, Molly. So you have a new nurse, do you?"

Lisa started to answer, but Molly forestalled her. "This is Lisa, she comes from T-Texas, she's been with me for two weeks and I won't have you s-scaring her away with your interrogations."

Lisa laughed, though she had to admit she was relieved. Questions made her nervous. Not that she had anything to hide, but...well, she did. Two words defined her existence since she'd left Houston. Low. Profile. It had been nearly a year, and maybe soon she'd feel completely safe. But not yet.

Mrs. Murphy's tinfoil quivered like a set of antennae as she eyed Lisa. If anything, she looked even more curious.

"I won't be in town for long," Lisa told her. "I'm sure you have better topics to discuss."

"Yes, like Evie's wedding." One of the other hairstylists jumped in.

Letting out a long breath, Lisa picked up a copy of a tabloid and casually leafed through it as the discussion swirled around her. She had no interest in weddings, having been in more than her share. Her mother had remarried three times and her stepsisters had already racked up five weddings. Everyone in her family liked to get married—multiple times, apparently. Except her.

A photo in the tabloid caught her eye. It was a red-carpet photo of a couple arm in arm. The woman was a willowy blond actress whose name Lisa couldn't quite place. The man looked like an Italian prince—dark-haired and stunningly handsome. And familiar. She stared at it, trying to remember where she'd seen him. In a movie? On a billboard?

Then her gaze dropped to the next photo. This one was taken in a hospital room. The same blond woman posed next to the bed—Lisa could tell it was a pose, having seen thousands of actual women next to real patients.

In the bed lay the same dark-haired man, except now the entire left side of his face was covered in red burn marks.

Annika rushes to bedside of wounded fireman hero, read the caption.

Oh please. Could their writers be any more overdramatic? She skimmed the story, which talked about a "burnover" in the Big Canyon Wilderness. Twenty firefighters had nearly died when a wildfire had changed direction and they'd taken shelter inside their emergency tents.

So the mystery man was a fireman. Had she met him last summer, when she'd volunteered at the Breton Forest Service lookout tower? A memory tugged at her.

An excited voice caught her attention.

"Oh my goodness. Would you look at that?" Mrs. Murphy jumped to her feet, bonking her head on the metal dome of the hair dryer. It didn't faze her one bit as she rushed to the door of the salon. "Finn's back. And he has that actress with him. They must be here for the wedding."

Finn. *Finn.* Now she remembered. In excruciating detail.

*

It had happened a few weeks ago, when she'd first returned to Jupiter Point. She'd decided the town would be a good place to stay off the radar. She knew the area because she'd spent all the past summer at the Breton lookout tower volunteering for the Forest Service—but hiding out, really. For six months, she'd been mostly alone in the remote wilderness looking for smoke that would indicate a wildfire. She'd loved every quiet, healing minute in that tower.

So the first thing she did when she got back to town was hike out to Breton, which wasn't staffed in the winter. But instead of the peace and quiet she'd expected, she'd stumbled onto an engagement party. Twinkle lights lit up the observation room, some of them spelling the words "Bri and Rollo 4 Ever." Brianna, the bride-to-be, had invited her to stay, so she'd accepted a glass of champagne and some cheese and crackers.

And then someone had planted himself in front of her. Someone extremely good-looking—and extensively scarred on one side of his face, from jaw to cheekbone. Burn scars, she knew from experience. Wide shoulders, lean build, thick dark hair, smoldering brown eyes with ridiculously long eyelashes—the entire package was breathtaking. And he was staring at her as if he never wanted to stop.

It made her so uncomfortable, she nearly swallowed a cube of cheese. She didn't want attention. Not even from an attractive man.

"So, do you come here often?" He winced as soon as he asked the clichéd question. "Don't answer that. What I mean is, I think I saw a picture of you on that corkboard."

He waved in the direction of the kitchenette where she'd cooked her meals last summer.

She nodded, making a mental note to confiscate that photo as soon as possible. She hadn't known it was there.

"So, I figure you've been here before. Not that I'm stalking you or anything. I didn't know you'd be here. I mean, I kind of hoped you would be." He clawed one hand through his dark hair, leaving it romantically tousled. With a pained—but charming—smile, he finished with, "I'm making a mess out of this, aren't I?"

She wrinkled her forehead, still not really getting it. "A mess of what, exactly?"

"Let me try again. I hiked out here a couple months ago with some friends. I saw that photo, which I now know is you, and I thought, 'I hope I meet that woman someday.' And here you are. Sounds like destiny to me."

"Destiny?" She finished her cheese and wiped her fingers on a napkin. "Sorry, I'm not much of a believer. I put destiny in the same category as cheesy pick-up lines."

"Are you a magician?"

"Excuse me?"

"Every time I look at you, everyone else disappears." He looked at her expectantly, waiting for her to smile.

She narrowed her eyes at him instead. "That's the cheesiest line I've ever heard. It's actually an insult to cheese."

He laughed. "Did you read Dr. Seuss as a kid?"

"What?"

"Because green eggs and *damn*." He shoved his hands in his pockets, raking her with an exaggerated, appreciative survey.

Finally, she laughed. It was an involuntary, incredulous laugh, but still. "Okay, you got me. *That* is the worst pick-up line I've ever heard."

"Oh, I've got more. I have an extensive collection."

Honestly, she was surprised he needed pick-up lines. A guy like him, with his looks and charm, could probably pick up a woman with half a wink of one eye. "Strange thing to collect."

"Yes, well, I grew up in LA." He gave her that flashing, groove-in-the-cheek smile again. "Misspent youth on Sunset Boulevard. How about you? Where are you from? I'm Finn Abrams, by the way."

"Well, Finn, I don't think we've reached the sharing-life-stories phase, sorry."

"I think I heard a 'yet' in there. We're not at that phase *yet*. But I know a good way to get there. So how about we back up and start again. Will you have dinner with me, mystery tower woman?"

She shook her head, bewildered by how quickly the conversation had morphed so it felt like she actually knew this stranger. Like she *wanted* to know him. Wanted to know how he'd gotten the scars, why pain still lurked behind his eyes. How he could still be so charming, despite such a recent—to her expert eye—trauma.

But she had to stay cautious. And she didn't go for the charming type anyway.

"We're in a tower in the middle of the wilderness. What exactly did you have in mind?"

"Leave it to me. We'll gorge on cheese and crackers and drink champagne under the stars."

Everything about him was so warm, so inviting, so enticing.

So not happening. "It's January."

He cocked his head at her. "Do you believe in love at first sight?"

She gaped at him.

"Because I can walk by again." Mischief glittered in his dark eyes.

She snatched her backpack off the floor. This engagement party was nice and all—Rollo and Brianna seemed great— but this was crazy. "Let's start over completely, shall we?"

"Good idea."

"We'll back up to the part where you're celebrating your friends' engagement and I'm about to walk in." She stepped backwards, pulled the door open, and slipped out.

"Wait. Don't leave. Just tell me your—" he called through the door, before she shut it tight.

She leaned against it, torn between laughing and wanting to run back in. It felt like there was a magnet behind that door, drawing her back into life and sparkling fun and bright possibility.

Sparks with a stranger—definitely not on her agenda.

She ran down the staircase, back to the trail, starlight illuminating the path. Forget that sexy, scarred charmer. She'd never see him again anyway.

Yeah, about that...

Lisa whipped her head around to look outside. The first thing she saw was the back of a photographer side-stepping along the sidewalk as he snapped photos. When he stepped out of her line of sight, she finally got a glimpse of the glamorous couple strolling arm-in-arm down Constellation Way. The very same couple she'd just been reading about. And the same man she'd met at the tower.

"It's Annika Poole," Mrs. Murphy was saying. "Molly, I can't believe an actual celebrity is coming to Evie's wedding."

Across the room, Molly sniffed. "Finn can do much better, in my opinion."

"With those scars?" Mrs. Murphy shook her head and hmphed. "It's a shame, it really is."

"Stop that." Molly's body was trembling. She always shook to some extent, but when she was upset it got worse. Lisa pulled her gaze away from the couple and hurried to her side. "I adore Finn. He's a sweet boy. He brings me flowers when he visits."

Sweet boy? Lisa nearly snorted out loud at that description. During her encounter with Finn Abrams, the phrase "sweet boy" had never crossed her mind. She'd pegged him as the flirtatious player type.

"And he's still very handsome," Molly added.

"Obviously, you're not the only one who thinks so," Lisa said dryly. "I spy a movie star on his arm." She glanced at Annie, who had pulled the scissors away from Molly's head of flyaway white hair. "How's the haircut coming?"

"Almost done. And Mrs. McGraw, I absolutely agree with you. He's still a hottie in my book. You don't have to worry about Finn Abrams. He's a charmer."

Lisa snuck another glance at the street outside. Annika had stopped to take a call and was speaking heatedly into her cell phone. Her other arm was wrapped tightly around Finn's elbow. Wearing a stocking cap, a woodsy brown sweater and trousers, with both hands in his pockets, he looked casual and mouthwatering and...bored.

Huh. He definitely hadn't looked bored when he'd flirted with her back at the Breton tower.

CHAPTER THREE

"Hasn't he gotten enough shots by now?" Finn asked through clenched teeth. "Do you think we could move on?"

"Do you think you could look a little more excited?" Annika snapped shut the little crystal-studded case of her iPhone. "It shouldn't be that hard."

"I'm not an actor. I'm a firefighter." Since he'd gotten out of the hospital, he had to keep reminding himself of that fact. Injured, still recovering, but damn it, he still had his red card. If he busted his ass, he could get on a hotshot crew, and that was all he wanted. Since the burnover, nothing felt right. As if he'd jumped off a cliff and was still falling. He couldn't get his bearings.

For instance, he used to think Annika was sexy. Now she just seemed whiny.

"Honestly, it's getting old, Finn." Annika rested her head against his chest and aimed one more dreamy smile at him. "When are you going to let that whole firefighting thing go?"

"Thanks for your support. I really appreciate it."

"Oh come on. Wasn't I the one who ran to your bedside during all those surgeries?" She waved at the photographer. "That's it for now, Mark."

The photographer nodded and put the lens cap back on his camera. He worked for Finn's father, Stu, who owned the studio that was producing the *Miracle in Big Canyon* movie, in which Annika was starring. Apparently, the publicity department thought that photos of Annika with the real-life "wounded hero" firefighter would get lots of attention.

Finn was going along with the charade for now, but his patience was wearing thin. Since the burnover, only two things mattered to him. Getting back into action. And learning the truth about the strange flashback he'd had during the Big Canyon wildfire.

But Annika had been sweet to him during his stay in the hospital, so he didn't mind helping her with a little publicity.

"I have to get going, Annika. I'll walk you back to your B&B."

She looked at him vaguely, as if she'd almost forgotten he was there. Maybe now that the photographer was gone, she *had* forgotten him. "Fine. I'm going to see if that spa will send a masseuse to my room." She used her phone to take a photo of the sign—as if remembering "Moon Glow" would be impossible.

He glanced at the salon. His gaze snagged on someone inside. A weird thrill traveled through his body—that feeling when you scan a crowd and know you've spotted a familiar face, but you can't quite pin it down. A pair of wide-set dark eyes, inky hair swept into a loose knot.

Holy shit. Even though he couldn't make out her features through all the obstructions—window, stylists, salon equipment—he *knew* it was her. The girl from the tower.

The girl who'd brutally shot him down without even telling him her name.

He stared into the salon, trying for a better look. Maybe it wasn't her. Maybe it was just his imagination. Did he even *want* it to be her? Christ, he had enough things on his mind. He didn't need another distraction.

Annika tugged at his arm, and he allowed himself to be dragged down the sidewalk toward the Goodnight Moon B&B. It didn't matter, anyway. He needed to keep his focus where it counted. Get back on the crew, get some answers. Simple.

Okay, so he did take one glance back at the Moon Glow. He couldn't help it. But they were too far away and he couldn't make out anyone's face.

His phone rang. It was Rollo, his closest friend in Jupiter Point. He was staying in the guesthouse on Rollo's property while he tried to get his shit together. These days, the only people he felt right with were the hotshots. They'd been in the wildfire, they knew what it felt like. Rollo was the only one who knew about the weird flashback, though.

"Are you still in town?" Rollo asked.

"Yup. Just about to drop Annika off. You need something?"

"There's a package for you at the post office. From that detective."

"Cool, thanks man. I'll swing by."

Finn had hired a private investigator to track down his real parents, since Stu had completely shut him down.

"You're Finn Abrams. That's it. Nothing else to know."

"That's impossible. There must be records somewhere."

"Records? It was an under-the-table adoption that cost a fuck-ing fortune. No records. Maybe Ellie knew, but she died the year after. Drop it, Finn. I'm warning you."

Of course he hadn't listened to that warning. He couldn't. He wanted answers. Stu got fed up and they had a big blowout. Finn had come here, to Jupiter Point. To his friends on the hotshot crew.

"Grab a couple of six-packs, too. Sean's last night as a single man. Figure that deserves a toast or two."

Finn's gut tightened. "He probably doesn't want me there."

"Bullshit. You need to talk to him, Finn."

"I know."

"You're running out of time, dude. The wedding's to-morrow, then the honeymoon. You want on the crew or not? You have a shot since I'm retiring and Josh will need time off for the baby. He's going to fill that spot one way or the other."

Rollo's voice rose, catching Annika's attention. "Is that Rollo? Hand me the phone, I want to say 'hi.'"

But Rollo had heard her. "Hanging up now," he said quickly, the phone going dead right afterward. Rollo couldn't stand Annika and avoided her whenever possible.

Finn shrugged an apology at Annika. "Sorry. You can say hi at the wedding."

"Sometimes I think he doesn't like me."

Finn snorted. He had no idea why she cared what a bunch of firefighters thought of her. But she apparently did. "You're Annika Poole. Why wouldn't he like you?"

Her eyebrows drew together at his non-answer. He braced himself for a deluge of resentful questions about who did and didn't like her, and why. Jesus. Sometimes he couldn't believe that he'd spent so much time over the years dating women like Annika.

Again, the girl from the tower flashed into his mind. That girl—she was different. She hadn't wanted charm or flattery from him. She was more the don't-bullshit-me type. Maybe that was why he'd been so attracted to her. With everything in his life thrown into confusion, she seemed...real.

Yeah, real—as in really, *really* not interested in him.

Luckily, Annika's phone rang just then. "Gemma." Her publicist. "Yes, it went great. Just the wedding left, then I'll be back in LA."

Finn couldn't lie; he was counting the hours.

CHAPTER FOUR

By the time Lisa drove home after her shift, she still hadn't forgotten about that near miss with Finn Abrams. If he was really coming to the wedding with Annika and a potential entourage of photographers, she'd have to be extra careful.

Not that she wasn't already. She was freakishly cautious. She hadn't even rented an apartment in Jupiter Point yet. When she'd first left Houston, she'd bought a small motorhome and made it as homey as possible. Now, all these months later, it *was* her home.

And when she was ready to leave, all she had to do was turn the key in the ignition and go.

Her mother and stepsisters would laugh their asses off if they could see her now. They all had five-bedroom houses and a new car every year. A diamond necklace for Christmas, a Caribbean vacation, and they were happy.

She'd always been the odd one out. Working in health care was strange enough. But then tossing her whole career aside to help Maria? As always, they'd thought she was crazy. They'd definitely think so if they could see her new home here in the Jupiter Point Campground. Instead of live oaks and bayous, she was surrounded by towering pine trees and friendly little nuthatches and chickadees.

Since it was the off-season, she often had the campground to herself.

Just how she liked it.

She parked her car on the road that circled through the campground. It was an old-model Mercedes that she'd bought when she started working for the McGraws. She'd chosen it because of its boxy, high-clearance design—the perfect height for helping Molly in and out of her wheelchair. Since then, she'd added a seat cushion and a kind of "lazy Susan" apparatus that made it even easier for Molly to get in.

A footpath led to her camping spot, which included a picnic table and a fire pit with a grill. With a grateful sigh, she stepped inside her motorhome and locked the door behind her. The familiar smell of motor oil and coffee and grilled cheese embraced her. She had exactly two appliances in the kitchenette, an espresso machine and a panini maker—which would also make her family laugh hysterically. No dishwasher? No ice cube maker? No microwave?

She made her way to the back of the motorhome, which was entirely filled with a platform bed. After plopping her tote bag at the foot of the bed, she dropped onto her back and gazed up at the swaths of indigo fabric she'd pinned to the ceiling. Whimsical stars and moons twinkled back at her. A down comforter as thick as marshmallows sank under her weight, along with over a dozen overstuffed pillows.

Home sweet teeny-tiny home.

Safe.

Alone.

A vivid vision flashed through her mind. In the salon, for one shocking moment, she could have sworn that Finn was looking right at her through the storefront window. He wore the same expression he'd had at the tower—intense, smoldering...*curiosity.*

Who was he, anyway? She reached for her tote bag and pulled out the old tabloid from the salon. They wouldn't miss it, and she intended to return it as soon as possible.

Well, after she studied every word about Finn Abrams, "wounded hero firefighter."

Okay, now her family would *definitely* be laughing at her.

A knock on the door sent adrenaline shooting through her. She scrambled off the bed. The campground was empty. No one visited her here. *Ever.*

She grabbed the baseball bat she kept as a weapon and hurried toward the front of the motorhome. Outside, she saw two men in police uniforms. She relaxed a tiny bit, recognizing Police Chief Becker from a picture she'd seen in the local newspaper. Not that having the police on her doorstep was *relaxing*...but it was better than a menacing stranger.

She discreetly stashed the bat and opened the door. "Yes?"

"Ms. Lisa Peretti?"

"Yes, that's me."

"I'm the Chief of Police here in Jupiter Point, Chief Becker. This here is Sheriff's Deputy Will Knight."

She made a quick survey of the two men. Chief Becker was an African-American man who easily cleared six and a half feet. He had a slow, quiet manner that managed to be imposing even when he didn't say much. Will Knight wasn't quite as tall. He had broad shoulders, dark gray eyes and an easy smile probably meant to put her at ease.

It didn't really work.

"You're a hard woman to track down," said the chief.

She stiffened. "You've been looking for me?"

"For a while now, as a matter of fact. Since last November."

Last *November*? Had something happened to Maria? She tried to figure out a good way to ask that question without giving anything away, but couldn't.

"Um...I've been traveling around. I just got back to Jupiter Point. What's this about?"

"Is this a good place to talk?" He glanced around the little campground. It was about six in the evening, and shadows were settling around the edges of the clearing.

"Well, I'd invite you in, but I'm not sure you'd both fit inside this thing." That was the truth; both men were big and tall. "How about we sit at that table. Can I get either of you anything to drink? I have cold coffee. Or I could make some hot coffee."

Will Knight grinned. "Cold or hot coffee. I like a menu with variety. Nothing for me, thanks."

The police chief also declined a drink, and they all trooped over to the picnic table. As soon as they were settled in, he began.

"Are you aware of the incident that occurred on the trail to the Breton lookout tower last November?"

A bolt of alarm went through her at the mention of Breton. "No, I wasn't here then. I left at the end of October. But I was volunteering there all summer."

She cringed at the way the words just flowed out of her. Damn it, didn't all the TV shows say not to volunteer any extra information?

Will Knight picked up where the chief had left off. "This past November, a man with a gun assaulted a group of hikers from Jupiter Point. They were about half a mile from the Breton tower. The assailant grabbed Merry Warren, one of our local reporters here in town. He claimed he was looking for a girl who had dark hair and lived in the tower. The other members of the group disarmed him and we took him into custody. He lawyered up right away and pled guilty to assault. But he refused to say anything more about who he was looking for or why."

Oh my God. Lisa's thoughts whirled in ten different directions.

"Was Merry...she wasn't the one he was looking for?"

"No. We did some process of elimination with everyone associated with the tower and the obvious target is you. The question now is why." Chief Becker looked at her in an authoritative way that demanded an answer.

She swallowed hard. Since she'd helped Maria escape, she hadn't told anyone what happened. She'd promised her silence, for both of their safety.

"Maybe it was a random mugger. If he pled guilty, that's the end of it, right?"

His steady gaze didn't waver. "I certainly hope so, for your sake. But my gut tells me otherwise. I'm protective of this town. One of our own reporters was nearly kidnapped, and I don't like that. The assailant knocked out Finn Abrams too. Nearly gave him a concussion."

She flinched. *Finn* had gotten knocked out? That made two people hurt by someone looking for her. "I'm so sorry they were hurt."

"It could have been a lot worse," Knight said, his tone deceptively easygoing. Each word felt like a stab in Lisa's heart. "Merry Warren's wrist was badly sprained. She couldn't type for two weeks."

Becker narrowed his eyes at Knight. "I didn't hear about that."

"She didn't report it. I pried the truth out of her. Gave her an on-the-record quote as bribery. Not bribery in the legal sense," he added quickly. He popped a piece of gum in his mouth and gave it a laconic chew.

Chief Becker rested one elbow on the picnic table and shot the other officer a long-suffering look. "They had to assign *you* to this, didn't they?"

"Yup." Knight grinned back.

Lisa wondered if they had some kind of good-cop-bad-cop routine going on. Or maybe it was more of a stern-cop-goofy-cop routine.

"Back to you, Lisa," Knight continued. "If you could just answer a few questions, that might help us figure this out. You came to Jupiter Point last summer, right?"

Scratch the "goofy cop" description. Knight was definitely using his casual manner as a smokescreen. "Yes, I came here last June and volunteered as a spotter at the Breton tower until the season ended."

"Why here?"

"I heard the stargazing is spectacular," she said blandly.

Knight and Becker exchanged a glance. "That it is," Knight agreed. "Right, Chief?"

"So I hear. I'm usually too busy protecting the citizens from gun-wielding attackers to notice."

Lisa laughed; she couldn't help it. She wanted to trust these two officers. And she didn't want anyone else to get hurt. Maybe it would be okay to tell them a little of her story.

"Listen, I left Houston because of an incident involving a very powerful local politician. It's possible that this mugger has something to do with that. I have no idea how or why, though. And I really can't say any more."

Both men were watching her alertly. "What kind of incident?" Becker asked the question while Knight took out a little notebook and pen.

"Domestic violence. The victim was a school friend of mine. I helped her leave, then we parted ways. I decided to take some time off before I went back. I needed a vacation anyway. My work is stressful and I was pretty burned out." She worked a splinter out of the edge of the table.

"So you left Houston to protect your friend?" Knight lifted one eyebrow as he scrawled a note.

"It's just temporary. As soon as I think it's safe, I'll go back."

"I'm guessing it's not safe yet."

Lisa looked away. A night moth flitted across the clearing, into the shadows. The chief was right. If someone was looking for her, she couldn't go back yet. Then again, she probably wasn't safe here either.

Knight leaned across the table, his gray eyes cool and penetrating. "If you tell us who we're dealing with, we'll have a better chance of protecting you."

She swallowed hard. Maria hadn't trusted the Houston cops because many of them knew her husband. But these guys were Jupiter Point police. Should she break her promise to Maria and tell them everything? "Has anything else happened since November? Any other people looking for dark-haired women?"

The two officers exchanged glances. "Not that we're aware of," said Becker.

"So they came looking, they didn't find me, and now they've moved on."

"That's one possibility." Knight leaned back and crossed his arms over his chest. "I can think of a few others."

So could she. A hard lump gathered in her throat. Crap. She couldn't stay in Jupiter Point. She just couldn't. No matter how good the stargazing was.

Chief Becker rose to his full height, which meant he towered over both of them. "We'll let you get back to your evening. If anything unusual happens, please call the station. Don't hesitate. And watch your back."

She nodded absently. Already her mind was sorting through her familiar departure routine. Pay the rest of her campground bill. Stow her clothes and kitchen items.

Deputy Knight stood as well, and handed her a business card as he shook her hand goodbye. "Put this number in your phone. Call it anytime."

"Thank you."

She watched the police cruiser pull out of the campground. Quiet fell across her little corner of the world, which no longer seemed quite so hidden. If the local police knew where she was, how long would it take for Senator Ruiz's people to find her? On the other hand, maybe they'd given up on Jupiter Point because they hadn't found her here in November.

Basically, either this was the safest place to be or the most dangerous. How the hell was she supposed to know which?

She couldn't take any chances. She had to leave Jupiter Point.

Leaning her elbows on the picnic table, she tilted her head back and gazed up at the famous Jupiter Point sky. And jumped a bit with surprise. The first brilliant evening star was twinkling at her as if it had been waiting for her to look up. It had to be Venus. In the Breton tower, she'd spent hours looking at the planets and constellations. Venus always appeared first.

"Hey you," she said softly. "I know you're just a gaseous rock, but what do you think I should do?"

The planet didn't have much to say. But she knew the answer anyway.

For now, Molly needed her, so she'd stay. At least through the wedding.

CHAPTER FIVE

Sean and Evie's wedding was just as romantic and beautiful as such a passionately in-love couple deserved. In the Chapel of the White Dove, Finn watched the two of them face each other before the minister. Evie looked like an angel floating on air, or a fairy queen. A crown of white and lavender flowers held back her hair. More flowers were woven into the rich mahogany locks that flowed over her shoulders. Her gown looked like something out of Regency England, with a princess neckline and a filmy cream skirt flirting with her ankles.

But the sheer beauty of the moment couldn't distract him from the throbbing up and down his side. He'd done too much PT last night, like an idiot. He'd been so frustrated by the package from the private investigator he'd hired. Nothing but old photos of people Finn didn't recognize. A few photocopies of twenty-year-old news articles. And a hefty bill.

Finn didn't care if it took all his savings. He wanted the truth. If he had another family out there, he wanted to find them.

After writing that enormous check, he'd thrown himself into PT just to release his tension. Stretching scar tissue created a special kind of weird sensation. Sometimes, he welcomed that pain. At least it was something concrete and real.

The rest of the evening was spent drinking beer with Rollo. Another disappointment—Sean never showed up. Which mean Finn *still* hadn't spoken to him about getting on the crew.

Maybe it was for the best. Finn wanted some answers first. Until he knew the full story, how could he be sure the same freak-out wouldn't happen again?

Today, feeling antsy as hell, he'd dragged an Armani suit onto his throbbing limbs. He'd picked up Annika, dressed in a gorgeous frock he couldn't be bothered to notice. And now he was numbly watching his former crew leader get married while Annika sniffled beside him.

"Give it a rest, Annika." Finn spoke out of the side of his mouth, without moving his lips. "You don't even know them."

Annika elbowed him in the ribs. "Don't be such a beast. I can cry if I feel like it. And now *you're* making me cry, so there."

He gritted his teeth. Why had he agreed to bring Annika to the wedding of two people he actually cared about? He'd been so numb since the burnover, he hadn't thought it would matter. But now that he was here, he found it *did* matter. This was Sean, this was his crew. It mattered.

He ignored Annika and fixed his gaze on Sean. For such a rugged guy, he wore that tailored tux pretty well.

His groomsmen—Josh, Rollo, Baker—didn't look too shabby either. They were all members of the Jupiter Point Hotshots. If Finn hadn't bolted during the burnover, he'd probably be up there too.

Sean had taken it personally when Finn had turned his back on the crew instead of deploying his shelter. As the crew captain, he'd felt responsible for all of them. Especially Finn, since he was a rookie. There was still tension between them, partly because Finn still hadn't told him the whole story.

The minister spoke the all-important words.

"Do you, Sean Adam Marcus, take this woman, Evangeline Mary McGraw, as your lawfully wedded wife?"

"I do."

"And do you, Evangeline Mary McGraw..."

Finn held back a sneeze. The entire chapel was overflowing with flowers. Peace lilies, larkspur, white peonies. Green vines were twined around the pews. Brianna, Evie's best friend and gardener extraordinaire, had gone nuts with the flowers. He hoped none of the guests had allergies.

Someone else sneezed across the aisle.

He glanced over and saw *her*. The girl from the tower.

Holy shit. It *was* her.

He gaped at her. She was sitting at the end of the pew, next to Molly McGraw's wheelchair. She wore a simple navy dress with a sheer polka dot bolero jacket over it. It wasn't especially flattering; Annika wouldn't be caught dead in something so demure. But something about the way she held herself, straight and graceful, with her chin at a proud angle, hit him right in the gut.

He nearly groaned as he remembered what a fool he'd made of himself at the tower. She'd totally knocked him off his game. His heartbeat had gone all wonky. His vision tunneled until all he could see was her dark eyes and slim form, the backpack slung over her shoulders, her look of dismay as she took in the group invading her tower.

Then he'd actually talked to her and made a complete ass of himself. She'd laughed at his attempts to charm her—and not in a good way. Then she'd disappeared down the trail from the Breton tower.

What was she doing here, sneezing at Sean and Evie's wedding?

Molly's shawl slid off her shoulders and Lisa bent to retrieve it. She settled it back into place as Molly gave her a shaky smile.

Holy shit. She was *taking care of* Molly. That meant she *lived* here.

Annika dug her elbow into his ribs, and he jerked his attention back to the wedding in progress. Ah hell. This was ridiculous. She was just a woman who'd caught his eye but turned him down. No need to get all crazy about it.

The minister was saying, "I now pronounce you man and wife. You may kiss the bride."

Sean gathered Evie into his arms. They held each other for an endlessly romantic moment. Finn was a sucker for romance, he had to admit. Before the burnover, he'd always been the guy who brought flowers and conjured up the perfect first date. Girls had always loved that about him, and yeah, he'd enjoyed the results.

That all seemed like a lifetime ago now.

He heard a general shuffling of feet as everyone stood up to applaud the newly married couple.

Evie, flushed and glowing, hand in hand with Sean, faced the crowd of guests. "We'll see you all at the Star Bright Shelter. The kids have gone all out to decorate it and my cousin Suzanne is in charge, so you know it's going to be perfect."

Everyone laughed, Finn too.

That was Jupiter Point for you. Everyone knew everyone, flaws and all.

Except him. He still didn't feel part of this town. He was just the guy staying in Rollo's guesthouse. The guy from Hollywood, with that actress. The guy who'd panicked during the burnover.

He still felt separate, apart.

And glancing across the aisle again at the girl from the tower, he saw a similar emotion on her face. She didn't really belong here either. So maybe they had something in common after all.

*

The reception was even more magical than the wedding. The Star Bright Shelter for Teens was situated on an old farm at the edge of town. Finn braked his Tahoe to a stop, marveling at the amazing sight. Suzanne and her helpers had transformed it into an enchanted fairyland. A huge white tent festooned with garlands of flowers took up most of the open grassy area between the outbuildings. Lanterns in shades like Chinese red and royal purple hung from every available tree branch. Twinkle lights lit the pathways from the tent to the dance floor and the bathrooms.

They left the Tahoe with a local kid volunteering as a valet and strolled toward the captivating scene.

"Wow. This is really something. I knew Suzanne had skills, but this is over the top." A motley crew of teenagers was circulating among the guests, carrying trays of appetizers—spanakopita, mini quiches, mushroom and brie puffs. He scanned the crowd, looking for the other hotshots. Or maybe for the girl from the tower.

He groaned inwardly. This *had* to stop.

Annika snapped a picture for her Instagram account. "Hashtag 'wedding for a good cause'," she murmured as she tapped the words. "I thought they were crazy at first, but I can get plenty of mileage out of this."

"That's not why Sean and Evie chose this place," he said sharply.

"Oh, get over yourself. I know that. I gave a donation, didn't I? Just like they requested?"

"Anonymous, of course?"

She laughed at him. "Close enough. There may be a leak to the press. It's a win-win, though. Good PR for the shelter. So don't go getting your panties in a bunch." She pinched his ass.

His entire body went rigid. This was Jupiter Point, not some pool party in Beverly Hills. His hotshot crew was here, along with half of Jupiter Point. Jesus, why had he agreed to bring Annika?

Just then, Molly McGraw called his name. He winced as he turned in her direction. Was the girl from the tower with her? Had she seen—?

Yes, she had, he realized, as soon as he met her dark eyes. Her eyebrows were raised, and she seemed to be biting back a smile.

"I have to say 'hi' to someone," he told Annika, who was forming her familiar red-carpet smile. One of the teenagers was in the midst of asking for a selfie—that explained it. "Be right back."

He made his way over to Molly. Her husband, the Dean, and the dark-eyed girl were standing close by. His skin prickled with energy as he approached them. He cursed himself and his ridiculous reaction to her.

He bent to kiss Molly on the cheek. Like Evie, she wore a crown of flowers on her fluff of white hair and beamed with joy. "Congratulations, Molly. That was such a beautiful wedding."

"It was," she agreed. "F...Finn, I want you to meet someone. This is Lisa Peretti. Lisa, this is F-Finn, the sweet boy I was t-telling you about."

He cringed at that description as he straightened. "Hi. Nice to see you again."

A smile tugged at one corner of her mouth, making a crescent-shaped dimple appear next to it. "Nice to see you too. You come here often?"

He grinned ruefully at her reference to his first pick-up line attempt. "I was kind of hoping you'd forgotten all that."

"I did try to block it out, true."

The Dean glanced between the two of them with surprise. "You two already know each other? Lisa's only been here two weeks. I guess you're living up to your reputation, Finn. The Mighty Finn, is that what they call you?"

Aaaaaand...more humiliation. Why not just keep heaping it on? "That was a long time ago, Dean. These days, it's more like the Unsightly Finn."

"No, dear. That's t-terrible." Molly shook her head, distressed, and he wished he could take it back. He didn't want to give the impression he felt sorry for himself. He didn't—he liked the scars. They reminded him that he was a goddamn wildland, kickass, highly trained elite firefighter. A hotshot. It was scrawled all over his face.

The scent of Annika's jasmine perfume wafted around them.

"And who's this?" Annika materialized next to him. She took in the sight of Molly in her wheelchair and crouched down in front of her. "Look at how precious you are with that hair of yours and those flowers. I absolutely love it. Would you like a selfie too?"

Molly drew back, a tremor jerking her body. It was the Parkinson's, Finn knew. He put a warning hand on Annika's arm, but she shook him off, her focus entirely on Molly.

"Oh, that's so cute. Are you nervous? Here's a little secret, just between you and me. Us movie stars are just like everyone else. I know, hard to believe, right?"

Finn got that watching-a-train-wreck-in-slow-motion feeling. "Uh, Annika, this is Molly McGraw, she's—"

But Annika ignored him and rose to her feet. "Are you her servant or whatever?" she asked Lisa. "Do you have her phone so we can take a selfie? Or maybe she'd rather have me sign something. I can sign her wedding invitation if you have it."

Lisa bit her lip and met Finn's eyes. Hers were brimming with laughter. Another of those unsettling thrills ran through him. "That is such a lovely offer. What do you think, Molly?" Lisa asked.

"Excuse us," Finn told them. He wrapped his arm around Annika's shoulders and steered her away. "Molly is the mother of the bride, and her son happens to be married to Starly Minx, the pop star. I don't think she's at her daughter's wedding so she can get your autograph."

Annika swatted his arm. "Get out. Starly Minx? Is she here?"

"Right over there with Evie and her brother Hunter." He tilted his head in the direction of the bridal couple. Hunter had Evie wrapped in a big hug while a beaming Starly Minx took a photo. The famous pop star wore her hair in a lavender French twist and wore a cream linen suit. She and Hunter had just returned from a tour of South America that broke all attendance records.

"Oh my God. I'm going to say 'hi'. We have the same agent, she won't mind. I have to get a shot with her."

Finn caught her arm. "No, Annika. This is a private family event, not a publicity appearance."

"Not for me."

"Oh God" The logic of Annika-world. He tugged her toward the bar. "Come on, we need champagne. You can stalk Starly later."

Despite a quick two flutes of champagne, the reception dragged on. Finn lounged next to Annika at a picnic table while she posed with fans and got buzzed. He would have given anything to be able to hang out with the other hotshots. Josh and Rollo were goofing around, downing beers and ragging on the other members of the crew. He caught Rollo's eye and jerked his head in a "please join us" gesture. But Rollo mouthed a "hell no."

Awesome.

Even his non-hotshot friends were busy. Brianna with the flowers, Suzanne with the caterers, Merry Warren behind the bar.

On top of all that, every time he looked up, he spotted Lisa Peretti. Or maybe it was more accurate to say he kept looking for her. He noticed when she skirted the dance floor in search of a drink for Molly. He watched her turn down three dance invitations from various members of the first-responder community.

He noticed when her hair came out of its twist and when she took off her jacket. At some point, she sat on a folding chair next to Molly in order to help her eat. She kicked off one shoe and rubbed her bare foot against the opposite calf.

He fantasized about giving her a foot rub. Or a full body rub while feeding her bits of wedding cake in bed. He imagined her eyes sparking with desire instead of rejecting him.

God, he was losing it.

Basically, he'd rather be doing anything than babysitting Annika right now.

But he was stuck. And his famous date was getting more and more tipsy. It didn't take much for someone with zero-percent body fat to feel the effects of three glasses of champagne.

CHAPTER SIX

After four glasses of champagne, Annika surged to her feet and grabbed his hand. "We need to talk. Somewhere private, no cameras."

"Not sure I've ever heard those words from your mouth before."

"Shut up." She pulled him along the edge of the dance floor. The band had launched into a fast-moving swing number that had dancers laughing and scrambling to keep up. She snagged another bottle of champagne on her way out of the white catering tent.

Outside, Finn drew in a deep breath of the fresh evening air. A breeze had sprung up, making the lanterns sway and shadows dance across the grass.

"Slow down, Annika. You're going to fall on your ass at this rate."

"If you care about my ass, you better start acting like it, mister." She whirled around and poked him in the chest. "I've gone out of my way for you, Finn Abrams. It's time for you to step up."

He caught her hand against his chest, mostly to protect himself. He knew this mood of hers. Any second now, she was liable to throw a chair at him. "Excuse me?"

She ripped her hand away from his grip. "I have to get you off my chest."

"What?"

"I mean...*it*. The thing. Get it off my chest."

"What thing?" Finn didn't know if he should be laughing or driving her home.

"The thing that's on my chest."

Totally confused, he dropped his gaze to her chest, where he saw nothing but barely there silk and a Tibetan symbol dangling from a platinum chain.

"I mean, the thing that's on my *mind*." Annika tapped the side of her head. "Eyes up here. God, what's wrong with you?"

"Christ, Annika. Whatever's going on, let's talk about it later. I don't want to make a scene at Evie and Sean's wedding."

"I. Will make a scene. Wherever I want to." She whirled around and stalked a few feet away. Folding her arms across her chest, she presented her back to him. "You need to fucking propose to me, like now."

"What?"

She spun around and stalked toward him. "Yes. Because my time is val-u-able." She drew out the syllables. "People pay mill-ions for my time. And I give it to you for free. But nothing is free, Finn. Not in Hollywood. And Hollywood's just like the real world except better."

"Okay, you're going off the rails here, Annika." He glanced around to see if anyone was watching or listening. He wanted to remind her their relationship was all an act, but he didn't want to take a chance on someone reporting this to the tabloids.

"Gemma has it all worked out. Beauty and the Beast."

It took a moment for her words to sink in. "What on God's green earth are you talking about?"

"I'm Beauty, because duh." She swept a hand down her side in a sensual move that would have turned him on in the past. "And you're the Beast, because duh." She waved at the scarred side of his face. "People will *love* us together. Do you know how much good press I got after you got burned? All those times I came to the hospital?"

A sinking feeling grabbed at his stomach. All those times she came to the hospital—was there a hidden agenda involved? "So Gemma sent you to visit me?"

"The woman's a genius."

Holy crap. All this time, he'd been thinking she'd come to the hospital out of kindness. What a fool he was.

"At first I didn't want to, because of...you know." She glanced at his scars again. "But I do care about you, Finn. So I've decided I can live with your deformity."

"Oh. My deformity." Sometime later, the meaning would sink in. For now, her words slid off without making a dent. None of it mattered anyway. Nothing could touch him in this numb state. "That's, uh...damn, Annika. Where is this even coming from? You seriously want to get married? Why?"

"Well, you are, you know. You *were*. A catch." The twinkle lights cast whimsical will-o'-the-wisp sparkles across the smooth planes of her face. Objectively, she was beautiful. No one could deny that. "With your father and all."

He shoved his hands in the pockets of his dress pants and stepped closer to her. "What if I told you he isn't really my father?"

"Shut up."

"It's true. Not only that, we had a big fight and now we're not speaking. He cut me off, or I cut him off. Not sure which."

"No. Way. I haven't seen anything in the news about that."

"Yeah, well, the news might have other things to report on. It's all true. Still want me to propose?" He took another step closer. "You want to look at this deformed face for the rest of your life? Or maybe just a couple of years until the divorce?"

"Stop it." She took a step back, eyes huge. "What are you going to do, Finn? You broke with Stu? This is serious."

Shrugging, he came even closer. "I'm not worried. I figure I'll marry a rich and famous actress and be set for life."

Her forehead creased. She thrust her bottle of champagne at him. "I'm out of here. I'll find Mark, he'll take me back to my room."

"Good choice." He took the bottle and tilted it to his lips. He wasn't nearly drunk enough for any of this.

Under a swaying Chinese lantern, she paused. "You can't stay in this little pit stop of a town forever, Finn. You can't be a fireman anymore. Not with all those burns and scars. You'd better make up with Stu or you'll be nothing. Nothing at all."

He watched her go, red lantern light glimmering on the ivory silk of her dress. Half a bottle of champagne slid down his throat.

Cheers, he thought. *Here's to nothing.*

He slumped onto a redwood bench at the edge of the clearing and closed his eyes. The champagne was making his head spin; he'd always been more of a beer drinker. Like his father, the thought flashed into his mind. His real father, who worked at a bar somewhere.

An image of his mother shimmered to life. Not Ellie Abrams, who he barely remembered. This was a young woman with dark, wavy hair like his, smiling at him with incandescent kindness.

*

"Finn? Are you all right?"

His eyes snapped open. Lisa Peretti stood before him, barefoot, her sandals held in one hand. Wary sympathy shone from her dark eyes.

Great. How much had she overheard? "Fine. How are you?"

Smooth. Very smooth.

"Not bad. For what it's worth, 'deformed' is a little over the top. As a medical professional, I wouldn't use that phrase."

"So you heard all that."

She nodded. Her glance flickered down his body, and it seemed she wanted to say something else. But she didn't. She probably wasn't one for empty expressions of sympathy.

"Fan-tastic. I'm trying to figure why I keep embarrassing myself in front of you and I'm coming up blank." He grabbed the champagne bottle and took another swallow. "Drink?"

"I'm good. I don't drink when I'm working."

"So I'm drinking alone, then. One more embarrassing moment, in case you're counting." He toasted her with the bottle then set it aside. Any more and he might throw up. That would definitely put him in the Humiliation Hall of Fame for good.

She came toward the bench and sat next to him. Not right next to him, but close enough so he could inhale her scent, something light and spicy. "So, uh...I have a question for you," she said.

"The answer is yes."

She laughed. "Do you ever stop flirting?"

"This? This isn't flirting. Believe me, you'll know when I get back into flirting." Suddenly he felt a hell of a lot better than he had a few minutes ago. In a flash, this wedding had gone from endless tedium to something more like exhilaration.

"Will there be more cheesy pick-up lines?" She clasped her hands at her throat and fluttered her eyelashes at him. "A girl can dream."

"Speaking of dreams... Do your legs hurt from running through my dreams all night?"

She groaned. "Worst ever. You keep topping yourself. It's a gift."

"Yeah, kind of like that gift from your great-aunt Gertrude that you can't return because she'd be insulted."

"Oh, I doubt it. I'm sure that kind of thing works on most people."

"That kind of thing?"

She smoothed out a wrinkle on her dress. The night breeze lifted the long strands of hair that had come loose. "You know, the charming thing."

"I've had nearly an entire bottle of champagne, but I'm pretty sure you just called me charming."

"*And* I said it doesn't work on me."

He squinted up at the night sky. The lanterns overheard swayed, sending shadows chasing across the lawn. "No, you didn't. You said it worked on *most people.*"

"But I'm not most people."

"Now that," he looked back at her, "is for sure. One hundred percent."

It was a little hard to tell in the light of the lanterns, but it looked like she was blushing under his gaze. "I'm never going to go out with you, Finn."

She sounded so serious that it took him aback. *Never?* "Why not?"

"I'm not interested in dating anyone. I won't be in Jupiter Point for long. Even if I were..." She bit her lip, glancing away from him.

With all that champagne in his system, he went for the joke. "Let me guess. I'm too charming, funny, handsome and irresistible."

"Exactly."

He gave a double-take. "I was joking. I figured maybe it was the scars."

Her eyes flew up to meet his. "Of course not. It's the opposite of that. It's all the other stuff. The Hollywood stuff."

The Hollywood stuff. The kind of thing that was catnip to the other women he'd dated was a turnoff for Lisa Peretti. Great.

Actually, it *was* kind of great.

"So if I dial back the charm and good looks, we can try again sometime?"

She smiled—there was that damn dimple again—then laughed. "You can't even offer to dial back the charm without being charming."

"Damn it. I'm going to have to talk to Aunt Gertrude about this."

"And there you go again."

For a moment, they grinned at each other like fools. Sure, she was rejecting him again. But it didn't feel that way. It felt as if they were wrapped together by the breeze, the starry night, the swaying lanterns.

He tilted his head back and took in the dark arch of sky overhead. Was it more majestic than usual, more stunning? Or was that Lisa's effect? He pointed to the brightest object in the sky. "Venus is in opposition. That's why it's so bright lately. Pretty good timing for a wedding."

"It's just a planet, millions of miles away. It has nothing to do with Evie's wedding."

"Oh, I see how you are," he teased. "All logic, no romance. No wonder I fell flat on my face with you."

She nudged him with her elbow, a quick touch that sent a thrill through him. "You didn't fall totally flat," she confessed. "You definitely made an impression. I didn't expect to see you again, though."

"Believe me, I didn't either. Maybe Venus is playing tricks on us." She shot him a look. "I know, I know, it's just a planet. But it's an especially beautiful, mysterious one. Its surface can't even be photographed. They have to map it with radar."

They both looked up at the planet in question, an enchanting spark of light in the velvet sky. He breathed in the fragrance of her hair, rosemary and mint, and felt more alive than he had since the burnover. Not numb at all, not even a little bit.

Then she broke the spell. "So, my question."

"'Yes' wasn't the right answer? Fine, go ahead. Ask away."

"Did you get the limp at the same time as the scars?"

And just like that, all the magic evaporated from the moment. He stiffened and pulled himself upright. He couldn't believe she'd noticed his limp. He'd slaved so hard in PT to get rid of it. Most people didn't pick up on it. But like she'd said, she wasn't "most people." She was a medical professional. She was also someone who'd just witnessed him being dumped by his movie-star girlfriend and labeled as "deformed." *And* she'd rejected him and informed him she'd never go out with him.

Yeah. No. He didn't want to talk about his limp with her.

"I did, yes. But it's fine. I got it handled."

"I'm an ER nurse, and I have some experience with that sort of—"

He cut her off. "Thanks, but that's okay."

"I just wanted to offer—"

"You'd better get back to Molly."

At his gruff tone, the sympathetic expression vanished from her face and she gave a tight nod. "Okay. You're right, they're probably looking for me by now. Maybe I'll see you around, Finn."

"Sounds good."

With her shoes dangling from one hand, she gave him a formal sort of nod and headed toward the white tent, where the band was deep into a bad cover of "Desperado."

Sounds good? What a moronic thing to say.

But at least no one could call it charming.

CHAPTER SEVEN

What on earth had she been thinking? Offering to help Finn with his limp was idiotic. She wasn't going to be around long enough to do anything like that. It had been an impulse based on...what? The horrible things Annika had said to him? The way he looked in that suit? Or maybe it was the vulnerability she'd seen in his face as he slouched on that bench, eyes closed, long legs stretching forever.

Finn might be sexy and charming, but there was a lot more to him than that. Face it, he intrigued her, and she liked talking to him. Time seemed to disappear when she was bantering with him. If she left Jupiter Point, she'd very likely never see Finn again.

It didn't matter. She *was* leaving. She had to. Just in time, too, she thought as she parked her Mercedes outside the McGraws' stately Tudor-style home. This town was starting to grow on her, with its gorgeous setting and quirky stargazing theme.

And handsome firefighters.

Yes, it was time to leave. Past time. She just had to give notice to the McGraws and then she'd go.

But when Molly McGraw's face lit up at the sight of her, she completely lost her nerve.

"How are you today, my dear? You look wonderful." She kneeled down next to Molly, who was already in her wheelchair. The Dean had been reading to her; he slipped a bookmark into place and put down the book. A mystery, Lisa noticed. Good choice; they helped keep her brain active.

"F...fine. Happy to...see you."

The Dean met her questioning gaze. "She wanted to wait for you to give her a shower. She says I don't do it right."

Lisa smiled and smoothed Molly's hair. "We have our little routine down, don't we?"

"Yes." She nodded firmly, though her head kept trembling when the gesture was over. "I love my husband, but he g...gets all w...wet and makes a big m...mess."

Lisa chuckled as she wheeled Molly toward the downstairs bathroom, where a special bathing stall had been added. "We all have our areas of expertise. I know the Dean has many."

"Yes. Just ask him."

Lisa burst out laughing at that zinger. Molly winked at her husband on the way out of the room. He was shaking his head with amusement. At least she hoped it was amusement. Sometimes the Dean could be hard to read.

She helped Molly undress and assisted her into the sit-down shower stall. Molly held tight to the grab bar while Lisa maneuvered the hand-held showerhead.

"Are you sad?"

She looked down to see Molly peering up at her through the layer of shampoo she'd just applied to her head.

"No. Of course not. Well, maybe. I—" This was it. The perfect moment to tell Molly she was leaving. *I have to leave town for a while. I'll find someone even better than me. I'll come back to visit someday.*

But she couldn't get the words out of her mouth.

Molly filled the gap. "You need more f-friends. Evie says you should t-take her place at the Orbit."

Lisa frowned as she rubbed the foamy bubbles across Molly scalp. "The Orbit? That bar? I've never been there."

"The g...girls are coming to pick you up."

"Oh no. No, that's really not a good idea. I—"

"It's too late. They're on their w...way. Evie made me promise. It's her g...gift to you. B...because you came to her wedding even though you h...hate weddings."

The thoughtfulness of the gesture made tears prick Lisa's eyes. "I didn't hate *her* wedding. Hers was just fine. Wonderful, in fact." She rinsed the shampoo out, holding her hand as a shield to protect Molly's eyes. She finished the rest of the shower routine, then helped her out of the stall and dried her off. "I bet they're having a fantastic time on their honeymoon. They're in Italy, right? Drinking wine and eating veal parmigiana?"

"And t-taking lots of photos. Two weeks in Italy, j-just imagine."

Two weeks. Yes! She'd wait two more weeks for Evie's return, then she'd give her notice. It would be too difficult to find a replacement now, and the Dean couldn't handle it himself. Who would help with Molly's shower?

No. The fact was, Molly needed her *now*. And Lisa loved her and couldn't possibly walk away from her. She refused to abandon her favorite patient because of some weird incident that had happened four months ago.

After all, nothing had happened since then. She could wait two more weeks. A sense of relief flooded through her.

Smiling now, she helped Molly get dressed.

She'd figure something out. She'd get a gun. A pit bull. Maybe a rabid raccoon. Maybe she could train the campground nuthatches to chirp at the approach of danger. Everything would be fine.

Brianna showed up in her ancient red truck when Lisa still had an hour left in her shift. Molly insisted that she was about to nap and Lisa should go ahead and have fun.

Fun?

Not a concept Lisa had dealt with much over the past year. She was definitely rusty in that area. But Brianna's friendly chatter during their ride to the Orbit put her completely at ease. They talked about the wedding, and all the work Brianna had put into the flowers. Lisa showered her with compliments, leaving out the sneezing.

At the Orbit Lounge and Grill, they slid into a black vinyl booth. The entire place was designed to look like outer space, with black walls and a curved ceiling decorated with glow-in-the-dark stars. Kind of like the ceiling of her motorhome, Lisa realized with a smile.

Brianna introduced her to Suzanne Finnegan Marshall and Merry Warren, who were both around her age. She'd seen Suzanne at the wedding reception—she was the extremely pregnant blond ordering people around. But she hadn't met Merry before. Merry had skin the color of almonds and warm eyes alive with curiosity. A headband held her dark hair back from her face.

"Hi. I'm Lisa."

"I know you." Merry toasted her with her margarita. "You're the Freak."

"Excuse me?"

"The Freak on the Peak. Rollo told me that's an affectionate nickname for the spotters who hang out in those lookout towers." Merry's eyes danced; she definitely lived up to her name. "You have no idea how much I'm dying to interview you. How did you not lose your mind up in there? Didn't you get bored?"

"No, not really. I liked it." She'd *loved* it. But she didn't want to sound like too much of a *freak*. "It was what I needed at the time, I suppose."

"Needed it? Why?" Merry cocked her head. Lisa could see why she was such a good reporter.

"Overworked and under-vacationed," she said lightly. "I was—am—an ER nurse. Pretty much nonstop stress. That tower was kind of like detox. It was so peaceful."

"I could use some time at that tower," Suzanne announced. Her long blond hair was twisted off her neck and her pregnant belly barely fit into the booth. "Josh is driving me crazy. If he offers me one more back rub... Just kidding. I'd marry him ten times over just for those talented hands of his."

Brianna waved a toothpick with a chunk of pineapple at her. "You can stop right there, Mrs. Marshall. I'm still recovering from the overdose of sappy we all experienced at the wedding."

"Oh please. You're the sappiest one of all. Didn't you find those white flowers that look just like stars?"

"She's my oldest friend. I have the right to be sappy."

"You're both a total embarrassment," teased Merry. "It's a good thing I've got enough cynicism for all of us. Anyone needs a dose, come see me."

"Or me," Lisa chimed in. She raised her hand. "Team Cynic over here."

The other women all looked at her with surprise. "Really? You?" Brianna asked. "But you're so romantic-looking."

"*Romantic*-looking?" Lisa laughed. She had no idea what that meant.

"Yes. Just ask Finn. He was tongue-tied at the sight of you. And foot-tied. I thought someone had literally tied his shoelaces together when he practically tripped over himself at the tower." Brianna's green eyes brimmed with laughter. "It was fun to see, after all the times I made a fool of myself over him."

A weird jealous feeling came over Lisa. Had Finn flirted with Brianna too? "You and Finn—"

"Oh no. It was just a crush. A misguided one. Not because he isn't crush-worthy," Bri added quickly. "He absolutely is. He was so nice and patient about my crush. But Rollo's the man for me. It just took a while for me to see the light."

"I can vouch for Finn. He's a very cool guy," said Merry, popping a chip into her mouth.

"So you and Finn..." Brianna asked, lifting her eyebrows at Merry.

Merry shook her head. "Too alike. We can talk up a storm together, but we don't have any sparks. Now Finn and *Lisa*..."

"No, no," she said quickly. Maybe too quickly. "No men for me."

"Amen." Merry reached across the table and high-fived her. "Team Cynic is on a roll."

Suzanne gestured between her and Brianna. "Speaking for Team Romance, some important information has just come to light. Did you hear that Annika Poole broke up with Finn? He's available."

Brianna bounced on her seat, making her drink slosh. "Rollo's so happy he wants to throw him a big bachelor-party-type thing. Like a 'congratulations, you're free' party. Rollo really didn't like Annika, by the way."

"If the Mighty Finn is back on the market, plenty of girls will be throwing a party," said Suzanne.

"I don't know, I think that might be the old Finn." Brianna chewed thoughtfully on her straw. "Rollo says ever since the burnover, he's been different. Like something's eating at him."

"Well, he did nearly die," said Merry logically. "And he had surgery and spent months in rehab. There's no way something like that doesn't change you. I heard he used to be kind of a player but he never acted like that with me."

"Or me, Lord knows," said Brianna mournfully. "I tried to get him to flirt with me but he was so sure I was with Rollo he refused."

"So only one person here has the scoop. Lisa, what's it like to be flirted with by Finn Abrams?" Suzanne lobbed the question so quickly, Lisa didn't have time to deflect.

"Disturbingly fun." She grinned.

The other girls hooted and Merry reached across the table to high-five her again.

Lisa laughed as their palms met. Then she saw a familiar figure push open the door of the Orbit. The rangy form of Deputy Will Knight emerged. She must have reacted, because Merry turned to look over her shoulder.

"Oh, crap on a cracker jack. Deputy Slow-Mo is here. This calls for a refill."

Suzanne gazed at her, fascinated, as she sipped at her virgin margarita. "Merry, I didn't know you had a thing for the hot cop."

"A thing? Like a can't-stand-the-sight-of-his-slow-ass thing? I guess you could say that."

"His ass looks pretty good to me." Brianna was watching him as he headed for the bar. She actually tilted sideways to get a better look. "Yup, looking good. You may go out with him if you choose, Merry."

"I don't choose. I'd rather date a cactus."

"You *are* kind of a cactus," Brianna pointed out. "Emotionally speaking. I should probably mention that he's coming this way."

"Mother—" Merry snapped her mouth shut as the detective strolled next to their table.

"Ladies," he said, nodding a greeting to them all. Did those gray eyes linger on Merry? Lisa couldn't tell. He ended up fixing his gaze on her. "I'm glad I ran into you, Lisa. I have a few more questions for you. Can we set up a time to talk?"

"I really don't—"

"You don't need to talk to him," Merry piped up. "He doesn't have any jurisdiction here. This is JPPD territory, he's with the county."

His eyes flickered to her, then lingered there. His tone was cool when he spoke again. "This is about *your* attempted kidnapping, Ms. Warren. You might show a little more concern."

"*You're* on the case?" She sank back in her seat and folded her arms across her chest. "Great. Might be solved by the time I'm eighty."

He showed no reaction, which earned him big points in Lisa's book. It sure looked to her like Merry was trying to get under his skin. He turned back to Lisa. "Well?"

"I really don't know what else I can do for you, Deputy. I don't know anything more."

"Call me Will. Just a few questions. It won't take long."

"Pfft." Merry snorted. "Won't take long? Tell my editor that. Maybe he'll forgive me for the four deadlines you made me miss."

"I like to do things right," Will said firmly. "They take whatever time they take. Thoroughness is my middle name. Comes in handy in certain situations."

Merry's brown skin turned a little rosier than before. To save her from any more embarrassment, Lisa made a plan to meet Will for coffee the next day.

When he was gone, Brianna and Suzanne both pounced. "Okay, time to dish some dirt here," Suzanne declared. "Merry, you have some explaining to do. You and Will Knight? Is there some sort of history there? And Lisa, what do you have to do with what happened to Merry—oh!" She sucked in a breath. "Hang on."

With a hand on her belly, she closed her eyes. They all held their breath while she rode out whatever sensation she was experiencing. When she opened her eyes, they were shining with laughter. "Just a little love tap from the little guy," she explained. "Don't let us interrupt the spilling of secrets."

"Sorry, Team Cynic is going to plead the fifth," Merry announced. "You'll have to find your gossip elsewhere."

"Boo," Brianna chanted. "This isn't gossip. This is *information*. You're the queen of information, Ms. Best Reporter in Town. Cough it up."

Merry muttered something inaudible into her margarita, so Brianna turned to Lisa. "Oh my God, I just figured it out. That mugger! He was looking for *you*, wasn't he? When he grabbed Merry? Of course he was! You were the girl in the tower he kept jabbering about."

Lisa turned to Merry. "I'm really sorry, Merry. I feel terrible that he hurt you."

"Pfft." Brianna waved her toothpick in the air. "She would have kicked his ass if Rollo hadn't done it first. You should have seen her face."

"I grew up in Brooklyn. No one grabs me without payback." Merry shoved aside her margarita and leaned toward Lisa. "But now you got me curious. Why was he after you?"

Lisa was seriously second-guessing her decision to come to the Orbit. "I probably shouldn't talk about it now that the police are investigating."

She had no idea if that was true, but it sounded plausible.

"Not just any police, but the very handsome Deputy Knight, for that matter." Brianna winked at Merry, who ignored her. She was still focused on Lisa.

"You're pretty new in town, right? How do you like it here so far?" Merry asked her.

"It's great. Everyone's been really nice and welcoming. I love working for Molly McGraw. She's a sweetheart."

Merry tilted her head. "Where'd you come here from? I hear an accent."

"Houston."

"Merry, why are you interrogating her like that?" Suzanne interrupted. "This is supposed to be a nice, friendly drink to welcome Lisa to town."

Merry twisted her face in apology. "Sorry, Lisa. I don't mean to be rude. It's the reporter in me. When I smell an interesting story, I can't resist following up. And the fact that I nearly got kidnapped by someone looking for you— that's definitely a story. Forgive me?"

Lisa stared at the other woman. If only she could explain. If only these were her *friends*. In ordinary circumstances, she could be friends with these women. They were fun, kind, funny, friendly. She missed having friends and being able to vent about anything and everything. "Nothing to forgive," she murmured.

Brianna clapped her hands, breaking the tension. "Let's talk about something else. Rollo and I came up with an amazing plan for a wedding present for Sean and Evie. We're all going to work on it together. Except Suzanne because sorry, babe, you're just too darn pregnant. Lisa, we'd love for you to join in. Are you interested?"

"Sure. Absolutely." She felt a huge smile cross her face. She couldn't share everything with them, but she could offer up her time. At least it was something. "What are we doing?"

"How are you with manual labor?"

CHAPTER EIGHT

Normally, Finn loved a good work party—the kind where a bunch of friends got together to help someone build or repair or clean or paint or move. But that was before the three skin-graft surgeries and months of physical therapy. Once again, he'd overdone it with the workouts and now everything hurt, even pulling on his work pants.

This is nothing compared to firefighting, he reminded himself. *Suck it up.* No way was he going to miss out on Sean and Evie's wedding surprise.

Since last year, the hotshot crew had been talking about helping Sean fix up the old airstrip his family used to own. It had been abandoned since Sean was eighteen, but he'd recently decided to fix it up and sell it. Without Sean's knowledge, his friends had decided this was the perfect time to make it happen. While the newlyweds were roaming around Italy, the crew would be repairing the roof and painting like maniacs.

Finn drove to the hotshot base, where he helped Rollo, Josh and Tim Peavy load one of the rigs with tools. They filled a cooler with ice and beer and headed out to the airstrip.

It was situated close to the shoreline, on an isolated stretch of wind-tossed meadow not far from Stargazer Beach. The constant breeze sent ripples through the high grasses and made the tattered old wind socks dance like raggedy puppets.

Finn strapped on his tool belt and stared dubiously at the ramshackle collection of buildings—two hangars and a reception building—that formed the airstrip. "People are actually willing to get on a plane here?"

"Once upon a time." Josh shrugged. "Sean's father did pretty good business here. Until the crash, obviously. And that turned out to be weather-related."

Finn scanned the buildings. They all looked like they needed some love, but the main reception building was the worst. "All right then. Where do we start?"

Josh pointed at the main building. "Right there. The roof. The inside's in pretty good shape but that roof's about to go." They all strode toward the reception building like some kind of wrecking crew. Jupiter Point Hardware had already delivered the supplies. A pile of roofing metal sat on the tarmac, along with some two-by-fours and other lumber.

"I volunteer to stay on the ground so I don't make the damn roof collapse," said Rollo. "The rest of you lightweights can get your asses up there." Since he had a good three inches on everyone else in the group, no one argued with that plan. Bracing for pain, Finn climbed up to the roof by way of an awning and squatted near the seam that ran the length of the roof.

That wasn't so bad. Not too much soreness. On the other hand, the roof was a mess. He couldn't see one piece of metal roofing that was salvageable.

"Demo time?" he called down to the others.

"Go for it," answered Josh. "Then we can check the boards underneath, see what needs replacing."

Finn took a hammer from his tool belt and worked the first piece of metal away from its screws. The heads were so rusty it came right off. "Head's up," he called down as he tossed it behind the building. He took a moment to look out at the ocean, which was so cheerfully blue it could have been a painting. The offshore islands held a smudge of haze that promised heat later in the day. A slight breeze lifted the hair off the back of his neck. It helped him ignore the soreness of the right side of his body.

It was just scar tissue stretching, he knew. The doctors said it was good to be active. The pain wasn't harming him, so he could bear it. As long as he could shove it to the back of his mind.

He didn't want the guys to know he was still dealing with the effects of his burns. He wanted to be active, to do all the things he used to do. So he was going to stay up on this fricking roof and rip metal away from wood until he was damn well done.

Josh and Tim Peavy joined him on the roof. Right away they got into the same kind of groove Finn remembered from the fire lines. Joking, teasing, real talk—all interspersed with comfortable silence.

Tim was doing his best to scare the crap out of Josh about the baby coming soon. "Treat it like a tornado's gonna hit. Like you gotta stock up on rations and find yourself some shelter. You better learn how to do laundry and dishes and anything the hell else she needs you to do. Changing diapers—that's the least of it. You know what helped us? You're not going to believe this, but get yourself some lavender oil. I'm not even kidding. Really calms you down."

"For the baby?"

"Nah, for you and your wife. Soothing as hell. Just spritz it on your pillows or something. And forget about sex, by the way. Unless it's a quickie. It's like the baby has a sixth sense, like it's nature's way of making sure you don't have another one too soon. You start thinking about sex, boom, baby starts crying. Weirdest thing."

Josh looked gloomily toward the ground, which was at least twenty feet down. "Are you trying to make me jump off or something? Finn, stop laughing. This could be you someday."

"Not laughing." Finn tried to straighten out his grin. "Just exercising my facial muscles. It's a burn thing."

"Riiiight. Speaking of which, the guys and I have been talking." Tim and Josh exchanged a glance. Josh pried off another sheet of metal and sent it sailing onto the pile.

"You're going to talk to Sean when he gets back, right? About getting on the crew?"

He tensed. Rollo must have let that slip. "I'm thinking about it."

"You should," said Tim Peavy. "We're gonna need someone, because ol' Josh here is about to be MIA in the BBL."

"The what?"

"Babyland. That's what Rosario and I call it."

Josh snorted as he pulled off the last of the roofing sheets. "The hell with that. I'm going to be back in no time. No baby tornado is going to stop me. I'll take some time with Suzanne, work on my hotshot YouTube channel, then get back to work."

"See, that's the thing. You're going to *want* to be home with them. You won't want to fly off to Montana at zero dark thirty." Peavy shook his head. "Nope, you'd better get your ass ready to jump in, Finn. And we're going to help you. We have two weeks to get you in top shape before Marcus gets back. Then another month until we have to report. You can do this."

"Yeah?"

"Dude." Josh slid a sheet of metal off the roof and wiped his forehead with the back of his hand. "You were rookie of the year. You're an animal when it comes to training. And with the rest of us kicking your ass, you're a shoo-in."

"I might have to go somewhere else if I want on a crew."

"Fuck that. You belong here," said Josh.

Finn had to look away, a surge of emotion catching him by surprise. Did he really belong here? For sure, LA wasn't home anymore. But he might have a better chance getting on a hotshot crew that wasn't run by Sean Marcus. Something in Alaska or Arizona.

But he didn't want to leave Jupiter Point. This was where he wanted to be.

Plus, there was Lisa.

In fact, literally—there was Lisa. Getting out of Brianna's red truck, which had just pulled up next to the reception building.

Surprised, Finn made a sudden movement that nearly sent him sliding off the roof. He clutched the roof beam to keep from tumbling at her feet in a pile of sweaty man. Jesus, was there no end to the ways in which he could embarrass himself in front of this woman?

He took another peek at her. God, she looked good in a pair of snug blue jeans tucked into hiking boots. She wore a dark green fitted hoodie that clung to every soft curve. Her dark hair hung down her back in a sleek braid and she wore an Astros baseball cap. She was smiling at Rollo, who staggered slightly as Brianna leaped into his arms.

She must have felt his stare, because she glanced up, her eyes meeting his from under the bill of the cap. Her smile dropped slightly, then came back—but different. More cautious.

Of course she was cautious. He'd been rude to her at Sean's wedding. Damn it. He didn't want things to be uncomfortable between them. He wanted her to smile at him with just as much ease as she smiled at Rollo, the big bastard.

He waved at her, hoping it came off as confident and casual, rather than terrified that he might lose his grip on the roof beam. Of all moments to see Lisa again. He had the worst damn luck with this girl. Maybe it really was destiny—karmic payback for all his misbehavior back in LA.

From behind him, Josh snorted. "Dude, if you're going to play Romeo, you need to be the one on the ground."

"Would you get off—" he started to snarl at his friend, then realized that was a bad idea. "Would you help me down from here?" he asked in a lower voice. "I might have overdone it a little."

Josh got it instantly. He might joke around a lot, but he was always there when you needed him. "Hey, Rollo! I got a cramp in my leg. How about you set up that ladder?"

Once Rollo had anchored the ladder into place, Josh gripped Finn's forearm and helped him get his left foot securely onto one of the rungs. "You got it?" he asked in a low voice.

"Yeah, I'm good from here. Thanks, man."

"No worries. I didn't know—"

"It's okay. No biggie, just some residual tightness in the scars. I'm working it out. Mostly it's fine, I just have to keep moving. Don't...don't say anything, okay?"

Josh hesitated. Finn knew what he was thinking. If his mobility was compromised, he shouldn't be working wild-fires.

"You know something, Josh? I'm going to take you guys up on that training offer. I could use the help."

The other fireman grinned broadly. "Now you're talk-ing. I can't wait to kick your ass up and down Heart Attack Hill."

"Keep dreaming, daddy-o. I'll be so far ahead, you'll be stuck in last week."

"Now get your ass down there and flirt with the tower girl."

Finn flipped him the bird. Universal sign for "we're cool now."

CHAPTER NINE

Lisa tried not to feast her eyes on the sight of Finn descending the ladder in faded work pants and a tool belt. A *tool belt.* That thing looked much too good on him. It wasn't remotely fair. It wasn't right that he should have extra color in his face from being out in the sun and that his hair was all rough and tumbled from the breeze up on the roof. And when he reached the ground, the smile he flashed her ought to come with an extra dose of oxygen. Because she couldn't quite catch her breath afterwards.

That smile was so potent, it almost distracted her from how much he was limping as he came toward her. But not quite. Not that she planned on mentioning his limp, after she'd put her foot in it last time.

"We're here to help out!" Brianna called from the safety of Rollo's embrace. "We brought snacks and our willing and able bodies."

Rollo growled something in her ear that made her blush. Despite her determination not to, Lisa glanced at Finn. He looked like he was trying hard not to laugh.

"You always know just how to put things," Finn told Brianna solemnly.

Brianna stuck her tongue out at him. "Watch out, or I'll explain the life cycle of the birch beetle again."

"At the larval stage, they're encased in a hard shell, which they lose upon reaching their adult stage," he recited with a wink. "And you thought I wasn't paying attention."

Brianna and Rollo burst out laughing. "I tend to get carried away when it comes to certain topics," she explained to Lisa. "Everyone knows to just tune me out if I start talking about biodiversity or other absolutely riveting subjects. Except Finn, apparently."

The funny thing was, Lisa could have told Brianna that would be the case. Even though she didn't know Finn, not really, she knew things *about* him. She already knew he paid attention to details. Just look at how he'd recognized her from that silly photo. She knew that he tuned in easily to other people's emotions. Even at the tower, when she thought she wanted to be alone, she was wrong. The highlight of that hiking trip was that brief encounter with Finn.

That was what made him so charming, in fact. The other day, Molly had listed off all the nice things he'd done for her—bought her an Audible subscription for her birthday, sent her postcards from LA, and of course, flowers every time he came to Jupiter Point. His charm came from his thoughtfulness.

Oh God. Please don't let her develop some kind of *crush* on the guy.

"So how can we help?" she asked the group. Josh and Tim had joined them on the tarmac.

"How much carpentry have you done?"

"Um...zero?" She laughed. "But if anyone has an injury, I'm your girl. Maybe I should just be the standby medic. How's everyone feeling so far?"

She saw Josh slide a glance at Finn, whose jaw tightened.

"Great," Finn said. It was perfectly obvious to her that he wasn't doing great. Macho men and their pride.

Josh snorted. "I may have gotten a splinter. It's a real pain in my ass. Or something is, anyway."

"Such a funny guy." Finn rolled his eyes. "No one needs medical attention, unless it's Peavy from postpartum male stress. And Josh from prepartum male panic."

"Damn, does that cause baldness? Cuz the world can't afford to lose a work of art like this." Clowning around, Josh grabbed at his shaggy blond hair. Finn cuffed him in the shoulder while Rollo and Tim Peavy laughed.

Brianna spoke to Lisa in a stage whisper. "In case you wondered, yes, they're always like this. It's a wonder they ever manage to put out a fire the way they never stop joking around. It's like they're in a sorority or something. Kappa Delta Dumbass." The affectionate way she wrapped her arms around Rollo's middle took the sting out of her teasing words.

The men laughed good-naturedly.

"Kappa Delta Dumbass, I like it." Josh mused, stroking his chin. "Join for the laughs, stay for the life-threatening situations."

Brianna made a face at him. "Great, make me feel bad. You know I'm teasing. And you can't be mad, because Rollo saved your life and I'm engaged to Rollo. So it's almost like I saved your life."

As they all continued to tease each other, Lisa once again found her gaze drifting to Finn. Even though he was laughing as much of the others, she knew he felt apart from them. It was his body language, the way he hung back just a little, the way he let Josh take center stage, the slight hesitation before he chimed in with a comment.

As a newcomer, she was the most apart. But Finn was too, and she couldn't imagine why. He was a fireman just like the others, just as fit and good-looking and confident. Why wasn't he right in the thick of things like Josh?

And why was she so curious about him anyway?

After much discussion, they decided to eat the sandwiches she and Brianna had brought, then figure out the next phase of the cleanup. Lisa volunteered to get the cooler from the truck, and before she knew it, Finn was walking beside her.

"Listen, Lisa. I want to apologize for my rudeness at the wedding. I didn't mean to brush you off like that when you asked about my limp. Most people never notice it, so you caught me off guard. I like to pretend it isn't there, but that's just stupid."

"It's not stupid. I can understand that. You're a physically fit guy who works with his body. It's no wonder it's hard to adjust."

Even that comment seemed to make him uncomfortable. "Yeah. I hope to be one hundred percent someday very soon."

She didn't say anything to that. Based on her experience, he'd never be *exactly* the same again. Scar tissue didn't behave the same as unmarred skin. But maybe that dream would motivate him.

"Don't hold back. I can take it," Finn said.

"Excuse me?"

"You look like you want to say something. Something I don't necessarily want to hear."

"You can guess all that? I didn't say anything."

"Not out loud."

At the truck, Lisa reached into the bed for the cooler. Finn did the same thing at exactly the same time, and their arms brushed. A spangle of sensation made her heart skip a beat. "I can get this," she told him.

"As can I." The stubborn set of his jaw made her draw back and cede the cooler to him.

"Look, you really don't have to prove anything to me. I'm a nurse. I can tell you overdid it on the roof and now you're trying to pretend everything's just peachy. But guess what? You can pretend all you want, but your body knows best. Your body knows exactly what's going on."

He swung the cooler over the side of the truck, then put it on the ground. With one arm braced on the truck bed, he narrowed his dark eyes at her. This close, she saw they were several shades lighter than brown, shot through with amber and copper. "Okay, then. You tell me. What's going on with my body?"

Her throat went dry. He smelled so good, like sunshine and sweat. "I'm not your doctor."

He leaned closer, voice lowering to a growl. "And I'm not your patient. I'm asking anyway."

She swallowed hard. She didn't know why Finn had decided to aim his incredible charm at her. Of all the women who probably wanted his attention, why her? She had no defense against it except to repeat her "low profile" mantra. And she could barely remember it when he was looking at her like that.

She scrambled for an answer. Her brain cells seemed to have left her high and dry. "I can't really give you a good answer without a thorough, hands-on," she swallowed even though her throat had gone tight, "evaluation."

He stared at her. Her blood pumped in her ears. Awareness jumped between them, vibrating like a bass guitar string.

She groaned silently. What had made her throw that "hands-on" in there? It sounded much too flirtatious. Which it wasn't. Or was it?

He flashed a sudden grin. "Damn, I just figured it out. I'm doing this all wrong."

"What are you talking about?"

"You win."

"I do?"

"You do. You just won yourself a patient."

She stared at him.

"I'm treating you like the medical professional you are. I need your help, Lisa. As you probably know, I was injured in a fire and suffered extensive burns along the right side of my body. My doctors are back in LA, so I've been on my own with the rehab. I haven't been doing so well with it and I'm worried that I'm backsliding. And I can't do that. I need to get back on a hotshot crew. I'm about to kick my training into high gear and I need your help. I need you, Lisa Peretti."

"I have a job."

"You have a part-time job. I happen to know you only spend three afternoons a week with Molly. I think you can squeeze me in. And the fact is, I was hurt in the line of duty. No nurse with a conscience could turn me down." Clearly, he believed he'd outfoxed her. His wide smile said it all.

But she had a few tricks up her sleeve.

"Fine." She folded her arms across her chest. "You're right, I can't turn down a request for my help, especially because I have some experience with burn scars. I helped my grandfather recover from a kitchen accident. You remind me of him."

He winced, but his smile only dropped a little.

"You're staying at Rollo's, right? I'll come to his place on my next day off, which is in two days. And now that I've accepted the job, you should know that I never date patients." Now it was her turn to smile at him triumphantly. Boom.

But all he did was raise an eyebrow. "That just proves how confident I am in your skills. I'll be cured in no time. Let's pencil in dinner for, say, a month from now?"

She laughed. Darn it, how did he always do this to her? "Let's start with the rehab for now. By the time we're through, you might hate me. They didn't call me Nurse Badass for nothing."

He bent down to pick up the cooler, his muscles flexing under the thermal fabric. The intense look he gave her from under those dark eyelashes made her shiver. "I almost wish I could hate you. It would make a nice change from wanting to rip your clothes off."

He headed back to the others while she stood there, her nerves jumping all over the place. Pretty soon, he'd be taking *his* clothes off and she'd be putting her hands all over his body. Heaven help her. Sure, she had experience with burn scars. But she'd never worked with anyone who radiated sex appeal the way Finn did.

CHAPTER TEN

When Finn got back to Rollo's guesthouse after the work party, an email from the private investigator waited for him.

I found a news article from Rhode Island that could be a good lead. Do you have the funds for a trip to the East Coast?

Finn scanned the article, which was very brief. A family by the name of Joao had been killed in a house fire exactly twenty-five years ago. They were an immigrant family from Portugal that lived in a rundown duplex that probably had expired fire extinguishers. A three-year-old child had been rescued from the scene. The photo accompanying the article showed a crying baby wrapped in a blanket, held in the arms of a firefighter in full bunker gear.

He stared at it, examining every detail, hoping it would jog his memory. Had that blanket belonged to him? Was that the firefighter who had burst into the room in an orange halo of flames? The one who had pulled him from the toy chest and run with him toward the window? In his memories, they'd flown out the window like birds, but his grown-up mind knew there must have been a ladder.

He couldn't be sure, but it was definitely worth a flight to Rhode Island. He emailed the go-ahead to Ericsson.

Then he went to the bathroom and popped some Tylenol for his soreness. He stared in the mirror as he swallowed it down. His scar ran from cheekbone to jaw, but it didn't touch his eye socket. One inch higher and he could have lost his eye. Or the scar could have changed the shape of his eye.

He knew how lucky he was that it hadn't been worse. He liked the scar on his face, as if he'd been marked by fire. The scars on his body, on the other hand...

He lifted his shirt to remind himself—or maybe to check if they had magically healed in the meantime. Nope. Still ugly as hell. Ridges of scar tissue made up a kind of topographical map of flesh. Some of the scars were angry scarlet, some were flamingo pink, others the color of mucus. The one time Annika had seen him without a shirt, she'd gagged. The doctors had suggested more plastic surgery, but he refused. He couldn't bear another stint in the hospital. They'd never fix all the scars anyway, and he wanted to spend his savings on a detective, not more doctors.

And now Lisa was about to see the whole gruesome sight.

He left his shirt off—the sensation of cloth against the scar tissue still unnerved him. Then he sat down at his laptop and did some searching for the name Joao. It turned out to be one of the most common names in the Portuguese language.

He remembered the voice of his mother, like the low murmur of a lullaby, but he remembered it in English, not a foreign language. Or was his mind automatically translating it into the language he knew best? Wouldn't he remember some Portuguese words if he was really Elias Joao?

He wasn't even sure why he was pursuing this. If this news article was correct, his birth parents had died in the fire that he remembered. What was the point of tracking down the truth, battling Stu, shelling out money for an investigator?

He squinted at the caption on the photograph. "Providence firefighter Joe Pike rescues child from house fire."

Ericsson would be pursuing this lead. He should just let the man do his job. But instead he pulled up a travel site and punched in a search for flights to Providence. Maybe that firefighter would remember a face better if it was right in front of him.

*

Rollo Wareham lived in a sprawling cliff-top property with a stunning view of the Pacific Ocean. Lisa had heard that he came from a wealthy banking family, even though she never would have believed it from his down-to-earth manner. When she knocked at his door, massage supplies in hand, he answered in bare feet and sweatpants.

"Sorry, Finn's not here." The big, bearded man scratched at the back of his neck. "He's been gone a couple of days. Want to leave a message?"

"Yes." *You're a jackass*, that was what she wanted to say to Finn. "No. That's okay, we must have got our signals crossed. He hired me to do some post-burn therapy with him."

A funny expression crossed his face. "Doesn't sound like something he'd want to miss. Lord knows he could use it. He's been a mess since the burnover."

"No, not that kind of therapy. I'm a certified nurse. I've had good success with some massage techniques...never mind." Why was she explaining herself to him? "Just tell him I came by and maybe we'll try again some other time."

But probably not. The fact that she'd been looking forward to this appointment was a big huge red flag. The fact that he'd missed it—even bigger. Finn had probably gone back to Hollywood and found another actress to date.

Rollo's kind blue eyes held hers. "I'm sure there's an explanation. Finn's a solid guy. Don't write him off."

She shrugged and turned away, back to her ancient Mercedes.

Just then, a silver SUV whipped around the curve of Rollo's driveway and screeched to a halt next to her car. The driver's side door flew open and Finn jumped out. With a thick growth of black stubble and bleary eyes, he looked as if he'd driven all night, or maybe just come off a bender. That was bad enough, but the fact that he still looked so good that her mouth watered—that was a problem.

"Lisa, you're here. Sorry I'm late," he said in a rush as he came toward her.

"It's no problem." She sidestepped him and heaved her bag into the backseat of her Mercedes. "Maybe another time."

"You aren't leaving, are you? We have an appointment."

"Which you missed."

"I only missed five minutes of it." He dug out his phone and checked the time. "I took the redeye to make sure I got here on time. Then I broke every speed limit between here and the airport."

She eyed him warily. "Why didn't you text me?"

"Maybe because you refuse to give me your number." He reached past her, dragged her bag out and slung it over his shoulder. "Come on, my gorgeous medical professional. I need you. A night without sleep in an airplane is definitely not what the doctor ordered."

She felt herself soften. He was just so irresistible with that puppy-dog look in his eyes. And he was playing on her soft spot—she couldn't turn her back on someone who needed her. "Fine. On one condition. You tell me where you went and what you were doing."

If he was attending a red-carpet premiere with a supermodel, she wanted to know. If he was on a date with Annika, she wanted to know. Sure, it wasn't the kind of information a medical professional would ask for. But this was Finn, and he was getting under her skin, and she had to put a stop to it.

A shadow crossed his face, but he shook it off. "All right. Your wish is my command." He took her hand and led her toward a cozy little building with black shutters at the other end of the lawn. "But it might take a while. And I need breakfast first."

Inside his little guesthouse, he downed a big glass of water and got some coffee going in a glass French press. The guesthouse was pure flowery Laura Ashley, as if someone's grandmother had decorated it, which was such a contrast to Finn's dark and masculine good looks it was almost comical. She settled into an armchair.

He handed her a mug of steaming-hot coffee, then lowered himself onto the couch, stretching out his legs with a long sigh.

She turned the mug in her hands and laughed. It showed a picture of a bare-chested fireman with the words "Let Me Heat That Up for You" printed on it.

"Cute mug." She gazed closer at the fireman. "He even kind of looks like you."

"He is me. One of my dad's girlfriends made it for me. She felt bad that my dad hated my career choice so much."

"Why did he hate it? Most people admire firefighters."

His smile dropped. "Long story. You know, I've been drawn to fire as long as I can remember. My father wanted me to be an actor or a producer or a screenwriter—anything in the movies. But I wasn't interested. I never liked Hollywood. My whole life, I wanted to be a firefighter. Fire was the most compelling thing in the world to me. And I never knew why until the burnover in Big Canyon. Something happened then. No one knows about it except

Rollo. But I know I can trust you. Doctor-patient confidentiality, right?"

She stared at him in surprise. "You could trust me anyway. I'm pretty good with secrets, although I'm terrible at lies."

He laughed and dug the heel of his hand into his forehead. She fought the urge to offer him a neck rub.

"I blacked out during that fire, when we were supposed to deploy our tents. I had a...well, I guess it was a flashback. Like a buried memory."

He told her the whole story, from the wildfire to his flashback, to his father's stonewalling, to his trip to Rhode Island to find a fireman from twenty-five years ago. It was like listening to the plot of a movie, except with all the real emotion Finn poured into it.

"Did you find the fireman?" she asked when he reached the end.

"I did. Joe Pike. He kind of squinted at me and said, 'well, maybe, couldn't say for sure.' But when I went to the neighborhood where the house was located, an old lady walking her Pomeranian thought she recognized me. Of course, she also thought I was the prince of Spain, so that could mean anything."

God, that grin. She wished it came with a remote control so she could turn it down. Last night, she'd lain in bed under her starry fabric sky, thinking about Finn. That killer smile. The wicked gleam that chased away the sadness in his eyes. His amazing physique. And more—his vulnerability. His determination. She liked that. A lot. It made her think he could be trusted. Finn might be funny and loose and charming, but underneath all that, she sensed a core of real strength.

She shook herself back to reality. "So you're back to square one."

"Yup." He blew on his coffee to cool it. "But my investigator is on the job. I'll get there. I'm persistent. But you probably know that about me."

And...there came that smile again. Her pulse fluttered and jumped. For some reason, his story made him even more appealing. Maybe because she too had always felt out of place in her own family.

"You know what I've been wondering?"

"What's that?"

"Well, you definitely are persistent. You've been asking me out practically ever since you met me. Why me?"

He squinted at her. "Seems pretty obvious to me. Why do you think?"

"I suppose because I seem like some kind of challenge since I turned you down the first time. Maybe you're not used to rejection."

He lifted one eyebrow. "You saw me get rejected at the wedding. By Annika."

"Yes, but, that was...that was Annika. And that's now. What about before? From what I hear, you've dated half the models in Hollywood."

The expression on his face made her shift uncomfortably. She hadn't meant to insult him. He tossed back a shot of coffee. "Don't believe everything you hear. Yeah, I liked to party back then. Anything to get out of the house. Depending on who my dad was dating, it was either a war zone or the loneliest place in LA. So yup. I partied. What about you?"

"Nope. I studied." She flashed a smile at him. "But I do know what you mean. My parents divorced when I was seven. Both of them remarried. I ping-ponged back and forth and it sucked. My mother divorced again, then again. She's on her fourth husband now. I acquired a few stepsisters and ex-stepsisters along the way. I know the whole war-zone feeling. And the lonely feeling."

Under his sympathetic gaze, she felt a wave of heat travel slowly up her face, from her neck to her hairline. Oh no, not The Blush. She hated when her emotions wrote themselves across her skin in living color. A mortifying shade of red, no doubt.

"You're blushing. That's...fascinating."

If anything, the heat in her face got more intense. "Why? It's a perfectly normal physiological process."

"Because you're supposed to be Nurse Badass. Nurse Badass, blushing?"

God, should she open a window or something? Maybe pour water over her head? "You don't have a freezer by chance, do you? If I could just stick my head in it for a moment, that would be great."

97

He laughed, teeth flashing against his stubbled jaw. "Believe me, it's adorable. I could watch you blush all day."

She closed her eyes and pressed her hands against her cheeks to cool them down. So much for being a medical professional. Jesus.

When she opened her eyes again, his expression was all business. "This is my fault, anyway. I didn't intend to hijack my appointment with all this personal stuff. We should probably get to it, but if you want to reschedule, I'll understand."

"No, no. I'm here. Willing and able." She seized onto his change of topic with a massive sense of relief, as if they'd stepped back from the edge of a cliff. Nursing, she could handle. "When my grandfather had his flan accident and got burned, he didn't trust the doctors to work on him. I took a course on burn-specific massage techniques. They worked really well for him and I imagine they would for you too. I suggest we start slow because it can be somewhat painful."

"That's nothing new," he muttered. "Isn't all PT painful? Bring it on, Nurse Badass. Where and how should we do this?"

"Well, I brought a yoga mat. You can lie on that, in whatever way feels most comfortable. We'll just clear a space next to you."

"I got that part." He stood up and lifted the coffee table out of the way, plopping it in a corner of the room. She spread out the yoga mat in the center of the living room, making sure there was plenty of room to move around it, then sat on her heels next to it.

He came back to stand near her. She glanced up, surprised to see him hesitate, a vulnerable expression crossing his face. "Shirt on or off?"

Ah, of course. He felt uncomfortable showing her the full extent of his scarring. She'd just have to be extra professional to put him at ease. It would be a lot easier in a more official medical setting, and without the sexual awareness that hung between them. But she could do it.

"Shirt off. Take everything off except your underwear. It's best if I get a complete picture of what we're dealing with."

He nodded once, his expression darkening. She saw his Adam's apple move up and down as he swallowed. "It's not a pretty sight, I should warn you."

"Believe me, I've seen it all. You don't have to worry."

After just a little more hesitation, he put his hands to the lower edge of his black t-shirt and lifted it over his head.

And she realized how wrong she was.

CHAPTER ELEVEN

Dead wrong. She did have to worry, not because of his scars but because of the rest of his spectacular torso. He looked as if he'd been chiseled by a master sculptor who had lost patience and flung handfuls of clay over one half of his work. Muscles rippled and flexed as he draped his t-shirt across the back of his chair.

What had she been thinking? This was lunacy. No way could she put her hands on this man and not lose her carefully achieved cool.

"It's bad, huh?" His face was turned away from her as he spoke in a low voice. "If you want to back out, I understand."

Yes, she wanted to back out. Because a certain sensation was vaulting through her lower belly right now. Want. Desire. *Sexual* desire. Crap. Crap crap crap. She cleared her throat.

"Of course not. It's not so bad. I've definitely seen worse." She focused on his scarring. It covered the left side of his rib cage, all the way down to his hip. It was probably tough for him to twist and bend. She was amazed that he'd climbed onto a roof and stayed in a hunched position for so long. He must have impressive pain tolerance, which wasn't necessarily a good thing. Healing took time, and patients with no patience could set back their recovery by months. "I'm going to ask the classic pain question. One to ten, with ten being the worst, where is it right now?"

"About a three. Pretty good, considering I've been on an airplane."

"What other activities aggravate it?"

"Exercise in general can be challenging. Running is fine unless I trip and have to twist or something. Swimming isn't too bad. It's more of a controlled environment." He put his hands to the fastening of his jeans and her mouth went dry again.

Oops, she'd told him to take his pants off too. She shouldn't have done that. Seriously, she wasn't made of stone here! She opened her mouth to rescind that part of the request, but nothing came out. That was because he was in the midst of revealing the most muscular thighs she'd ever witnessed up close. Every inch of his physique was fit and honed and bronzed. Under his jeans, he wore a pair of black boxer briefs that were filled in a snug way that had her turning red again.

She averted her gaze before it became too obvious that she was staring. As she took out the salves she worked with, she kept taking little peeks from the corners of her eyes. Almost as if she couldn't believe what she was seeing. Were his abs really that ripped? Were his shoulders actually that wide and solid? He wasn't overly buff, not like someone who spent a lot of time pumping iron or juicing up on steroids. He was just...perfect. His long torso was a graceful V, his waist narrowing from those wide shoulders into slim hips. Not one particle of flab appeared anywhere on his body. He was all lean, sleek perfection. And his legs looked so insanely strong, as if he could run up the side of a mountain without blinking.

Which he probably could.

She wondered why the scars didn't detract from his appeal, at least to her. She remembered Annika's description of his "deformity." How could she see someone like Finn, a brave, injured, gorgeous fireman, as deformed just because of some damaged skin?

She must have been muttering something about that, because Finn said, "What was that?"

"Oh nothing, I was just thinking bad things about Annika."

He lifted one eyebrow. "What, that she'd walk away from all this?" He struck a muscle-man pose. "Nah. It was all an act anyway. Maybe you didn't pick up on that part."

"What do you mean, an act?"

"To promote the movie. You know, injured firefighter, angelic actress. I went along with it because she was a sweetheart to me after the burnover. Another act, though I didn't know it." He rubbed the dark stubble on his jaw. "The tabloids loved it. Not that you would know about that, because you probably never read that trash."

And...there went The Blush heating her face again. If he only knew how many times she'd read that article about him and Annika. She still hadn't returned it to the

Moon Glow, as a matter of fact. She made a mental note to do that immediately. Well, as soon as she read it one more time, with this new knowledge.

Finn had never been with Annika at all? Wow. That changed things. She wasn't sure how, but it did.

Lisa made herself stop ogling his body and switch into Nurse Badass mode. "It's none of my business anyway. You don't have to explain anything to your massage therapist."

"Right." He smiled wryly. "I forgot for a minute and thought I was just standing here in my underwear for the hell of it."

She smiled at him. "Come on, let's get going before you freeze. Please lie down in whatever position feels best to you."

He whooshed out a deep breath then lowered himself onto his knees on the mat. Gingerly, he stretched out on his side, with the burned area facing her. He dragged a pillow under his head and shifted around until he found a position that worked. Instead of watching his body, she kept her gaze on his face, noticing every wince and twitch of pain.

When he was still, she scooped a dollop of cream into her hand. For her grandfather, she'd developed a mixture of Vitamin E oil, Calendula, aloe vera, and lavender to keep the scars soft and moist.

"One great thing about massage is that the pressure helps take away that itchy feeling. Have you had much of that?"

"Oh yeah."

Starting at the outer edge of the scarred area, she gently stretched the scar tissue with small, steady movements. He didn't react beyond tightening his jaw and closing his eyes.

"When I did this with my grandfather, he used to curse at me in Spanish. That's how I knew how much pressure to use. If he started in on anything related to 'porco,' or 'dios,' I had to ease back."

He grunted, his right eyelid twitching. "I'm not going to curse. I'm a big strong mother-effing fireman who doesn't curse. Not fucking ever."

She laughed. It was truly amazing how easily he made her laugh. "I know it hurts. It's okay, you can just let it out."

"That's okay. I'm still trying to impress you. Can't you tell? Why else would I show off my scars? I'm being sarcastic, by the way. And I'm trying to distract myself from your...mother of God!" He moaned. "I'm pretty sure this is banned by the Geneva Convention. Or it ought to be."

There went one of her grandfather's telltale words. "I'll lighten up."

"Fuck no. If your grandfather could take it, I can. Big strong tough fireman here."

She shifted to the area along his laterals, trying desperately not to focus on the bronzed washboard abs just inches from her fingers. "Haven't you heard the news, Finn? This is the twenty-first century, it's okay for men to show their vulnerability. You don't always have to be the Mighty Finn."

"I'm pretty sure I'm winning the gold medal in showing my vulnerability right now. I look like raw hamburger. Come on, help me out here. Distract me. Tell me something good."

"Something good?" She applied more oil to her hands and smoothed her fingers down his side. Touching someone, even in a medical capacity, always created a connection. This was what she loved—tending to people, taking care of them. In the months since leaving Houston, she'd missed it. First Molly, now Finn—it felt good, like getting her life back.

"I can recite a delicious recipe for flan. That's good."

"Do it. I beg you."

She rattled off the instructions for her grandmother's specialty.

"God, that sounds incredible. Someday maybe you'll invite me over for flan." His jaw clenched as she stretched an especially tender spot.

She laughed. "I don't date patients, I told you."

"It's not a date, it's flan. How many times have you eaten flan in your life?"

"I'm part-Cuban, so probably hundreds." Her gaze slid across his broad shoulders to the dark hair curling over his ears. She wanted to run her hands through it, but kept them where they belonged.

"Were all those flan-eating occasions dates?"

"Of course not."

"There you go. No date. Just flan." He sighed and shifted his position, making his muscles flex under his olive skin. "So who do you date, Lisa Peretti? No patients, no strangers in lookout towers. Who's left?"

"Well..." She hesitated, wondering if this was too personal a direction to go in. "Actually, I haven't dated much. I've been mainly focused on my nursing career."

"Huh. What are you, late-twenties? Mid-twenties?"

"I'm twenty-eight. I've been busy with school, the ER, and so forth. It's a draining profession." Getting defensive, she dug her fingers too deeply into his muscles. "Sorry."

"I can take it as long as you keep distracting me. Keep talking. What inspired you to become a nurse?"

She gave a maniacal laugh. "So I can have big strong firemen at my mercy, bwahaha."

He snorted. "Seriously. I want to know."

"Well..." She thought back on her time in the ER, all the highs and the lows—and her breaking point. "As a nurse, you're the person who's there when people are going through some of the scariest times in their lives. They're in a crisis and they're terrified. They're at their most vulnerable. And to know that I have the skills to help, even if I can't cure whatever they have, just to be there for them, it's very satisfying."

"Then you're just like firemen. You run into the crisis, not away. Fires for us, medical disasters for you nurses. We're just alike, underneath."

She laughed. "I never thought of it that way."

They fell silent as she worked on the lower perimeter of his scar mass, where it impacted his hip.

"But now you're not working in the ER anymore. What happened?" he asked.

"Oh..." Better keep this answer vague. "I needed a break. It's emotionally overwhelming. Right now, I have one patient and that's all I can handle. Well, two, I suppose, counting you."

He tilted his head to smile at her, but she gently pressed it back to the mat. "So you're a beautiful, intelligent, kind-of-secretive, badass ER nurse with divorced parents who spends all her time at work and never dates. It's all starting to make sense now."

"It is?"

"Yup. You have intimacy issues. Textbook case."

She laughed out loud. "Thanks for the diagnosis. Aren't you supposed to be the patient in this scenario?"

"I am. I'm very patient. I'm patiently figuring you out, piece by piece. You care about people, or you wouldn't be working in a healing profession. But you like to keep them at a distance. You have that electric fence around you for a reason."

"Right, better watch out or you'll get zapped," she teased.

"You think I'm afraid of getting zapped? I'm not." He twitched his shoulder to draw attention to his burns. "Big tough fireman, remember?"

She was having a hard time forgetting, with all his chiseled muscles and scarred skin.

"You'll see, one of these days you'll turn off the electric fence and invite me over for flan," Finn said.

"Not a chance. There's no space. I live in a motorhome." She sucked in a breath, stunned by how easily that secret had slipped out. Not even Molly knew about her motorhome.

"A motorhome?" He rolled over onto his back and snagged her wrist in mid-stroke. "You fascinate me, Lisa. Why are you so fascinating?" Her eyes widened. She was still on her knees, leaning over him. Electric attraction sizzled between them. Her ponytail slid off her shoulder and brushed his chest. Even that contact gave her a jolt, as if she had nerve endings in the strands of her hair.

"I'm not fascinating. I'm perfectly ordinary."

"Not to me." His intense gaze captured her and refused to let her go. "I want to know everything about you. What you think, what you feel, *how* you feel, how you taste."

He tugged her closer. A drumbeat of desire pulsed between her thighs. Oh, this was not good. Not good at all.

"I'm insanely attracted to you, Lisa. And unless I'm crazy, you're attracted to me too."

She bit her lip. Too bad she was such a bad liar. If she tried to deny it, he'd know in a flash. He could already read her so well. "Yes," she admitted. "Fine, I'm attracted to you. You're attractive. There's chemistry. Sparks. And of course I feel them. I'm a nurse, not a nun."

He studied her face intently. "Then what are you afraid of? It's not the scars. They don't bother you. We're not in some kind of real professional setting with rules. No one's going to care if we kiss."

If we kiss.

The idea set off wild sparks in every direction. Kiss Finn? *Oh yes.* Her body was practically throwing a party at the thought. Her nipples tightened, liquid heat spread through her lower body. She imagined his sexy mouth pressed against hers, his scruff scraping against her soft skin. Her tongue tingled. She pressed it to the roof of her mouth.

This was crazy. She shook her head to break the spell.

Then her practical side took over. Kissing Finn would be just like kissing anyone else. Anti-climactic. After all, kissing was tricky. It was so easy to overdo it. To be honest, kissing had never lived up to her expectations. Not once. In her opinion, it was an extremely overrated activity.

Yes, that was it! The answer came like a flashing neon sign. If she kissed Finn, she could shake this silly attraction-slash-crush she was developing. If he was at all slobbery or overeager or clumsy with his kiss, she'd be over him—just like that.

And really, the chances were good that she'd find *something* to object to. The last time she'd kissed someone—a doctor she'd dated briefly—all kinds of thoughts had wandered through her head. *I don't like how his teeth feel. Did I get Mrs. Carter her meds yet? What's the world record for longest kiss? What about shortest? Can we go for that?*

Kissing Finn was the perfect solution.

"What's going on in that brain of yours?" Finn asked, amusement curving his lips. She took in the scruff around his mouth. It would probably scrape her skin and break the mood. He still looked tired from his redeye flight. This was the perfect moment; the kiss would suck, and she could forget about Finn.

"I was just...thinking..." Instead of finishing her sentence, she drew in a long breath and dove in. *Bad kiss coming up.*

Her lips met his. *His breath is so sweet.* That was her first thought. And then, *Sweet mercy, that feels good.*

And then, *Oh crap. Big miscalculation.*

It took him no time to catch up with her. He went from surprise to kissing the hell out of her in about half a second. He took charge of the kiss immediately, his lips warm and firm. His tongue urged her lips apart, gently touched hers, drew her in, intoxicated her with every smooth sweep and tug. His hands came to her head and held her still. She melted into his grip, feeling all hesitation and tension drain away. She closed her eyes and lost track of where she was.

Finn kissed like a champion, as if he'd been born and bred for it, as if he could read her mind and know exactly what would feel best. He kissed as if they had all the time in the world, as if nothing mattered except the two of them, right now.

It felt as if she were flying through a velvet-dark sky lit up with sparks. She could soar forever like this, coasting on wings of pleasure.

Then it shifted, the kiss going deeper, as if Finn was telling her a story in this other language, the language of lips clinging, of hands kneading, of erections rising.

Erections.

Sharp excitement seized her as the ridge of his arousal pressed against her thighs. Her wet, trembling thighs. *Oh my God.* She could come right here against him, with all their clothes still on. And she wanted that, so badly.

What the hell?

She ripped herself away from the kiss and realized she was now straddling him. When had that happened? She'd been kneeling next to him when the kiss began. Now she was riding him like a rodeo queen.

"Oh my God." She scrambled off his body. He groaned and scrubbed a hand across his face. His erection made a steeple in his boxer briefs. She held a hand up to block the sight so she didn't get any more crazy ideas. "That wasn't supposed to happen."

"It wasn't? But you kissed *me*."

"I know I did. I kissed you on purpose, but you weren't supposed to be so good at it." She glared at him accusingly. "It was supposed to be a *bad* kiss. The kind of kiss I'd never want to repeat."

His bewildered look dissolved into laughter. "Maybe you should have clued me in to the bad-kiss thing. I would have done my best, because I always give one thousand percent when it comes to kissing."

"I noticed. Damn you." Her hair had come loose from its ponytail. Viciously, she swept it back into place and twisted her hair tie around it. "You're an amazing kisser. And I know exactly why. Because you've done it so much. You're a player, just like I thought. Of course you wouldn't be a bad kisser. You're the Mighty Finn. I don't even want to think about what sex with you would be like."

"It would be a disaster, I'm sure," he said dryly. "Incredibly good, and a total disaster."

"Exactly."

She shoved her salves back into her bag. Now that she was coming back to her senses, she had the need to get out, to get back to her own place, her own little haven in the woods.

"So that's it? Kissing and leaving?"

The Blush marched across her face like a blow torch. "I'm sorry I kissed you. That was completely unprofessional of me. I promise it won't happen again."

She focused on packing up her bag while he got up from the yoga mat. She couldn't handle the sight of his body anymore.

"Maybe it was a good kiss because we're good together," he said softly.

She rolled up the yoga mat willy-nilly, so it ended in a lopsided shamble instead of her usual tidy roll. "Don't say that. This can't happen. I don't even know how long I'm going to be here."

He tugged his shirt over his head. She gave him one last look, scorching the image of him into her brain. Strong thighs emerging from his tight briefs, t-shirt clinging to his torso, scruff darkening his jaw. Eyes burning with frustration.

"And there goes that electric fence. Zap."

She shouldered her tote bag and hurried toward the front door. "Oh, wait." She turned back and pulled a sheaf of papers from her bag. "I printed out some exercises for you. Just in case you see good results from what we did today."

He took the pages and leafed through them. "I'd say the results so far are interesting and definitely deserve further exploration. But that's just me."

She had no answer for that, and since his magnetism was drawing her like gravity, she escaped out the door before she gave in to temptation again.

With her entire body still tingling, she dashed across the open lawn to the driveway where she'd left her car.

Finn had it all wrong. If anyone had gotten "zapped," it was her.

CHAPTER TWELVE

After that session with Lisa, Finn buried his frustration by throwing himself even harder into his training. Every morning at dawn, he went running along the cliff trail with Rollo. Then he met Tim Peavy at the gym, where they lifted weights for a couple of hours. In the afternoons, he and Josh took his dog Snowball to the beach. While Snowball chased the foamy waves up and down the sand, Finn plunged into the waves and swam at least a mile out, until the ocean salt nearly brined his skin.

None of his nonstop training made him forget Lisa's cool hands or her hot kiss. Even while battling the surf, he remembered the slippery glide of the salve she'd used, or the heady scent of it. Lavender, maybe, and something like cedar. Soothing and relaxing—nothing like that kiss. That was pure passion. The sparks had ignited in a flash, as soon as she'd touched her lips to his.

And *she'd* initiated the kiss. Not him. Hallelujah. Now he *knew* he wasn't the only one feeling this attraction.

He'd been drawn to her since the first moment he saw her. Even before, really. That photo at the tower had first caught his eye. But now that he'd tasted her full lips, felt the passion behind her practical exterior, he wanted her even more. With one kiss, she'd turned everything upside down. She challenged him, threw him off-balance.

And pushed him away.

She hadn't given him her number, and she didn't call him. Was she even thinking about him? She must be. That kiss had been too incendiary to forget. Jupiter Point only had a few campgrounds, so he could probably find her motorhome. But that seemed too stalker-ish.

The hotshots put in two more days of work at the airstrip. Finn and Josh nailed down the new roofing metal while Rollo, Tim and Brianna painted inside.

Lisa was a no-show. Somehow, he didn't think it was a coincidence. He'd gotten too close, so she'd stepped back into her safety zone.

At the beginning of March, Sean came back from his honeymoon. The hotshot crew sprang their big surprise on him on a crisp morning soon after that. At first Finn hesitated to join them, but Josh and Rollo insisted. They all drove together in the Ford Super Duty, tools loaded in the back. To keep up the pretense, Finn and Josh spent the entire drive complaining and groaning about all the work ahead of them.

"You ought to junk the whole place," Josh said. "There ain't enough paint in the world to make it sellable."

"Yeah, just turn it into a skateboard park. Or use it for paintball," Finn agreed. "No point in wasting our time."

Sean scowled at them from the front seat. "Damn, I miss Italy."

In the driver's seat, Rollo shrugged his massive shoulders. "Guess the honeymoon's over, bro. Back to reality."

Then they made the turn into the airstrip parking lot. The new roof metal glinted in the sun, and the fresh blue exterior paint gleamed. Sean's jaw literally dropped.

"Holy fucking shit. It's done. What the fuck happened?" Finn and Josh bumped fists, while Rollo grinned so widely his face looked like it might split.

"It's a little something called a wedding present," said Josh, cackling gleefully.

"You guys did this?" Sean jumped out of the Ford and planted his fists on his hips. "I can't believe it. It's done!"

"Brianna helped too, and so did Lisa Peretti. Merry even put in some time. Suzanne sent sandwiches." Josh stood next to him and bumped his shoulder. "You did register for a new airstrip, right?"

"We can always get you one of those awesome fondue makers instead," Finn added, joining the others. "Or a KitchenAid. Those things rock."

"No. Nope." Sean shook his head. "It's the perfect gift. I can't believe you guys. This is above and beyond."

"What else are brothers for?" Josh clapped a hand on his shoulder. "Through thick and thin, right?"

"Right." Sean fixed his gaze on the building as if he couldn't believe what he was seeing. Or maybe so no one could see the emotion on his face. "I can't wait to show Evie. This is something else. Beers are on me, guys. Barstow's Brews, who's in?"

Josh shook his head. "Sorry, got a birthing class."

Finn snorted, earning a glare from Josh. Birthing classes were no laughing matter, apparently.

"I can't either, bro," Rollo said. "My sister Sidney's coming out for spring break and I have to pick her up at the airport tonight."

So much for that, thought Finn. No way would Sean want to go with just him. He turned to get back in the Super Duty, but Sean stopped him with a hand on his forearm. "How about you, Finn? Grab a beer?"

Shock kept him from answering right away. The guys all waited as he tried to get his mouth to move. "Sure. I'm in."

"All right." Sean glanced at the other two hotshots. "I'll catch you two another time. When you aren't birthing or babysitting. You know, when you're men again."

"Low blow, bridegroom. Low blow."

"I heard you've been training pretty hard," Sean said as they nursed their mugs of Guinness in a dark corner of Barstow's.

"Yeah." Finn drew in a deep breath and steeled himself. "I want on the crew, Sean. I need to get back to work, back on the line."

"You do, huh? Screenwriting didn't work out so well?"

Finn laughed. He'd taken a crack at the *Miracle in Big Canyon* screenplay and basically sucked at it. He'd spent several months holed up in Rollo's guesthouse sweating it out over his computer before throwing in the towel. "I gave it a try. Writing's a lot harder than it seems. I'll take a Pulaski over a laptop any day."

"How are you doing physically?"

Finn took a swallow of the smoky dark ale. "There's still some pain. But it doesn't hold me back. I'm still doing my rehab PT and I got some extra exercises from Lisa."

"Lisa?"

"Lisa Peretti. Molly's caregiver."

"Oh right. The hot brunette. The one who's about to leave."

Finn nearly spewed his Guinness over the table. "*What?*"

"The McGraws mostly needed her during the wedding and the honeymoon. Now that Evie's back, she'll probably move on."

"Probably. So it's not for sure?" Maybe patience was the wrong approach, if that meant Lisa slipped away while he wasn't looking.

"You should ask Evie. Or, you know, Lisa."

Finn scowled at his Guinness. Sure, he could ask Lisa. If she ever bothered to hand over her phone number. Would she really leave town without saying goodbye? Why not? All they'd done was kiss. She didn't owe him anything.

If she left, he'd probably never see her again. Maybe it was time to find out which campground she lived in and go pound on her door.

"Why, are you interested? Good luck with that. Evie says she's kind of cagey. Never talks about herself. Didn't even give a home address. But she's great with Molly, so they let it go."

"She doesn't have an address because she lives—" He broke off. Maybe Lisa didn't want people to know about her motorhome. "Forget it."

Sean lifted his eyebrows. "Sounds like you know more about her than the McGraws do."

"I doubt that. They interviewed her, didn't they?"

"Sure. She gave them all her credentials, and everything checked out. She's way overqualified. The Dean quizzed her hard about why she wanted the job. She said she wanted something temporary and slower-paced than the ER. It sounded like she had some kind of bad experience and that's why she left."

A bitter sensation gathered in the pit of Finn's stomach. Sure, Lisa had kissed him. But she hadn't given him more than crumbs of information about herself. "That's definitely more than I know."

Sean shot him an amused look. "Running into some roadblocks?"

"You could say that," Finn muttered into his beer. "Electrified roadblocks."

"That's new and different for the Mighty Finn. You've never had to work for a woman's attention before, have you?"

Finn glared at him, and Sean put up a hand in surrender.

"Changing the subject now. Back to where we started. You were saying that the hot nurse gave you some exercises and..."

Finn allowed himself to relax. Usually he didn't mind getting teased about his love life, or anything, really. But with Lisa, everything was different. "They're helping. I'm probably about eighty-five percent now. I'm aiming for ninety."

"Eighty-five percent of Finn Abrams is still a damn good firefighter."

Finn let the compliment wash over him like a warm ocean wave. "Thanks."

Sean put down his tankard and speared him with a hard stare. His green eyes looked even smokier than usual in the dimly lit atmosphere of Barstow's. "You know, Finn, you were always a standout. I never saw you lose your nerve. And I was watching because you were the first rookie I was ever responsible for. I paid *close* attention. You were smart, you kept your head, you worked hard. We all thought you'd be the spoiled type, coming from your background. But you weren't. And then..."

Here it was. The moment he'd been dreading for months. "Yeah. Then I lost it. Look, Sean. I don't want to make excuses. Anything I say is going to sound like some kind of lame justification."

"Don't worry about how it sounds. You know how it is out there on the fire lines. We have to trust each other. It's life or death. How can you work on my crew if you don't trust me?"

Finn stared at the crew leader, thunderstruck. Did Sean really believe that Finn had panicked because he didn't trust him? "It had nothing to do with trust. It wasn't about that. Ah, Christ."

He scrubbed a hand through his hair. Every time he remembered that damn flashback, his head pounded.

"I was hoping I'd have more answers before I told you all this. But there's still a big fat blank spot."

"What blank spot?"

"Me."

He told Sean the entire story. It took two more Guinnesses to get through it. Sean absorbed every word without any sign of calling for a psych consult.

"Damn, Finn. That's some story. So you still don't know anything about your origins?"

"Nope. The latest lead from the PI is another dead end. Every other day he has something new, but they never pan out. I'm starting to think I might never know. I had this idea that if I remembered everything, if I knew who I was, I could guarantee that nothing would sneak up on me again the way it did in Big Canyon. But I can't say that. I'm ashamed of how it went down. I want to get back out there and, I don't know, redeem myself."

Sean gave a slow nod. "I appreciate your honesty."

Fuck. That sounded like a windup to a "no." Finn looked down at his beer. He could try another crew. Anywhere but Jupiter Point. Someone, somewhere, would want his skills.

"We start training drills in mid-March. Why don't you join in and we'll see how it goes? I'll have to talk to Vargas about it, but I can probably keep a spot open for you. But I want daily reports. Twice daily."

"No problem." Finn could barely believe this was happening. A grin threatened to take over his face. He tried to keep some kind of stoic tough-guy attitude going, but it just wasn't his nature. "Woot!" He hooted out loud, causing heads to turn. "I'm back."

Sean laughed and lounged back in his seat. Since getting married, he looked more relaxed than Finn had ever seen him. "You're lucky I just got back from my honeymoon and I'm feeling generous. Don't expect any more breaks."

"Don't want any."

"You're a lot tougher than you look, Hollywood."

Finn pointed at his own face. "Hey, I got a face full of ugly-ass scars now. No one calls me Hollywood anymore."

"Really? When did that happen?"

"Might have been when Annika dumped me. I don't know, but I'm glad it's gone."

"If you get on the crew, they'll probably come up with a new one."

"When, Magneto. *When* I get on the crew, not *if*."

Sean grinned and lifted his tankard to click it against Finn's. "Sing it, brother."

CHAPTER THIRTEEN

Finn didn't know Lisa's phone number or where she lived, but he did have one piece of information. He managed to pry her schedule out of Sean—Mondays, Wednesdays and Fridays. At least until she left town.

So the next afternoon, after an especially punishing workout with Tim Peavy, he drove out to the airstrip where Molly's favorite wildflowers grew. He picked a big armful of bachelor's buttons and Queen Anne's lace, then drove to the McGraws'.

At the sight of Lisa's Mercedes, relief so strong it felt like exultation filled him. *She hasn't left yet.*

He rang the McGraws' doorbell, feeling like a teenage boy showing up for prom. When Lisa opened the door, her dark eyes widening, his heart did a slow, happy somersault. God, it was good to set eyes on her again. Her hair was caught up in a clip and she wore a casual fitted hoodie. Warmth rushed through his body as he remembered how she'd felt pressed against him as they kissed.

He cleared his throat. "Hi. I brought these for Molly."

She dropped her gaze to the flowers. "Very pretty."

"She likes wildflowers best."

One corner of her mouth lifted. "Yes, she told me you always bring her the best flowers. She's a big fan of yours."

He grinned. At least Molly was on his side. That counted for a lot.

She let him in and he followed her into the living room where Molly spent most of her time. Along with the hoodie, Lisa wore crushed velvet leggings and Vans sneakers. Either she liked to dress comfortably when she worked or she was hitting a yoga class after this. Either way, he wasn't complaining. The way those leggings hugged the curves of her fine, fine ass was a sight to behold.

"Apparently you have a not-so-secret admirer, Molly. Does the Dean know about this?"

Lisa tossed a teasing smile over her shoulder at him. She seemed more relaxed here with Molly, not worried about putting up that electric fence. Maybe the wildflowers were working on her too.

Or maybe she was more relaxed because she was leaving. His stomach tightened at the thought.

"The Dean's gotten used to me and my flowers." He handed Molly the bouquet and dropped a kiss on her cheek. She sat in her recliner, a blanket over her knees. Her hair was damp at the hairline from a recent shower.

"F...Finn!" Her delighted tone made his heart warm. "These are lovely." She buried her face in them, even though the petals trembled in her shaking hands. "I know what you're up to, you d...darling boy."

"You do?" Was it that obvious that he was practically stalking Lisa?

"You're celebrating. You're J-Jupiter Point's newest hotshot."

Lisa lifted her eyebrows at him. "What happened? Have I missed something?"

"Finn is joining Sean's c-crew." Molly's face dimpled. "Lisa, my dear, will you bring some of that c-cake from the kitchen? Finn, you help her."

Yup, it was definitely good to have Molly McGraw on his side. Finn hid a grin as he followed Lisa again, this time into the kitchen. He reached for the high shelf where the McGraws kept the vases. When he turned around again, Lisa was frowning at him, her arms folded across her chest.

"Are you sure that's a good idea?"

"Flowers live longer in water," he said mildly as he filled the vase.

She rolled her eyes, even though that smile tugged at the corner of her mouth again. "I mean being on the crew. Do you really think you're ready?"

"Believe me, Sean will make sure I'm ready." He put the yarrow in the vase and arranged the pretty blue Bachelor's Buttons just right. When he looked up, she was watching him, her face lit with amusement.

"You know your way around flowers, don't you?"

"Your point being?"

"Nothing. It's kind of cute, that's all." She opened the refrigerator door and took out a domed cake platter.

Cute. That didn't sound promising. Better change the topic back to firefighting. "I'll have to pass a battery of tests before I go out on a fire. I've been training like a demon so I'll be ready."

"Have you been doing those exercises I gave you?"

"Oh yeah. They bring back all kinds of good memories."

Color washed across her face and she looked away. His heart sank. This woman was never going to let him in. The fact that she'd let down her guard so much last time—that she'd kissed him with all that fire, that she'd been so obviously turned on—none of that meant anything. She was still just as cautious as before.

God, he wished he could shake this fucking infatuation with a woman who was so determined to shut him out.

He picked up the vase of flowers and headed back toward the living room.

"Wait." Lisa's voice stopped him halfway to the door. "Why are you walking like that?"

"Like what?"

"Like your legs hurt even more than your side."

He turned back to see her staring at his lower half. His cock stirred. *Don't get excited, buddy. She's in nurse mode right now.* "I told you, I've been training."

"It looks like you're overdoing it. What's the rush?"

"The rush is that I'm not about to sit out another fire season. I'm a firefighter, that's what I do. I'm ready to go back."

"As your physical therapist, I highly recommend against it."

His smile dropped. First she blew him off for two weeks, now she was going to dictate his career decisions? "We had one session, Lisa. Then I didn't hear from you."

She flushed even more deeply. "I've been busy with Molly. But I didn't know you were already joining the crew. You should think about this seriously, Finn."

"I've been thinking about it ever since I got out of surgery. I need to get back on the job. Anyway, why do you care? Sean said you're leaving town. I thought you might already be gone by now."

She stared at him. He couldn't make out her expression. Surprise? Hurt? Guilt? "I...well, obviously I haven't left yet."

Yet.

So she was intending to leave, and she hadn't even tried to say goodbye. What was the point of this? Time to hand off the flowers to Molly and get to the gym. He could get his ass handed to him by a hundred pounds of iron instead of a prickly nurse.

He shrugged and turned to go again.

"My shift's almost over," she said abruptly. "If you wait, you can follow me back to my place."

"Your place?"

"All my stuff is there." Irritation edged her voice. "If you're going to be fighting fires, I want to make sure you're in peak condition. It's a public safety issue."

The second her meaning sank in, a huge grin spread across his face. "Absolutely. An urgent safety issue."

She shot him a wry look, then brushed past him with the cake plate.

He stood for a moment, inhaling the sweet fragrance of the yarrow.

Flowers. They worked every time.

*

She must have lost her mind completely. What was she doing, inviting Finn back to her private sanctuary?

Stupid, stupid, she chanted as she drove her Mercedes into the campground, Finn following in his dark green Tahoe. She should have left Jupiter Point the minute Evie came back from her honeymoon. Before she laid her eyes on Finn's sexy self again.

His sexy, *sore* self. As soon as she saw how gingerly he was walking, her resolve melted away. He needed her help and she couldn't turn away from that.

Okay, so that wasn't the only reason she'd invited him back. Ever since their kiss, she'd lain in bed fantasizing about every inch of Finn Abrams's body. She'd pictured his smile, she'd replayed some of the funnier things he'd said. She'd come up with brilliant responses she hadn't thought of at the time. She'd relived every moment of that unforgettable kiss.

When Sean and Evie had returned from their honeymoon, she'd fully expected to give her notice. Every time she walked through Molly's door, she intended to say the words. But they never came.

Face it, she didn't want to leave Jupiter Point. She didn't want to leave Molly. And she didn't want to leave Finn.

And why should she, when nothing else suspicious had happened? No other armed weirdos had been spotted in Jupiter Point or around the tower. She hadn't gotten any strange phone calls or emails or Facebook messages. There was no reason to be paranoid.

All the sleepless nights in the motorhome were lonely. What was the harm in having a little fun? Finn wanted her, she wanted him. There wasn't a single photographer snapping photos of him anymore. Why couldn't she indulge herself for a short time with a handsome, sexy, charming firefighter who set off fireworks inside her?

They both parked along the main road that circled through the campground. She led the way down the short footpath to the clearing where the motorhome was parked. Now that he was about to see her home away from home, she actually felt nervous about it. What if he had the same reaction her family would probably have? Hysterical laughter?

"It's a pretty small spot, and there isn't really room for cars unless I move the picnic table," she explained. "That's why I park out there. As you can see, the motorhome takes up half the space, even though it's only twenty-two feet. Sometimes I wish I had one of those big Airstreams, but this is perfect for me."

Finn wasn't laughing at all. Hands in his pockets, he eyed her little motorhome with appreciation. "I practically lived in my car during my first wildfire training. I never got around to buying a tent, so I kept crashing in my backseat. Believe me, this is luxury compared to that summer."

She unlocked the door and stepped inside, sniffing to make sure no strange smells had accumulated during the day. Nope—nothing but black coffee and the sweet candy smell of the chocolate croissant she'd had for breakfast. She stepped aside to let him mount the stairs. "I bought this motorhome from a woman I knew in Galveston. She was an artist who used to travel around painting water-colors. She said every woman ought to live alone at some point in her life and answer to no one."

Was she babbling? She folded her lips together to make it stop. Finn stepped into the tiny strip of space be-tween the pull-down table and the cushioned love seat. He had to bend his head to fit inside. He looked out the win-dow at the tall pines moving in the wind, a shifting wall of deep green.

"I love it," he said sincerely. "I really love it. How long have you had it?"

"About eight months." She beamed at him. "I'm glad you like it. It's not exactly the kind of home you usually show off. I can pack up and leave in about five minutes, give or take. The gas mileage isn't great and I've broken a few mugs that I forgot to stash somewhere safe. Otherwise, it's been just about perfect."

He flattened his palm against the motorhome's ceiling as he looked around. And suddenly his proximity was almost too much for her. His wide shoulders seemed to fill the space, or maybe it was the magnetic energy he carried with him. She took a little step toward him before she even realized it. Then she caught herself.

Aiming for professional, she cleared her throat. "I didn't really think this through. The only place I can work on you here is in the bedroom. I mean, on the bed, which is back there. But I don't want you to think..."

"I get it. Don't worry, we'll keep it appropriate. I'll control myself, even though those leggings of yours are practically killing me." He flashed her a rueful, one-sided smile.

Her knees went to Jell-O. If he had any idea what that smile did to her insides... When she was around him, none of her higher functions seemed to operate properly. She got all impulsive and spontaneous and...well, stupid.

"It's actually not you I'm worried about."

At her words, he glanced up sharply and the space between them seemed to evaporate. They stood in exactly the same positions, with the same eighteen inches between them. But those seemed to have shrunk down to a sliver of space vibrating with sexual tension.

"I see." His voice scraped like sandpaper. The intent look in his eyes made her chest tighten. Want rocketed through her system, starting with her heart. Whatever this pull was toward Finn, it was much more than physical.

But the physical part was what made her step toward him. That's what made her pulse flutter and her breathing hitch.

"Hi," he said softly. The way he looked at her, as if she were some kind of sixth wonder of the world, made her shiver.

"What..." She trailed off, pulling her bottom lip between her teeth.

He reached for her hand. As soon as it slipped into his warm grip, a sweet sensation flooded through her. She wanted to wrap herself up in him, let him surround her with all his strong, funny, charming Finn-ness. It was like being hypnotized.

"What are you thinking when you look at me like that?" she whispered.

"That it's only, what, ten steps to your bed?" His answer came so promptly she had to laugh, and the mood between them shifted from intense to teasing.

"Probably about five steps for you, with those long legs."

"You think?" As she squeaked with surprise, he scooped her off her feet and, holding her in his arms, edged down the narrow walkway toward the back of the van. "Only one way to know for sure."

Setting Off Sparks

CHAPTER FOURTEEN

Still dizzy from being swooped off the floor, Lisa clutched Finn's chest as they made their way through the motorhome. They passed her tiny bathroom, her microscopic closet. And then her bed was pressing against the backs of her legs. He put her down and stepped back, shoving his hands in his pockets. She shot a quick glance down at his crotch, where the bulge of his arousal made her giddy.

"I thought you were here for a physical therapy session," she teased, still catching her breath.

He lifted his eyebrows. "I am. You said your bed was the best place. I'm being expeditious."

She flushed, wondering if she'd jumped to the wrong conclusion. But the heat in his eyes told her otherwise. Not to mention the ridge in his pants.

"Very efficient." She scooted to the edge of the bed and got onto her knees. "Let's get this show on the road, then. Come lie down."

He started to pull off his shirt but she stopped him. "Please leave it on."

"Why?"

"It's just easier for me, that's why." No need to spell it out that she found him impossibly attractive when shirtless. But of course, he knew exactly what she meant. He raised an eyebrow at her, but left his shirt alone. He stretched out on her bed with a sigh, then rolled onto his back and flung his arms to the sides.

"This might be the best place in the entire world, right here." He gazed up at the ceiling of the motorhome, with its swaths of deep blue silk scattered with silvery stars. "Did you install the stars before or after you came to Jupiter Point?"

"Before, believe it or not."

She loved her bed any time of day or night, but Finn's presence made it even more irresistible. He folded his arms behind his head, his biceps swelling from under his t-shirt. The fabric rode up on his torso and exposed the lower part of his abdomen. She caught a glimpse of bare skin and a swirl of dark hair before she dragged her gaze away. He was still looking at her starry motorhome sky.

"So when you got here, you must have thought it was destiny," he said. "Since this is the stargazing capital of the West Coast."

"You know how I feel about destiny." She reached for the crate where she stored her oils and other medical supplies. After rifling through to find the mixture she'd put together for Finn, she scooted back over to him. He had rolled over onto his side, and was resting his head on his bent elbow, watching her with sensual heat in his dark eyes.

"I have an idea. You've been working hard. How about you give me a turn with the oils?"

"Excuse me?"

"Lie down." He reached around her waist and tugged her to his side. She tumbled against him. The heat radiating from his body felt like the best spa treatment in the world. She instantly relaxed with a long sigh. He was right. She had worked hard at Molly's.

He nudged her legs and arms into position next to him, so she lay on her back, rag-doll style. He smoothed the hair away from her face. His deceptively gentle strokes made her eyes drift halfway shut. They might be light touches, but there was passion behind them. She felt it sparking between their bodies, ready to ignite and light up her tiny star-filled bedroom.

Her body went languorous under his slow, deliberate caresses. He smoothed her hair across the pillow, then curved his hand into the soft space between her neck and her shoulder. Tingles followed wherever he made contact. She couldn't see his expression, but the angle of his head spoke of complete focus. Complete attention. Complete absorption.

One by one, her muscles relaxed. He stroked a finger down her upper arm to the crook of her elbow. The sensitive skin there jumped with awareness. Her fingers twitched and her palm fell open under the feathery glide of his hand.

No one had touched her like this in so long. Ten months of being alone, on constant guard, watching over her shoulder. Maybe she'd forgotten the joy of simple physical contact.

To her shock, a tear ran down her cheek. Why was she crying? She didn't mind being alone. She *liked* being alone.

Finn kissed the tear from her face and his warm lips made her heart tremble.

"Are you okay?" he whispered in her ear.

"Yes. It's just...it's been an interesting few months, that's all. It has nothing to do with you. I like you being here."

"I'm here for as long as you want. But I might have a hard time keeping my hands off you." He interlaced his fingers with hers. The rough warmth of his palm pressed against hers felt so reassuring. To her complete dismay, another tear ran down her cheek and dripped onto his arm.

"Do you want me to stop?"

"No. I'm not crying. I swear I'm not. This is some kind of bizarre physiological thing. Pretend it's not happening."

"Sure. I can do that. I can also pretend I'm not kissing you under the stars." Finn's whisper tickled her ear. He kissed his way down her cheek, along her jaw, until he reached the corner of her mouth. "I swear I'm not."

A lightning bolt of lust streaked through her lower belly. She drew in a long, shaky breath of air that smelled like Finn. His skin held the faint trace of aftershave with some kind of citrus note, warm from the outdoors, with an overlay of the wildflowers he'd been carrying. She wanted to lick him, to nibble her way along the rough grain of stubble.

But she ordered her muscles not to move, not to interrupt what he was doing, because it was magic.

She kept perfectly still as he brushed his lips across hers. Sparks crackled between them. She touched her tongue to the surface of her own lower lip, tasting the trail of fire that followed every movement that he made. And then his tongue captured hers. The kiss went instantly to a deep place she'd never experienced before. It felt as if she were swimming down a fast-moving river, being tumbled around until she didn't know what was up and what was down.

She rolled toward him so they could press more closely against each other. His chest felt hard and solid against hers, his chiseled muscles radiating heat all the way through her clothes, into her skin. She wanted to rip off her own shirt, feel his flesh against hers. And still they were kissing, swept away in the current of lust drawing them deeper and deeper.

His hands went under her shirt, fanning across her spine. She arched under his touch, lit up by the electric charge passing between them. She wriggled close to press against the hard bulge between his legs.

He groaned deep in his chest. "I don't know how long I can take this, Lisa."

"I'm sorry," she murmured with a gasp. "This feels so amazing. I don't want to stop."

"Are you serious about that? Because I'll go as far as you want to. But I'll stop as soon as you say."

Stop? That sounded like the worst idea she'd ever heard. She shook her head, squirming as far into his arms as she could. He pressed his big hand into the notch between her shoulder blades. Her head fell back and he kissed her again. He sent her soaring into a world of wild heat. Need pounded through her veins.

Her hands scrabbled against his shirt, trying to rip it off him. He helped her strip it away, then did the same to her shirt, and finally they were skin to skin. He ran one big hand across her ass, shaping it to her curves. An itchy restlessness seized her. She pushed her mound against his erection in urgent little movements. Heat built between them until it felt like fire. Sweat sprang to her face, hot air fanned against the back of her neck.

She'd always thought the way people referred to sexual heat was more of a metaphor, or an exaggeration, but the interior of the motorhome really did feel hot. It even smelled like smoke...

*

She froze in his arms and sniffed the air. Definitely smoke. She sat up so abruptly that her elbow knocked Finn in the chin. "Do you smell that?"

Looking dazed, he sat up next to her and pushed hair out of his eyes. "Smoke." He shook his head to clear it, then pushed aside the curtain that covered the little window.

Outside, she saw nothing but darkness. She blinked, completely confused. How had it already gotten to be night? The sun hadn't even set when they'd arrived at the campground. Could the time really have passed that quickly?

Then she saw that the darkness wasn't black, it was a deep, swirling gray with flashes of orange.

Finn was already flinging himself out of bed with a muttered, "Fuck."

He grabbed her hand and pulled her from the bed, then tossed her shirt at her. "Pull it on. How about a blanket too?"

"What are you talking about?"

"Your van's on fire. We have to get out of here."

She shook her head, still not understanding. Her brain didn't seem to be operating right. How could her motorhome be on fire? She hadn't even started it lately. "It only smoked once, when there was an oil leak. But I got it fixed."

"Lisa." He gripped her by the shoulders. "Grab what you need. We're leaving."

"What I need?" She looked around helplessly. "This is what I need. All of it. Everything I own is in here."

"Then choose what you need the most. Come on."

Her mind raced, thinking of her crate of medical supplies, her laptop, her grandmother's book of recipes, the stuffed panda she'd grabbed on impulse on her way out of her Houston apartment. What else did she need? What else did she refuse to lose?

When she still didn't move, he plucked her off the bed. As he whisked her toward the front of the vehicle, she reached up and snagged the starry fabric that covered the motorhome's ceiling. It came away with a ripping sound as the double-sided sticky tape gave way. As silly as it was, she wanted those stars.

Her heart nearly stopped when they reached the front of the van and saw the flames leaping on all sides.

"Someone did this," Finn said grimly. "The fire's on both sides. Someone torched it."

"What?"

He set her on her feet, then grabbed his leather jacket from the driver's seat of the van, where he'd tossed it when they came in. He wrapped the jacket around his right arm.

"What are you doing?" She coughed as smoke filtered up from the floorboards.

"We can't go out either door. The flames are too thick there. I'm going to bust open a window."

"Be careful—" But he was already ramming his arm into the window. The entire motorhome shook with the force of his blow, but the window didn't break. It took two more full-force punches before a crack appeared. Then a tremendous smashing sound hit her ears as the glass shattered. A hissing roar came in from outside. Was that the fire? Did fires really make that much noise?

She clutched at her head. Nothing was making sense. Her brain was moving at the pace of a slug. In the ER, she'd always been coolheaded and calm, but this was different. This was her home.

Finn used the jacket to knock out the jagged pieces of glass that remained, then spun back to her. He bundled the leather jacket around her and shepherded her to the window.

"You're going out first. You have to do exactly as I say. No hesitation. The motorhome isn't safe."

He shot an uneasy glance toward the flames licking the other side of the vehicle. Although he didn't say the words, she'd seen enough TV shows to know what he was thinking. If the flames hit the gas line the right way, or the propane tank that fed her fridge and cook stove, her motorhome would blow up.

"As soon as you hit the ground, get away from here. Call nine-one-one. I'll be right behind you."

She nodded. Finally her brain was clicking again. "There's a flat metal box next to the sink. I need it."

"I'll grab it. Ready?" He picked her up and maneuvered her feet-first out the window. "Don't hold onto the edge, there's still glass there. I got you, just trust me." With his hands under her armpits, he lowered her toward the ground. Heat fanned from her left, where flames were jumping in an arc around the van. Finn's steady grip felt like the only solid thing in the world. Her feet searched for the ground. She could touch her toes to it, but no more.

"I'm going to drop you now, okay?" Finn called to her. The van wasn't especially big, but it sounded as if he was shouting from far away. The din of the flames mingled with the roar in her ears.

"Okay." She hoped she sounded brave and strong, though she definitely didn't feel that way. He released his grip and she dropped the last few inches to the ground. She stumbled, then got her balance and swung around to look back at Finn. He had disappeared back inside the motorhome. Smoke swirled in big gusts, blocking her vision. Through the far side window, she saw flames flickering in the thick gray billows.

Finn reappeared with her purse. He tossed it toward her. "Run, Lisa. Please!"

But she couldn't. She bent down to pick up the purse, then stayed rooted right where she was. "Get out of there!" she shouted to him. "Right now!"

He held up a finger, then disappeared back into the interior. The next time he appeared, he was carrying her portable safe. Tears surged into her eyes. That metal box held all her personal papers, birth certificate, passport, and maybe most importantly, some files she'd brought from the hospital to back up her suspicions.

He leaned out the window and dropped the box on the ground. "Anything else?" he called.

"No! Just get out!"

He stuck his upper half out the window, then twisted so his back faced her. He reached up and gripped the ridge of steel that formed the upper rim of the window. With some kind of amazing combination of strength and flexibility, he maneuvered the rest of his body out the window. Then he hung in midair, muscles bulging, until he dropped like a cat onto the ground.

"Come on!" Lisa screamed. Every nerve in her body was telling her to run, but she refused to move a step until Finn came too. She couldn't abandon him. He bent to pick up the box, and in that moment, a finger of flame burst from the window above him. "Duck!" she shouted.

He dropped to the ground, right on top of her box. He scooped it up and, staying low, scrambled across the grass toward her. As soon as he was a few yards away, he rose to his feet and ran. He grabbed her hand as he passed her. Hand in hand, they fled toward the woods.

Then a percussive burst of sensation pushed against her back. She stumbled but Finn didn't let her stop. A loud clap of noise made her look back.

Sure enough, there was her motorhome—now a brilliant orange fireball setting off sparks in every direction. She screamed and nearly dropped to the ground. Finn wrapped his arms around her and spoke into her ear.

"We have to keep moving. This whole forest could go up. We haven't had rain in two weeks. We need to get out of here and call the fire department. Take this."

He shoved her portable safe into her hands, and then her feet were off the ground and he was carrying her past trees and branches, the smell of smoke chasing them through the woods. She buried her head in Finn's chest so the branches didn't slash her face. And because she just couldn't bear to watch her last remaining possessions go up in flames.

CHAPTER FIFTEEN

Finn's entire body was throbbing by the time the two of them got back to the road where they'd left their cars. He'd carried Lisa far enough into the woods that he felt sure they'd be safe, then the two of them had circled back around. Adrenaline still coursed through his system. What a terrifyingly close call that had been. If he hadn't been there...he didn't want to think about what could have happened.

From the direction of her camping spot, he heard the voices of firefighters—casual enough to tell him the fire was out. The shadows of the pines were lengthening, darkness gathering in the woods. The air held a chill it hadn't when he first drove up. It would be full night in less than an hour and Lisa had no home.

Finn knew where she was staying tonight, even though she didn't yet. She was going to stay with him.

"I'm going to talk to the firefighters," he told Lisa when they reached her Mercedes. "Want to wait here?"

"No way. I want to hear what they say."

He nodded, glad she had her spunk back. Even though she still looked pale and her eyes were red from smoke and tears, she wasn't about to collapse anymore. She unlocked her car and stashed her purse inside, along with the metal box and the fabric she'd grabbed from the ceiling. He'd seen that reaction before, fire victims who refused to let go of their one remaining tie to the home they'd lost.

"Come on then." Hand in hand, they approached her campsite. A Jupiter Point ladder truck and a paramedic van blocked the footpath to the smoldering hunk of metal beyond. He heard Lisa's breath catch at the sight.

A paramedic came jogging toward them.

"You two okay?"

"I'm fine," Lisa said quickly. "But you should check Finn out. He's limping."

Finn started to protest, but Lisa wrapped her arm around his and pulled him toward the van. "If you try to stop the nice man, I'll kick you," she whispered fiercely. "You carried me about half a mile."

"Fine." He allowed the paramedic to check his vitals and drank down the electrolytes they offered him. Lisa stayed next to him the entire time, still holding his hand. He wondered if that was for him or for herself—but either way, he loved it.

His heart ached for her. Who would do this? Was it a random attack or had someone targeted Lisa, and if so, why? Secrets were one thing, but this was dangerous.

"What are they saying about what caused the fire?" he asked the paramedic.

"Don't know. The motorhome was pretty much toast by the time we got here."

Lisa winced at the EMT's bluntness. Finn shot him a glare.

He tugged Lisa closer and murmured into her ear. "I'm so damn sorry this happened."

She turned her face away, her dark hair swirling around her shoulders. Trying to hide her emotions, he guessed.

"Why do people say they're sorry for things they didn't do?"

He liked hearing that feisty edge in her voice. She wasn't going to let this disaster keep her down for long.

She stole another look at her motorhome, then shuddered. "Sorry. I don't mean to be a bitch. I'm just...shaken up. You saved my life. I wouldn't have known what to do." She turned to the paramedic. "Take very good care of him. He got us away from the fire. He's a hotshot, did you know that? I bet you didn't know that."

Finn exchanged a look with the EMT. Maybe Lisa was more affected that he'd realized. He took her hand and rubbed his thumb across her pulse point. It beat with a rapid, jagged rhythm. "Are you sure you don't want him to check you out too?"

"Unless he has a bottle of vodka in that van, I'm good. Just a little shaken up."

The paramedic, in the midst of wrapping a blanket around Finn's shoulders, laughed. "It sounds like you're going to be fine. It's always a good sign when people can still make a joke."

Another official vehicle drove into the small lot. Deputy Will Knight unfurled himself from the driver's side and came toward them. Finn had seen him at Barstow's Brews a few times but didn't know him well.

Finn nodded a greeting. "Knight. Who called you into this thing?"

"Chief Littleton. As soon as I heard Ms. Peretti was involved, I hopped in my rig and came on out."

"Involved? What do you mean, *involved?*" Finn asked sharply. "Her home got destroyed, that's her only involvement."

"Right. Pardon my phrasing." Knight glanced from one to the other of them. "You were both here at the time of the incident?"

Lisa stepped in to answer. "Yes, we were both here, we didn't hear anything or notice anything strange until I smelled smoke. At that point, Finn knocked out a window and got us out."

Knight made some notes on a little pad of paper, then looked at Finn. "You're a firefighter, right? Did you notice anything unusual?"

He'd been so caught up in Lisa, he wouldn't have noticed a bomb going off outside. "No, but that fire was deliberately set. I'd stake my career on it."

Knight didn't look surprised. Finn shot a glance at Lisa—and noticed that she didn't either. "What am I missing? Why are you here, Deputy? What's going on?"

"Good question." Knight tapped his pencil on his pad. "If we had a little more information from Ms. Peretti here, we might have some answers."

Finn looked at Lisa. "What's he talking about?"

"I'll explain later," she said in a low voice. To the Deputy, she said, "Can we talk tomorrow?"

"Absolutely. Do you have a safe place to stay tonight?"

For a crazy moment, Finn thought Knight was going to invite Lisa to stay with him. The thought made him absolutely nuts. "Yes, she does," he said quickly. "She's going to stay at an exclusive cliff-top mansion with a full-time bodyguard on the premises."

"What are you talking about?" Lisa stared at him. A smudge of soot on her cheekbone made his fingers itch to brush it off.

"Your accommodations. What else?" The burning sensation along the side of his body made him irritable. "Just like the Deputy said, you need to be somewhere safe tonight. And that's with me."

She tried to pull her hand away, but he refused to let her go. "Finn, that's completely unnecessary. What if it was just a freak accident? Will's probably just being alarmist."

Will? She was calling him "Will" now? Finn shot the deputy a glance, wondering if he was going to have to take some kind of measures here. Something short of attacking an officer of the law.

"I'm not being alarmist." Knight might have rolled his eyes, though it was hard to tell under his official deputy's hat. "I'm being smart. Which is what you should be too."

"Exactly. You should be smart," Finn told Lisa. "And stay with me."

"We have many fine bed and breakfasts in the area," continued Knight blandly. "I'd be happy to provide you with a list."

"She doesn't need the fucking Chamber of Commerce," Finn snapped.

"All right, then. Maybe you have a friend you can stay with. Would you like me to contact Merry Warren? She's left me her number many times with permission to call her. More like a command to call her, in fact."

"She's not calling Merry. Merry's probably on deadline." She usually was, Finn knew. And while she'd be happy to take in Lisa, Finn didn't plan to give her the opportunity. "I have a perfectly good place for Lisa to stay. So butt out, Knight."

Knight looked about a second from bursting into laughter. "I'm giving you a pass here because the paramedics might get on my ass, but—"

"We'll figure something out," said Lisa firmly. "You don't have to worry about it, Will."

"Right, *Will.* We got this."

Knight was still laughing as he ambled off to talk to the firefighters. As soon as he was out of earshot, Lisa turned on Finn. "Look, Finn. I'm a grown woman who can take care of myself. I don't need some knight on a white horse to rescue me."

"How about a knight in a green Tahoe?"

"No knights. No Tahoes. I just want to check in somewhere and lock the door and sleep until noon tomorrow."

Which made sense, and he wouldn't have a problem with that, except that he kept thinking about the possibility that someone had snuck up on them and lit her motorhome on fire. Even if her door was locked with ten deadbolts, Lisa was only one person. She couldn't notice *everything* going on around her. And she was new in town, so she might not recognize someone as a stranger.

No, everything in him refused to let her be alone tonight. It was time to play dirty.

"So...are you really going to abandon me after I carried you through the woods? I'm shocked, Peretti. I really am."

"*Abandon* you?"

"I'm injured. In the line of duty. And I wasn't even on duty. I could have internal injuries, maybe a concussion. Or a long-buried allergic reaction to superheated automotive paint. I'm really surprised you're willing to leave me alone tonight."

She stared at him, her dark eyes glimmering in the light from the fire engine. "You're really playing the patient card?"

"Playing? I *am* a patient." He adopted a virtuous tone. "A very good patient. I'm doing everything the nice paramedic said to do. I'm sitting and resting like a good boy.

It's too bad not everyone does as they're told by first re-sponders. By the way, I'm technically a first responder. You should listen to me."

"Oh my God. You are seriously demented."

"Nope. Just determined. You're staying with me to-night. In fact, you can have the whole guesthouse. This is perfect. I need a house-sitter for when the fire season starts. I just got a, uh...pet, and I need someone to take care of him."

"Really? A pet?"

Not yet—but he would as soon as humanly possible. "Yes, poor little thing." What kind of pet could he possibly acquire at this point? A cat, a dog? He'd figure something out. "It needs a kind human to take care of it while I'm gone." He blinked at her with his best puppy dog eyes— which were damn good, he knew from twenty years of experience.

"You are shameless."

"You know, shame is good for things like crimes. But for little stuff like wanting to keep someone out of harm's way? Try another word. Like 'heroic.'" He grinned at her.

She stood up. Soot smudged her leggings, and a large smear of sap spread across one sleeve of her hoodie. Even so, he had no defense against her. He wanted to shield her, to make her laugh, to strip her naked and roll her around in his sheets.

None of that now, he warned himself. Making a move on her wasn't on the agenda. He just wanted to be sure she was safe. Somewhere between her bed and the woods, that had become the most important thing in the world to him.

"Okay. I'll stay at your place tonight. But it's only because I'm truly afraid that you damaged your brain when you climbed out of the van."

He didn't argue. He'd gotten what he wanted. And maybe he could use the brain-damaged thing to his advantage. "Brain damage requires long-term care, right?" he murmured.

CHAPTER SIXTEEN

Finn didn't want her to drive alone, so he left his Tahoe at the campground and rode with her in the Mercedes, sitting on the odd little contraption she'd installed for Molly. He jumped at the chance to question her about what Knight had said.

"You said you'd explain later," he reminded her.

"It's only about ten minutes later." She laughed as she took the turn out of the campground.

"Right. That means it's later. Why was Knight there? Why is he interested in a vehicle fire at a campground?"

She let out a soft sigh. "Because there's a chance that it's not the first time someone has come after me."

"What?"

"You know that guy with the gun who knocked you out on the trail up to Breton? The one who tried to kidnap Merry?"

He swiveled his head to stare at her. "He was looking for *you*?" Jesus, that made so much sense. The guy had ranted on about dark hair and the tower. At least, that was what Finn remembered before he'd gotten clocked on the head.

"It's possible. So far, he hasn't really explained himself. He pled guilty."

"I know all that. I followed the whole case. But why you?"

She worried at her bottom lip. She was gripping her steering wheel so tightly that her knuckles showed white. On the road ahead, her headlights shone across a jackrabbit skipping across the center divider. She swerved to miss it, a little more sharply than necessary. Even though she quickly corrected her course, he got the message.

"Let's talk about this when we're not in a moving vehicle," he said.

Relieved, she nodded. They both stayed quiet, lost in their own thoughts, until they reached his guesthouse.

Luckily, he'd done some minimal cleanup that morning, so he spotted only a small pile of sweaty training clothes on the floor. He kicked it under the dining table, hoping she wouldn't notice.

She pretended not to, anyway.

"I'll take the couch." He gestured toward the back of the house, where the bedroom was located. "The bed is all yours. The sheets were just changed, but if you want fresh ones, check the closet in the bathroom. There's about a hundred variations of pastel-flowered sheets in there. By the way, I have nothing to do with the decor of this place. I think someone's grandmother lived here."

She attempted a smile, but he sensed she was still uncomfortable. Time to put her at ease. Make crystal clear his intentions were honorable, at least for tonight. He dropped onto the couch and yawned deeply. "If you want to take a shower, go for it. Lots of hot water, courtesy of Clan Wareham. I promise I'll be a much better host tomorrow. I'll even bring you breakfast in bed..." He trailed off, eyes drifting shut.

And then it wasn't an act. All the stress and exhaustion of a full day's training and a dramatic fire rescue overwhelmed him. His body felt like one solid throbbing sore spot.

The sound of her soft laughter woke him up a little. He dragged his eyes open as she lifted his legs onto the couch and helped him stretch into a more comfortable position. Her movements were competent, sure, as if she'd assisted many couch-bound patients. She draped a throw blanket over him. It smelled like potpourri, as did everything in this little guesthouse.

"And here I was, worried that this was all a ploy."

"Definitely a ploy," he mumbled as he snuggled into the couch pillow. "Worked, too. Don't tell Nurse Badass."

She laughed and ran a light hand across his forehead, so quickly he might have imagined it. "I won't. Sweet dreams."

And he was out.

When he woke up, sunshine was streaming through the living room window and the smell of rich dark coffee floated from the kitchen. He sat up with a jolt and looked down at his chest. His shirt was missing.

The events of the day before flipped through his brain. Lisa. Fire. Lisa. Here.

He jumped off the couch and strode into the kitchen. Lisa held a mug in both of her hands as she stared out the window at the Pacific Ocean stretching to the hazy horizon. She wore one of his old Fighting Scorpions Hotshots t-shirts over the leggings she'd worn yesterday.

"What the hell is going on here?" He folded his arms across his bare chest as she turned. Steam from her coffee mug made her skin look dewy and fresh. "Someone took my clothes. And made coffee. I'm the host around here, that's my job."

"You were indisposed," she said primly. "And your shirt was sweaty and dirty. That's not good for your scars. It was a medical intervention."

Her eyes sparkled as she scanned his torso. He decided he'd take all the medical interventions she cared to offer.

"And the coffee?"

"There might be enough for you. If you hurry." She winked as she took a sip.

He laughed. He liked her like this, all loose and relaxed and wearing his t-shirt. He walked to the coffee maker and poured himself a cup. "How are you feeling today?"

She made a face. "Besides homeless, motorhome-less and clothing-less? Not too bad."

He winced. "You've still got attitude. That's a big plus. And you're not homeless. This is your home. I'm handing it over to you, free and clear. I can stay at the base if it makes you uncomfortable. I'm serious."

"Finn, I'm not going to chase you out of your home. I'll find a place."

"A place in Jupiter Point?"

Her hesitation told him all he needed to know. The fire was the last straw for her. She'd probably be leaving as soon as she finished her coffee.

"Don't leave, Lisa." The request came out more seriously than he'd planned. "I mean, don't leave before you have a solid plan. You still need clothes, and I have to get my Tahoe back, and we should see what's left of your stuff from the motorhome. And didn't you say you were going to talk to Deputy Knight today?"

"Right. I guess I did." Her expression tightened and she looked away. He wanted to ask her a million more questions about the fire and the Breton incident and Knight, but didn't want to scare her off first thing in the morning. Especially when two minutes ago, she'd been enjoying the sunshine and making herself at home in his kitchen.

He lightened his tone and leaned his hip against the countertop. "Besides, I need you here, remember?"

"Right. That pet you mentioned. Funny thing, I don't see any sign of a pet. I've been looking everywhere."

Busted. He ran a hand across his jaw. "On a related note, I need to run a quick errand. Can I borrow your car?"

She burst into laughter. "Did you make up a pet to encourage me to stay here?"

"If someone did something like that, how wrong would that be? Asking for a friend."

She threw back her head and laughed even harder. "You are really something. Actually, I'm touched that you would go to such lengths to get me to come here. And I know your motives were perfectly innocent. You just want to keep me safe. That's just...really nice."

He lifted an eyebrow at her. Nice? Was that really the right word? Well, it was better than many other words she could have chosen. He put his empty mug on the counter. "I'm going to take a shower. You're welcome to—"

"Join you?"

His mouth snapped shut. She batted her eyelashes at him, all sweet cream and innocence. Jesus, now she was playing with him. Or was she serious?

"Uh...sure. You're also welcome to help yourself to cereal. It's in that cupboard up there. Somewhere." He waved a hand at his kitchen cabinets, then turned and pretended to run into the doorjamb.

The sound of her laughter made him grin. As he stepped into the shower, he realized he'd do anything to keep her sounding like that. Not wary and cautious, but joyful, carefree and happy.

*

After his shower, they rode together down the long, winding road into town. She drove while he fired off a bunch of texts.

"Swing by Josh and Suzanne's first, would you?" he asked her.

He directed her to the new house they'd recently bought. It was a sunflower-yellow ranch-style house with a walled-in backyard perfect for kids.

Suzanne opened the door. Her belly seemed to fill the entire doorway. Her hair hung in a long braid over one shoulder.

"Wow," said Finn. "Won't be long now, huh?"

"Only about a hundred more years," she grumbled. "I have a bag here next to me but I can't bend down to get it."

"I got it." Finn reached past her for the giant tote bag filled to the brim with clothes. He handed it to Lisa, who peered at it curiously.

"What is this?"

"*This* is all the clothes I will never be able to wear again thanks to Buster here." She patted her belly affectionately. "Even if I could wear them, I wouldn't want to get spit-up on them. I'm handing them off to a worthy heir."

"Suzanne, I can't take this."

"Take it," she snapped, making Lisa jump. "You have to, I'm like one entire nerve ending right now. If you don't, I'll cry, and once I start I can't stop. Just ask Josh."

Meekly, Lisa tucked the handles of the bag over her arm. "Thank you, that's very nice of you."

"It's nothing. Really. You can buy me a margarita at the Orbit someday."

Finn noticed Lisa didn't say "no" to that, though she didn't say "yes" either.

"Was that your idea?" she asked after they'd gotten back in the Mercedes.

"Suzanne has a great sense of style and she loves dressing people. Seemed like a good match."

"Very thoughtful," she said neutrally.

After that, they stopped at a discount store, where she picked up a toothbrush and underwear and a few other essentials. Then he directed her to the Frisky Business Pet Store.

"Seriously? You're actually getting a pet?"

"Yup. Don't want you to think I'm a liar. Wait here, I'll be right back."

Since he'd already made the purchase via text message, it took no time to pick up his new pet and proudly bring it out to the Mercedes.

Lisa burst out laughing again. "A turtle?"

"A painted tortoise, if you don't mind. They don't like to be called turtles."

"Really? How do you know?"

"We've already started to bond. We have a lot in common. We both like feisty brunette nurses."

She peered at the small creature in the carrier. "What's wrong with his leg?"

"He's a rescue turtle. His bandages will need changing every couple of days for the next few weeks."

Her gaze skidded back up to meet his. "Oh, that's low. You chose an injured turtle on purpose."

"Of course I did, Nurse Badass with the Soft Heart. I told you I was starting to figure you out." He grinned at her. "I dare you to walk away from the poor little guy."

"He's a turtle. He's slow. Even slower than slow because he's injured. He'd never catch up with me."

"Because you won't have the heart to leave him."

"You are going to pay for this." But her voice had gone soft. She inserted her finger through the wire mesh and touched the turtle's shell. He cocked his head at her with a bright, inquisitive look.

Finn did a silent air punch of triumph.

After that, they drove back to the campground.

With her hands still clamped onto the steering wheel, she jerked the car to a stop. She stared at the spot where her motorhome had been. What had been an idyllic grove of pines now looked like a bomb had dropped. A scorched skeleton of a picnic table stood to one side of the pile of smoldering metal wreckage. Her whole body started to shake. "Oh my God. It's real. Someone literally tried to kill me."

"We don't know that for sure yet." Finn extracted his arm from around the tortoise's cage and touched her shoulder.

"You don't understand. I *do* know. And he tried to kill you too, just because you happened to be with me. Holy shit, Finn. This is insane. Oh my God, oh my God!" She reached over and punched the locks on the door, as if that would stop any bad guys nearby. She shrank back into the seat, wrapping her arms around herself.

"He?" Finn stared at her. "You say that like you know who it is."

"No. I don't. Not really." She shuddered, her entire body shaking.

"Lisa. Listen to me." He put both hands on her shoulders and turned her to face him. Her eyes refused to meet his. She scanned the campground, the woods, the backseat. Anything except him. "Take a deep breath. You need some oxygen. Passing out isn't going to help anything."

"I'm not going to pass out," she snapped. "And telling someone to take a deep breath is just so *annoying*. Why are you so calm? You shouldn't be calm. He almost killed you too!"

"I'm calm because I have a plan. Several plans, in fact."

"Plans. *Plans*? It's not your job to think of plans for me. I can do that myself. I've been doing it since I left Houston. And before that. I'm an independent, self-sufficient woman. Damn it all."

"Of course you are. You're amazing. But you don't have to do everything alone. You have friends here. People you can trust. You have *me*. Here." He grabbed a t-shirt from Suzanne's bag of clothes and handed it to her. She used it to blot the tears on the upper curves of her cheeks.

"This is crazy. I'm usually the calm and collected one. You should see me in the ER. I never lose control. I don't know what's wrong with me."

"I do." He pushed her hair away from her face. "You've been through a traumatic experience. Your home burned down. And now you have a pet tortoise. Of course you're upset."

She gave a shaky smile, then rested her head against his hand, giving its entire weight into his keeping. It was such a trusting gesture that his heart skipped several beats.

They stayed like that until his wrist started to cramp. But he'd rather chop it off than make her move.

Finally, she shook herself and sat up. "Let's go see what's left of my glamorous life."

CHAPTER SEVENTEEN

Lisa felt as if she were moving in slow motion as she got out of her car and walked toward her former haven. She'd been avoiding this moment all day. Her original plan had been to get up early, take Finn to his Tahoe, keep her promise to Will Knight, then drive like a bat out of hell in the general direction of Canada.

Why Canada? Why not? It had always stuck her as a safe kind of country.

But Finn had changed that plan just by walking into the kitchen that morning, all tousle-haired and stubbly and irresistible. She'd never forget the way he'd rescued her from the fire yesterday. Now she felt anchored to him. Tethered, like a kite on a string. As if he was the only thing keeping her from floating off into panic.

Driving around Jupiter Point with him, picking up clothes and toothbrushes and turtles, made it even harder to separate from him. She found herself sticking close to his side as they approached the wreckage.

Finn squatted down and poked through the cinders with a stick. He found a few window handles and a cracked mug, and then, like a miracle, her panini maker. He used the sleeve of his hoodie to pick it up.

Completely unharmed.

"Looks like lunch is on me." By some miracle, she actually managed a joke.

Finn shot her a proud smile. "You really are a badass, aren't you?"

She didn't want to admit what an act it all was. Sure, in the ER she knew what she was doing. But she wasn't equipped for this kind of situation. Ever since she realized that her home was on fire, she'd been shaking like a leaf on the inside, where no one could see. "Not nearly as tough as this panini maker. I wonder if it still works?"

He hefted it in one hand and examined it. "It's a stovetop version, right? Just a hunk of metal. I don't know why it wouldn't work. Grilled cheese and ham, that's my vote." He put the panini maker down and sifted through more smoking, formless debris.

Her heart expanded as she watched. Was Finn skipping his training today so he could help her out? She'd never even asked. He'd dropped everything to help her without a second thought. And that was *after* he'd rescued her from a burning vehicle. He'd offered his home, he'd gotten a pet for her. Finn was a rock-solid man.

She could trust him.

"I helped a friend escape her abusive husband," she said abruptly. "He's a prominent politician in Houston. That's why I left. I was afraid he'd send someone after me because he's very well connected. She kept coming into the ER, and I kept reporting what I saw, but nothing was done. The police never even questioned her, even when she finally agreed to call them. I had to break about a dozen hospital rules but I knew there was no other way she'd ever be able to leave him."

He set his butt on the ground, resting his elbows on his knees. She fixed her gaze on the panini maker next to him, its familiar stainless-steel casing grounding her.

"Start at the beginning," he said softly. "So I make sure I understand."

"I knew Maria in high school. I saw her on the news over the years so I knew she'd married an up-and-coming politician. But I wasn't really in touch with her. Then she came into the ER one night for a sprained wrist. She used her maiden name, which was a red flag right there. She refused to tell me anything, so I followed protocol and wrote up my notes. She kept coming in with new injuries every other month for about a year. I worked the night shift, so I saw her a lot. Every time I'd write my notes, but nothing would happen. It was like my reports were disappearing into nowhere."

Finn frowned, making his scars stand out even more. "Was someone making them disappear, do you think?"

"I don't know. I talked to my supervisor but still nothing changed. Finally, she came in with a broken arm, and I was like, you can't keep doing this. By then we'd gotten to be really close friends. She asked me to help her. I didn't have any expertise in that kind of thing."

It felt so good to finally share this story with someone. Now that she'd started, she didn't want to stop. She wanted to share every detail, although she knew that would be a mistake. No last names, that was her red line in the sand. Everything else, she could tell him.

"I switched her paperwork with someone else's, then snuck her out of the hospital to my car. We just drove off. I told my family I was taking an extended vacation. Maria had family in Mexico, so I drove her across the border. Then I headed to California because it seemed like a good place to lose myself. In San Luis Obispo, I saw a notice in the newspaper about the Forest Service looking for volunteer spotters. It seemed like the perfect way to be useful but hard to find. I didn't know if her husband would be looking for me, but better safe than sorry."

He watched her with dark eyes that didn't miss a thing. "You left everything, just like that? For your friend?"

"It wasn't just for her. I was so stressed out, losing weight, not sleeping. I needed a break. I didn't trust anyone at the hospital because it seemed like something fishy was going on. I figured I'd take a little time off, do some traveling, and go home when things had died down." Tears started in her eyes, but she blinked them back. "I didn't think anyone was going to search for me, but if they did, they'd never look in a motorhome. Or so I thought." Sadly, she kicked at a piece of scorched metal. "Or a lookout tower, for that matter."

He frowned, as if working through her whole story, trying to make sense of it. "Did you ever get any hint that someone was looking for you?"

"No. At first I was nervous about that, of course. That's why I chose the job in the tower, because I could see all the way around me, three hundred and sixty degrees, all directions. There was no way anyone was going to sneak up on me. But no one ever tried."

"Well..." He pulled a rueful face. "There was that one time..."

She knelt down on the ground next to him. His dark eyes tracked every move. She touched his hair, the soft thick waves like velvet. "I'm so sorry about that. Where did he hit you?"

He shook his head impatiently. "Nowhere. It's not important."

"It is to me." She slid her fingers over his scalp. "If you think about it, you were protecting me before you even met me."

He laughed. "I got knocked on my ass. How do you figure that?"

"I heard the whole story from Molly. You stepped between Merry and the gunman. Okay, so you weren't *technically* protecting me. But I'm going to count it anyway. If I had still been there, you would have stopped him. With your head."

He tilted his head under her touch. What started as the kind of gesture she'd use with a patient quickly morphed into something else. Something more electric.

"I really had no idea it had happened. I feel terrible that you and Merry got hurt because of me." She touched the scar on his face, his neck. His eyes darkened.

"You can't take the blame for that. Christ, Lisa. You have to tell Knight everything you just told me. And Chief Becker. They're both smart, I trust them. They can protect you."

She didn't answer. As much as she wished that were true, she didn't really believe it. The only way she could be totally safe would be to leave Jupiter Point and disappear. Saskatchewan. Winnipeg. One of those weird, cold Canadian provinces that were too far away from Houston for anyone to bother.

"I know what you're thinking," Finn said. He stood up, pulling her with him. "Running isn't the answer. If they found you here, they can find you anywhere."

"You know, the funny thing is, I don't even know what they want with me. I assume Maria's husband is behind this, but I don't know where she is now. We agreed to not communicate. And why would he want to kill me? It just doesn't make sense."

He cupped his hands around her face. "This is exactly why you should stay. Let Deputy Knight and Chief Becker do their jobs. Tell them everything and let them investigate. Find out what's really going on. In the meantime, stay with me. You have people who care about you here. That's important."

"I do?" A shot of pleasure ripped through her.

"You know you do." He scowled at her. "Isn't it obvious by now? I don't want you to leave. What do you think that damn turtle is all about? I care about you. Open your eyes, Lisa. Let me in."

Let Finn in... She was doing that already, by telling him about Maria, by staying at his house, by dreaming about their kisses, wanting more, wanting him...

"Let's go back." She stepped close to him, pressing the length of her body against that solid wall of Finn-ness. "To your place." She tilted her head and gazed up at him, knowing her desire must be clear in her eyes.

No matter what he said, leaving town was the best course of action. But before she did, she wanted one night with Finn first. Just one. Not enough time to get attached, just enough time to explore the chemistry that sparkled between them.

"One condition," he told her in a husky voice. "You should refer to it as *your* place. You're the one who's going to be staying there. Rollo's expecting you to. He's one thousand percent behind the idea. He's retired from the crew so he'll be around more than I will. And he's Rollo— you've seen him. He's huge and intimidating and more than happy to take on anyone who looks sketchy. It's the perfect place for you while I'm gone. Please. Say yes."

"Yes, I'll come home with you."

He squinted one eye at her. "That's not exactly what I asked. Say yes that you'll stay."

Instead of a "yes," she rose onto her tiptoes and pressed a kiss to his lips. Instant heat seared between them. *Oh my God.* Her head swam and stars danced across her vision. She must have swayed, because his arms wrapped around her, keeping her upright. Her knees quivered as desire thundered through her veins.

And then they were back in her Mercedes, he was at the wheel, and they were racing out of the campground.

"Your car!"

"Fuck my car," he growled. "This is more important."

His urgency amped her lust even higher. She wanted to touch him, put her hand on his thigh, feel the bulge surging between his legs. Was this the feeling that had propelled her mother into all those marriages? She'd never felt anything like it. She thought she might be going crazy.

Why was she thinking about marriage anyway? This wasn't about marriage. This was a one-time surrender to attraction, end of story. One single night. She'd probably leave tomorrow. Or maybe the next day. Soon, anyway. As soon as she could find someone for Molly, and as soon as she told the full story to Will, and said goodbye to Suzanne and Brianna and Evie and Merry. Maybe she could give Merry an exclusive or something.

Finn reached over and laced his fingers through hers. "Don't think," he murmured. "It's going to be all right. I promise."

She held on to his hand as if it were a towline in a stormy sea. Finn was right. Everything would be okay, as long as they were together and they were touching and the road wound through the starry night to the top of the hill, where heaven on earth awaited.

CHAPTER EIGHTEEN

Finally...finally...that was all Finn could think as they tumbled through the door of the little guesthouse. Finally he could touch Lisa the way he wanted, without holding back any of his wild lust for her. As soon as the door thudded shut behind them, he whirled against the wall and kissed her with the intensity of a tornado. He ran his hands down her sides, reveling in the feel of every sweet curve.

He cupped his hands around her ass, digging his fingers into her firm flesh. God, she felt good. Better than he'd even imagined all those nights. He pulled her legs around his waist, bracing his thighs to hold her up.

The sound of her rapid panting in his ear made his pulse rev even higher. "God, I've been craving this moment for so long," he groaned. "I have no control over myself. I want to just touch you everywhere. All at once."

A tremor ran through her body. "Me too. My God. This is insane." Surprising him, she wriggled from his grasp. "You can't hold me up like this. What about your scars?"

"Don't even feel 'em. What do you think all that training's for?" He helped himself to a handful of her long hair. It slid through his fingers in a silky waterfall. "But that's fine, I can adjust. Come on. Bedroom. Let's go." He tugged her hair back, gratified to see her eyes haze over with the same lust raging through his system.

"Make me," she murmured.

"Is that a challenge?"

"It's whatever you want it to be."

He walked her backwards in the direction of the bedroom. All day long he'd been thinking about the fact that she'd slept in his bedroom. He'd pictured her naked body against his sheets, her hair spread out on his pillows, her skin flushed with sleep. "I think it's an invitation. I think it's you wanting me as much as I want you."

"Maybe even more," she teased, gliding her hand down to his crotch. He groaned loudly, the sheer pleasure of her touch almost too much to bear. She ran one finger under the waistband of his jeans. "Why don't you check and see?"

He did as she said, sliding his hand between her leggings and her soft, sweet pussy. "Oh my God. No underwear."

"I haven't had a chance to open my new undies yet."

He maneuvered her through the open door of his bedroom. "It's too late now."

Her legs hit the edge of the bed. She sat down abruptly, then lay back. He bent over her, lifting her legs as if she were a doll. He peeled off her leggings then tossed them over his shoulder. He gazed down at her bare legs and the soft nest of hair at the juncture of her thighs, so dark against her pale skin.

She laughed self-consciously. "I know what you're thinking."

"You do?"

"You're thinking 'there's no way she comes from Texas. She must be the palest person in the Southwest. Everyone always laughs at me."

"That's not even close to what I'm thinking. I'm thinking you're fucking beautiful and there's a strong chance I'm hallucinating this entire thing." As she laughed, he put one knee on the edge of the bed between her thighs. "But you still have too many clothes on. I really need that t-shirt back, if you don't mind."

"Oh, so that's how it is. You take in a helpless fire victim, clothe her, then take it all back. Nice going, hotshot."

He snorted loudly as he lifted the shirt over her head. "Helpless fire victim? Not hardly. I'm the helpless victim in this scenario."

"Excuse me? How are you a victim?" She spoke from behind the fabric. When her head popped free, static electricity clung to the long strands of her hair, plastering them against her face. She tried to push them away from her eyes, blinking madly. She was so adorable, his heart hurt.

"Because from the first moment I saw you, I couldn't think of anything else. That's still true. You keep pushing me away, but it doesn't make any difference. I'm starting to feel sorry for myself, I really am."

"Oh stop." She reached for him with a soft look in her eyes. "Does it look like I'm pushing you away? Come here."

He braced himself over her while she ran her hands up and down his arms. She didn't even flinch when she passed the ridge of scar tissue along his right biceps. Something in him relaxed, and he realized he'd been holding on to the fear that his scars made him sexually unappealing. He hadn't slept with anyone since the burnover.

But Lisa was touching him as if she couldn't get enough. She pulled off his t-shirt and feasted her eyes on his torso. Her hands ran across his abdomen, dipping between the ridges of muscle, making him go hard as a fricking rock. Then she planted a hand on his chest and pushed him into an upright position. "You can come back down here when your pants are gone."

He snorted. "You're kind of a mean nurse, you know that?"

"Nurses always know best," she tossed back, all saucy. In mock revenge, he lifted her foot to his mouth and nipped her big toe.

"No arguments here." He nibbled her foot until she squirmed and gasped. Then he released her foot and dropped his hands to the waistband of his jeans. His cock was so engorged with arousal that he actually had trouble with the zipper. He struggled with it, finally managing to get it over the massive bulge underneath. "If I injure myself because I'm so turned on, you'll take care of me, right?"

She laughed, a flush coming and going in her cheeks.

Finally the zipper slid down and he shucked his jeans and underwear. He stood naked before her in all his scarred, aroused glory.

She scanned his body, the moment stretching until it felt endless. A faint trace of smoke still clung to them both, and it mingled with the perpetual potpourri smell of the guesthouse. He realized that from now on, for the rest of his life, this smell would bring back this exact moment. The moment when he and Lisa were completely naked together for the very first time.

"I don't want to rush you, but there's an urgent situation I need to address." He slid back over her body, hovering over her the way he had before. But now, with no clothes on, the electricity crackling between them felt a hundred times more intense.

Her dark gaze captured his, so he felt like he was falling, falling. "I just want you to know that I don't usually do this."

"This?" He lowered his head so he could touch his tongue to her nipple. She trembled as he circled it tenderly, using the sharp point of his tongue to tease the little nub into a hard peak.

"Or maybe this?" He moved to the other nipple. She tasted so sweet against his tongue that he lost track of time as he lavished attention on her beautiful breasts, with their deep red areolas and responsive tips.

He didn't stop until she was squirming and moving her legs restlessly against his. He shifted lower down on her body, nipping his way along her torso, tasting the softness of her belly, the sleek curve of her ribs.

She whimpered and dug her fingers into his hair. "Finn, we don't need foreplay. I'm ready. I want you. I want this."

"You keep saying that." He reached her intimate curls and dropped a kiss on the downy mound. "I'm just trying to figure out what 'this' is. Is it maybe something like..." He set his hands on her upper thighs and spread them open. The glisten of moisture between her legs went right to his head, and he had to take a deep breath. His erection pounded with arousal. He wanted her with every cell of his body. But he wanted to make this so spectacular she'd never want anyone else.

So he dipped his head to her clit, using the gentle, warm pressure of his tongue until he felt it swell. She tasted so amazing, like honey and passion all intermingled in one intoxicating flavor. He lapped at her, exploring with his tongue and lips and mouth. Her hips were making little bucking motions and her inner thighs trembled. The muscles strained against his grip, but he held firm. He wasn't ready to end this feasting yet. He loved this, loved having her open beneath him, loved hearing her soft whimpers and moans.

"Finn," she begged. "Please, Finn, please."

He loved that even more. His name on her full lips, the heavy flush in her pale skin, the dark wine of her nipples standing at attention. She was a feast for every one of his senses.

Then her movements got more rapid as she pushed against his mouth. She wanted to come. She was ready to come. And he could explode right this second. Instead, he stayed with her on her roller-coaster ride to orgasm. He increased the friction and pressure of his tongue, moved with her rhythm, tuning into the speed she wanted. He felt as if all his senses were synced with her, and all he had to do was listen, watch, smell, respond, touch, lick, gorge, and hang on for the ride when she cried out and arched against him.

Looking up, he drank in the dazed expression on her face, the rise and fall of her chest. Even though his cock ached with need, he knew *this* was what he really wanted. This intimacy, this closeness. He wanted to reach past her defenses and make her come apart. He'd wanted her to fly free and forget all the worries that made her keep her distance.

"Wow," she finally murmured. "That was...thank you."

He smiled. He could still taste her sweetness on his tongue. "My pleasure. Seriously. You have no idea what a pleasure it was."

He rolled over and rested his head on his bent arm. His cock brushed against her hip, make it ache even more painfully. Seriously, he'd have to get the thing looked at if the pressure didn't get relieved soon. But his satisfaction could wait. He wanted her to come again, maybe a couple of times, before he took his own release. He wanted this to be the best ever for her. The kind of "best" she'd never forget.

If he had to bury his cock in an ice bucket to bring down his erection, he would.

She rolled over onto her side and frowned at him. Not the reaction he was expecting. "Don't you have a condom around?"

"I do." He grinned at her. "But maybe I'm not done making you come yet."

She sat up, her hair falling around her shoulders. A damp sheen of sweat covered her chest. "Half an hour ago you looked like you might explode if we didn't go to bed."

"I can control myself."

She swung her legs over the side of the bed and would have jumped off if he hadn't wrapped an arm around her waist.

"Hang on, buttercup. What's going on here?"

She kept her back to him. "I thought you wanted me."

"Have you seen my hard-on? Fuck yes, I want you. Why would you have a single second of doubt?" Just to prove it, he took her hand and wrapped it around his cock, even though there was a big risk he'd come all over her hand if it moved so much as a millimeter. "Yeah, I want you. Like crazy. I might lose it if you so much as breathe on me. So what's the problem? Walk me through it."

She took her hand away and scooted around to face him. "This doesn't feel right, Finn. You're trying to prove something to me. You're trying to impress me with what an amazing lover you are. The Mighty Finn."

His jaw clenched tight. "That's not me anymore. I just want this to be good for you."

"Finn, listen to me. I don't want to be impressed. I want *you*. When we came in here, I thought you were going to take me against the wall. And I wanted that."

She put her hand back on his cock and slid it lightly up and down the length of his erection. He gritted his teeth to keep his focus.

"But honey, you deserve more than some screw against the wall. You've been through a lot the past couple of days. I wanted this to be incredible. Something you'll never forget."

Was he apologizing for that? Christ, she had him all mixed up. And all he could think about was her hand on his cock. Focusing on her face, her words, was nearly impossible.

She scooted on her knees right up close to him and smoothed her hands gently down his shoulders, his upper arms. "It *was* incredible. You're incredible. But this is sex, not romance. I can't start a romance right now. My life is nuts. You've seen it yourself. I have to figure out what I'm doing, where I'm going, how to handle this mess I'm in."

He started to speak, but she put a finger on his lips.

"I want hot, reckless, crazy sex. I want to get down and dirty and wicked and wild. I want you to lose your mind like I just did."

She gripped his cock again and ran her thumb around the tip. His eyes nearly crossed from the blinding pleasure of it. It blocked the sting of her words about "no romance." That hurt, he couldn't lie. But right now, with her hand on his shaft, he was fine leaving that conversation for another day. Now that he had her in bed, he could work on the rest of it.

"Lose my mind," he murmured. "I can do that." He reached for her, but she held up a hand to show she wasn't finished.

"Also—stop treating me like some fragile person who just lost her entire home and all her possessions and is really quite frankly kind of pathetic."

He stared at her. Message received. Lisa was a strong, resilient, kickass, sexy woman who gave as good as she got. And damn it, he'd give it to her.

"I think I've heard enough here." He flipped her onto her back. She squeaked in surprise, eyes going wide.

He reached for the nightstand next to the four-poster bed and felt around for a condom. "If I want to try to impress you, I'll do it. If I want to make you come before I get a chance to put on a condom, I'll do it." He rolled the condom onto his dick. "I don't think you're pathetic, you haven't lost all your possessions, and I don't think you're fragile. But if I want to help you stay safe, I'm going to *fucking do it.*"

She stared up at him, her pupils so dilated her eyes looked midnight black. "Unless I tell you to fuck off."

"Right." He hefted his cock in one hand. With the other, he stroked the insides of her thighs and across her soft mound, still damp from her orgasm. "So what's it going to be? Can we fuck? Or should I fuck off?"

She burst into laughter even as her legs fell open under his touch. "You really have a way with words, you know that?"

"Words are just one of my talents. Make the call. Because if I wait another goddamn second to get inside you, I will lose my mind." His blood pounded in his ears, his cock pulsed inside its latex sheath.

"Fuck me," she whispered. "Fuck me the way you want to. However you want."

Like water bursting through a dam, his control snapped. He spread her legs apart. He touched her clit with the pad of his thumb, feeling an answering pulse of heat. Still wet, still juicy and swollen. Grabbing onto every last bit of his willpower, he inserted the tip of his cock inside her and gritted his teeth against the intense pleasure. *Don't come, don't come. Hang on, you motherfucker.*

He must have muttered part of that out loud. "What did you call me?"

"Nothing. I was talking to myself. God, you feel good. Fuck."

She arched back so he could ease himself into her, inch by thick inch. "Do you always swear this much during sex?" she gasped.

"Fuck if I know."

She choked out a laugh as he seated himself fully inside the deep warmth of her channel. The walls fluttered around him, little pulses surrounding him with electric thrills. "Goddamn," he breathed.

"I'll take that as a yes." Her head fell back on his comforter. He bent her legs back toward her chest and put his hands on her knees so he could deepen his strokes. Her breath came fast. Her eyelids closed halfway, her lips parted. She was a wet dream spread out beneath him.

And he couldn't hold back. He pumped into her, dizzy with pleasure from the tight clasp of her body and the way she met each thrust with a tilt of her hips.

"I'm not going to last long." His vision went starry at the edges. "Fuck, Lisa. You feel so good. So damn good."

And then he was plunging down the final drop of the roller coaster, going faster and faster, the wind rushing past his face, pleasure jolting through his spine, and when she stiffened and cried out, he lost it. He detonated into a blinding, soaring orgasm, almost like a leap off a cliff at the end of a bungee cord. Even when it seemed to end, the spasms kept coming, little aftershocks of ecstasy. He kept his eyes shut tight. He wanted to collapse on top of her, but he didn't want it to be over.

Because with Lisa, there was never any guarantee there'd be a next time.

CHAPTER NINETEEN

As a medical professional, Lisa tried to look at sex in a practical way, as nothing more than a biological function. Its only real purpose was to reproduce, after all. The reason orgasms existed was to encourage people to have sex. She'd enjoyed sex in the past, but had never gotten carried away with it. After watching her mother treat love and marriage like a competitive sport, she'd chosen a different path. She didn't want her life to be a series of dramas and heartbreaks. Sex was fine, but she'd skip the romance and flowers. "Friends with benefits"—that was the way to go.

She'd made it to the age of twenty-eight that way. Then she'd left Houston, met Finn in a tower, and now everything felt different.

"Friends with benefits" had absolutely nothing to do with what she'd just experienced with Finn. That wasn't just an orgasm. It was an earthquake. It completely shook up all her ideas about sex and intimacy.

"Friends with benefits" was so much less confusing than this.

How could Finn Abrams, with his easy charm and ruined face, make her feel something so powerful? She wanted to do it again, as soon as possible. But she also wanted to run for the hills. Literally.

Maybe she could hide out in the Breton lookout tower again. No one would find her there—except possibly an armed thug with a can of gasoline.

She slept uneasily that night, curled under the covers of Finn's bed, soaking in the unfamiliar bliss of a male body radiating heat next to her. She kept waking up, panic flashing through her, imagining someone outside the window with a match.

But every time, Finn would mumble something and fling his strong arm across her waist, and its heavy weight would soothe her back to sleep.

In the morning, she stole out of bed and got dressed while he was still sleeping. The covers twisted at his waist, exposing his long torso and muscular shoulders. Maybe some women would fixate on the grotesque scars riding his rib cage. But she barely noticed them anymore, except to find patterns in them, as if they were clouds. A rearing dragon. An erupting volcano. That sort of thing.

She left a note next to his coffeemaker.

Went to talk to Knight. Xo Lisa.

She deliberately left out any mention of her plans after that. She didn't know what would happen next. At this point, everything she owned would fit into her car and still leave room for a family of four. It would be so easy to slip out of town.

And yet, so hard.

She drove down the long, winding road that led from Rollo's cliff-top house to the valley where Jupiter Point was nestled. On the way, she called Will and asked him to meet her for coffee.

The Venus and Mars Café was just opening when she pulled up to the curb. Someone had washed the sidewalk and the front patio with its ironwork fence, so it sparkled in the fresh morning air. A jasmine vine spilled over the black-painted bars, the pink-edged flowers still closed, awaiting full sun. Under the cheerful blue awning, the front door was propped open to welcome the first customers of the day.

Lisa sighed sadly as she got out of her car. It was going to be so hard to leave.

From the moment she'd first set foot in Jupiter Point, she'd felt safe. The little town was just so cheerful and charming, with its historic downtown and quirky star-themed business names. She'd driven the twenty miles from the Breton tower for supplies and found herself enchanted by the cedar-shingled buildings and vintage lampposts lining Constellation Way. The highlight had been a tour of the observatory. After all that time watching the stars from her perch in the lookout tower, she'd wanted a closer look.

How had the senator found her here? She had no idea. The man had resources she couldn't even imagine.

"Morning, Lisa," Will's voice rumbled behind her. He was dressed in cutoff sweats and a faded t-shirt from the athletic department of Florida State University. She wondered if he used to be a football player, with that long-boned, powerful build. Then it occurred to her that he probably wasn't even on shift yet.

"I'm so sorry, I wasn't thinking. This is your time off, isn't it?"

"Always on the job, that's me." His slow smile put her at ease. "In a town this size, we have to be. There are only a few of us. Anyway, I always have coffee before I run. Have you ordered?"

She shook her head and followed him inside. They both ordered black coffee and a muffin, then sat down in a corner table as far removed from the other early customers as possible.

Will didn't waste any time. He fixed his penetrating gray eyes on her. "So what do you have for me?"

"A name. Senator—" She swallowed hard. Taking this step, revealing names—after this, she couldn't go back. "Senator Tom Ruiz. He's a senator from Texas. I helped his wife get away. He was abusing her but she didn't want to go to the police. I don't know where she is, but maybe he thinks I do."

"Hm." He flipped open his notebook and scribbled the name. "So your theory is that this senator hired people to track you down so you can tell him where his wife is?"

She broke off a piece of muffin and crumbled it between her fingers. "I suppose so. It's all I can think of."

"Why not just hire people to find his wife?"

Trust a police officer to put his finger on the exact same question that had bothered her. "Maybe he did that too. I really have no idea. I'm not in touch with Maria now."

Knight pulled a smartphone from his pocket and tapped at it. He scanned through the results of his search. "It says in Wikipedia that Senator Tom Ruiz is recently divorced. He's a sponsor of a new bill to help domestic violence victims."

"Ugh, what a hypocrite. When did he get divorced?"

Knight was still staring at his phone. "Back in Houston you worked in an ER, right? Houston Memorial?"

"Yes." So he'd done his research. Of course he had.

"Says here he's funding a new wing of that hospital."

"Wow." Her mind raced with this new information. "So maybe he made a deal with Maria during the divorce that she wouldn't bring charges against him if he sponsored this bill and gave money to the hospital."

"Sure. That all fits." He closed his phone and frowned in concentration at his notepad. "The only piece of the puzzle that doesn't fit here is you. Why the gunman at Breton? Why the fire?"

"Maybe the fire was an accident."

He shrugged his broad shoulders. "It was no accident. It was definitely arson, but it might have had nothing to do with you. I called around and two other campgrounds have had incidents like this over the winter. No injuries, just damage. There's a chance the perp thought the motorhome was empty and just wanted to make some crazy firebug statement."

Lisa's heart soared with a sudden surge of hope. If Senator Ruiz wasn't behind the fire, maybe she wasn't in any danger. If the Breton gunman had reported back that she wasn't in the area, maybe she wouldn't have to leave Jupiter Point. Maybe she wouldn't have to leave Finn. Maybe she could stay in his guesthouse and take care of the turtle and see him when he came back from fighting fires and they could dive back into bed and gorge themselves on more mind-blowing sex...

Almost as if he'd read her mind—but hopefully not the X-rated bits—Will said, "I'd prefer it if you didn't leave town. I have a buddy from law school who works in the Houston DA'S office. I want to find out what I can about Ruiz, and the more we know, the safer we can keep you. This is a small town where people watch out for each other. If you're staying with Finn up at Rollo Wareham's place, that's a pretty good setup. The hotshots are good guys and they take care of their own."

She felt her face heat. "Their own?" She wasn't anybody's "own."

"If I stay, I'll probably try to find another place."

He smiled slightly, as if he didn't quite believe her. Which made sense, since she didn't quite believe herself either. "Whatever you decide. Just make sure I know where you're staying." His gaze drifted past her, and she turned to see Merry stroll into the coffee shop, her laptop under one arm, her other hand covering up a huge yawn. A purple headband held back her curly hair and she wore the kind of sweat suit you wouldn't dream of getting sweaty.

She spotted them and came toward their table, bending down to give Lisa a hug. "I heard about the fire, Lisa. If you need anything, you be sure to call me, okay?"

"Word to the wise, Ms. Peretti." Will closed his notepad and stuck it back in his pocket. "That's a ploy. It's a trap to get a scoop out of you. Merry Warren lives for scoops. She'll do anything for them."

Merry narrowed her eyes at the officer. "I'm not falling for your bait. I have work to do, unlike certain law enforcement types who get to roam around town in sweats."

"Matter of fact, I *am* working," Will said. "Which means you're interfering with a police investigation again."

Lisa nearly laughed at the outraged expression on her friend's face. No doubt, Will really knew how to get under Merry's skin. "Actually, I think we're pretty much done here, right?" She collected her coffee cup and rose to her feet.

Will followed suit, unfolding his long body from the little table with impressive grace for a man his size. Merry definitely noticed the same thing—or at least she was looking in the same direction. "If anything comes up, be sure to call. And let's keep this out of the news for now."

"Thank you, Will." She and Merry watched him stride out of the coffee shop, tossing his muffin wrapper into the trash on the way out.

"Keep what out of the news?" Merry asked as soon as he was out of earshot.

Lisa raised an eyebrow at her. "Aren't you the news?"

"I don't have to be. I can just be a friendly ear. I can put you in the Cone of Silence. I'm pretty good at separating my reporter side from my friend side."

Her *friend side*. Warmth bloomed in Lisa's heart. Having a friend would feel so good right about now. Not a "friend with benefits." Just a friend. Someone to help her decide what to do. Stay in Jupiter Point? Get into her Mercedes and leave?

"Maybe I just wanted a few minutes with the hot cop," she said lightly.

"He's not that hot," Merry grumbled. "Definitely not as hot as he thinks he is."

Lisa laughed. "He's been great, actually. Don't rope me into your anti-Will club. Team Cynic is one thing. But Will's a good guy. And he was looking pretty fine in that workout gear."

"Didn't notice." Merry smirked.

"Uh huh. Look, I really shouldn't talk about it right now. But as soon as I can, you'll be the first, I promise." She changed the subject. "What are working on today? Anything exciting?"

Merry's phone rang, and she fumbled with her laptop to get to it. "I'm doing a big feature on the Star Bright Shelter. Suzanne's supposed to meet me here for the interview."

She finally got her phone to her ear. "Sure thing, girl. Yeah, I totally get it. Hey, can I bring someone with me? Great."

She hung up and tucked her arm into Lisa's elbow. "Suzanne's feeling too bulky to leave the house. Says she's afraid she'll make the sidewalk cave in. Want to come with me and see how a future Pulitzer Prize-winning reporter does her thing?"

Lisa hesitated. Her Mercedes was right out there, waiting for her to hop in and steer it north. But hanging out with Merry—that would be fun. And she should really thank Suzanne for the clothes. And what about Molly? She should at least say goodbye.

One more day in Jupiter Point—what harm could it do?

"Sure. I'll bring the sticky buns."

CHAPTER TWENTY

When Finn woke up to find Lisa gone, with nothing but a note left behind, his thoughts went right to the worst conclusion.

She was gone. Skipped town. She'd given him the best night of his life, then headed for the hills.

But at least he now had a turtle.

He pulled on some boxers and his running shorts, then turned his attention to his new pet. He filled the little guy's food bowl, gave him fresh water, then cleaned out his cage. "I'm going to have to make you a better home, dude. Maybe a sandbox or something. And you need a name, don't you? You're a beauty, you know that?" The tortoise ignored him and toddled right for the bowl of food. His shell really was spectacular, with a deep crimson and olive-green diamond pattern.

A familiar knock came on his door. He flung it open to find Rollo in his running clothes.

"Hey bro. I'll be ready in a second." He turned to grab a t-shirt, only to realize his big bearded friend was staring at his torso. "What?"

"Nothing. I've never seen them before, that's all."

"Sorry. I forgot."

"Fuck, Finn. Don't worry about it. Leave the shirt off, for all I care. It's already pretty warm out there. I let you sleep in as long as possible." Rollo grinned broadly. "Brianna's idea."

Finn hesitated, then decided—why not be comfortable while he ran? If Rollo didn't care, why should he? He tossed the t-shirt away. "Can you give me a ride to my Tahoe later? I left it at the campground."

"Sure, dude. Let's get moving." He peered at the tortoise in its cage. "What's that?"

"That's Sparky." The name came to him out of the blue. "My pet tortoise. He might be my mascot too. I find him inspiring. Do you see him complaining about his injured leg? No, you don't."

"I'm sorry, Sparky the Tortoise?" Rollo's face wrinkled with mirth. "Did I catch that right?"

"Yup. Sparky the Tortoise. He may be slow, but you should never count him out." With that, Finn sprinted past Rollo to get a head start in their race along the clifftop trail. Rollo thundered after him, yelling about unfair tricks.

After their run, he had coffee with Rollo and Brianna and fended off two million questions about the status of things between him and Lisa.

"She's staying in the guesthouse for now, that's all I'm saying."

"But *with* you? Or without you?" Brianna was practically dancing with delight, her red hair catching the midmorning sun. "I vote for 'with.' I like Lisa, she's a cool chick."

"No comment. But when I'm at the base today, I'm claiming a spot in the barracks just in case."

Brianna's face fell. "That's so unromantic. I expect more from you, Finn. She should be head over heels for you by now."

"Yeah, no kidding," he muttered. "Don't count me out yet."

After that, Rollo drove him to his Tahoe and he headed for the base for the crew's first training drill. When he drove into the parking lot, he got a shock. A movie trailer was parked near the reception area.

He'd seen similar vehicles his whole life, every time his babysitter took him to visit his father on set. But what was a movie trailer doing here at the Jupiter Point Fire and Rescue compound?

Inside, he found Josh and Tim Peavy pretending to do stretches while they eavesdropped outside the closed door of the superintendent's office.

"What's up?" Finn whispered, joining them.

Josh shushed him. Finn focused on the rumble of voices behind the door—a male voice and a female. The male voice was definitely Sean. And the woman's voice sounded vaguely familiar too. But he couldn't quite place it.

"Something about a movie," Peavy hissed. "Sean's pissed as hell."

Finn got a sinking feeling in his gut. Why would a movie crew come to their base? It couldn't possibly be—

The door swung open. They all instantly snapped back into their various stretches. Josh went for a lunge, but he was completely off-balance and toppled over on his side. Tim Peavy did some kind of random yoga tree pose, arms overhead, balancing on one foot. He even hummed "om," as if that would fool anyone. Sean glared at the entire group of them.

At the sight of the woman with Sean, Finn dropped the arm stretch he was pretending to do. "Jill?"

"Finn Abrams, is that you?" Jill was a production coordinator who had worked with his father for years. Even though she was in her forties, her body was thin as a wire and she spoke like a Valley girl, every sentence ending in a question. She came forward and pecked an air kiss near his good cheek. "If any of you boys wants to be an extra, you just say the word. We pay SAG minimum." She darted past them with the speed of a hummingbird and was gone before they could answer.

They all looked at Sean's thunderous expression. "What's going on?" Josh asked.

But Sean was focusing all his fire on Finn. "Did you have anything to do with this?"

"With what? I thought we were doing drills today."

Sean studied his face, which always made Finn a little uncomfortable. "You really don't know?"

"Swear to God. I know that's Jill, and that she works for my dad. But that's all."

"Your father has gotten permission to shoot part of the Big Canyon movie here at the Fire and Rescue compound." From the unhappy way Sean made that announcement, he hated the idea.

As did Finn. "That's ridiculous. This is an active base. They'll be in the way."

"They're only shooting interiors here, whatever that means. And they're using the empty wing, not ours."

Finn sucked in a breath. The compound was a decommissioned Army base and some sections hadn't been allocated yet. The Fire Ranger had moved in first, then the Jupiter Point Hotshots. The hotshot crew had the use of one wing and its barracks. Finn had heard rumors about a Search and Rescue squad sometime in the future.

And now, apparently, a frickin' movie crew was moving in. Along with all the equipment and grips and staff and trailers that entailed. And...oh hell. The talent.

Annika.

"When is shooting going to start?" he asked.

"What's her name, Jill, is going to send me the schedule. I'm hoping they start soon, so they'll be done by the time the fire season starts. Here's what we're going to do. Our job. We train, we stay out of their way. They shoot their movie, then they leave. Any questions?"

Finn had lots of questions. But only one man could answer them. His father. Good luck getting answers out of him.

*

Instead, he called Jill as soon as training was done and he was back at Rollo's. No sign of Lisa's Mercedes, which just added to his rotten mood.

As he waited for Jill to answer, he paced next to the koi pond Brianna had recently installed.

"What the fuck is this about?" he asked as soon as she answered.

"Hi Finn. Somehow I knew you'd be calling."

"What's Stu up to?"

"It's so cute how you call him Stu instead of Dad. I've always wondered about that."

"Don't change the subject. Why did you change the location of the shoot?" He watched the brightly striped koi weave their way between the strong stalks of lily pads.

"Why don't you talk to the man who actually has the answers? I just do what I'm told."

"He doesn't tell me anything."

"All I know is our other location fell through, and he got on the phone and voila. Maybe this will be good? Give you a chance to heal the Abrams family rift?"

He crouched down next to the pond for a better look at the koi. "For us to have a rift, we'd have to actually be a family."

"Oh stop that. You have another family lying around somewhere?"

He didn't answer that directly, because yes, he did have another one—if he could only find them. "I consider the hotshots to be my true family."

"Listen, I'm glad you called because I could use your help."

"No. I'm not getting roped into this bullshit. I'll be *working*. My real job. Fighting fires."

The glint of metal caught his eye. A vehicle was driving up the road to Rollo's. His heart leaped. Was it Lisa?

"This won't interfere with your hero job. I need referrals. Support staff?"

"I want nothing to do with it. I'd rather live through another *actual burnover* than the damn movie version."

The car came into view—a tan Mercedes. Lisa. The relief made him lightheaded and he lost all track of what Jill was talking about.

He let her keep talking as he watched Lisa park her car and get out. She spotted him by the koi pond and waved, flashing a smile. He waved back, eating up the sight of her. She wore a white cotton shirt open over a black camisole that revealed the soft tops of her breasts.

She came close, standing next to him by the pond. He inhaled her scent—sunshine mixed with the light spice of her skin. She was still here. She hadn't left as he'd been assuming all day.

He cupped his hand around her calf, giving her a little squeeze. Her lips parted in an answering smile, and emotion shot through his heart like a dagger. He didn't want her to leave. It would drive him mad with worry. He wanted her in his bed, his body wrapped around hers. He wanted her safe, somewhere no bad guys could lay their hands on her.

He cut the coordinator off in mid-sentence. "Jill, I have to go."

"But wait—"

He switched off the phone and rose to his feet. "Hi."

"Hi."

He didn't know what to say. Everything or nothing? There didn't seem to be anything in between.

"I, uh, talked to Will Knight."

"Yes, you said that in your note."

A quick expression of guilt fluttered across her face. A-ha. So he was right. She had thought about running away. "He's not sure what's going on. The fire might be part of a campground crime spree. But he still wants me to be careful."

His gut tightened. Did "being careful" equate to leaving town? "He's right. You should be careful."

"I also went to see Molly. I told her I can't work with her any longer."

He looked away, trying to hide his reaction. If this was her decision, he'd have to respect it. "I know she'll miss you."

"Yes. But I can't take any chances. I started thinking about it. If someone's still after me, they might follow me to Molly's house. I couldn't stand it if something happened to her."

He took her hand and squeezed it. She was absolutely right, and he should have thought of the same thing. There was no reason for Molly and the Dean to be mixed up with whatever was going on. *If* anything was going on. Maybe the camper fire really was a random attack that had nothing to do with Lisa. "You're an outstanding person, Lisa Peretti. Molly's not the only one who's going to miss you."

A flush rose in her cheeks. "Oh, don't be silly. No one's going to miss me."

He scowled at that very suggestion of that. "Look, leave if you have to. But don't pretend I don't care about you. I dreamed about you all night. I woke up humming 'Love Will Keep Us Together,' and I haven't heard that song in decades."

A smile broke across her face. "No one's going to miss me, Mr. Romantic, because I'm not going anywhere. I'm staying, if you'll still have me as your guesthouse guest."

CHAPTER TWENTY-ONE

Finn lifted her off her feet and spun her around. She laughed as the sunset sky swung in wild arcs overhead. When her feet were back on the ground, he took her hand and dragged her toward the guesthouse, which was fast becoming one of her favorite places in the entire world.

"That would be a yes," he said as he ushered her inside. "Welcome home."

"Thank you, it's nice to be—" She gasped when he spun her around so his front pressed into her back. She felt his erection rise thick and hard against her. In a flash, hot need gathered between her legs.

"Nice to be what?" he breathed in her ear. He ran his hands all over her, molding her waist and hips, curving up her front to cup her breasts. She leaned her head back against his chest. Her body relaxed into him as if she had no say in the matter. He slid one hand inside her camisole and found a nipple. A light pinch of his fingers brought an electric pulse to life inside her body.

How did he know just how to touch her? Just the right degree of roughness, the perfect pressure and friction. She closed her eyes against the flood of sensation.

"Nice to be what?" he asked again. He nibbled her earlobe and her breath came faster.

"Nice to be here..." She caught her breath as he cupped both of her breasts in his warm hands and pulled at her nipples. "With you. I really appreciate everything you've do-one," she finished with another gasp.

"Appreciate?" He squeezed harder. The pleasure was so acute she wanted to scream. "So formal."

With one hand firmly fondling her breasts, he slid the other down her body, under the waistband of her pants. "Okay, I *really* appreciate—" His hand found her panties and another sentence trailed off in a moan.

"So wet for me," he growled.

She didn't answer, having given up on words by now. Her body was telling him everything he needed to know. She didn't need to say anything.

He bunched her underwear in his fist. The action tightened it against her mound. The slight friction drove her mad, and she began thrusting her hips forward, wanting more.

"I appreciate your appreciation, but that's not what I want from you, Lisa." He pulled the fabric tighter. "I want your arousal. Your screams. Your surrender."

Surrender...she wasn't good at surrender. She was too wary, too practical, too logical. But even so, she parted her legs under the pressure of his strong fingers, giving in to his unspoken demand. Her hips twitched, the need for closer contact nearly unbearable.

"That's what I want. What do *you* want, Lisa?" he murmured. "Tell me."

"Just...you. Touching me."

"Touching you? Where? How about here?" He slid her panties to the side. She bit her lip and writhed against him, waiting desperately for the relief she craved. Where were his fingers? What was taking him so long?

She glanced up and saw what was causing the delay. He was gazing down her body with an expression of such urgent lust that she nearly came from that alone. Her heart rolled over in her chest. This wasn't just sex. This wasn't just enjoying some physical release. This was something real.

And then his finger touched her clit and her thoughts scattered like petals in the wind. He stroked through her slick folds, finding the hot kernel where all her need was centered. At the first pressure, fireworks exploded at the edges of her vision. "Finn," she cried. "Oh my God."

"That's right, baby. I want you screaming my name." He rubbed a little faster, teasing, arousing, taking her up and away, into a place of bright, hot need. His finger was everything. It owned her. It promised the world, everything, right over the horizon, pure pleasure calling to her, just out of reach, beckoning, commanding...

She twisted in his arms, out of her mind with want. He was muttering in her ear, hot words that urged her on. "That's it, get it, girl...God, you're so sexy, so beautiful, you're going to come against my hand and it's going to be the best thing you ever felt and I'm going to watch you come apart."

Then he shifted his hand position, leaving her exposed and alone for half a moment. She moaned and jerked back against him.

"Don't you worry, Lisa. I will never leave you hanging. I swear it. I'll always take care of you." And his hand was back, not just the pad of his finger this time, but his whole hand, hot and rough and big enough to take her entire pussy into his palm. He pressed down just so against her clit and teased her breasts with his other hand.

Oh my God.

The first convulsion ripped through her body, so powerful she nearly jerked out of his grip. But he was so strong, so present. He held on tight as her orgasm erupted with the force of a volcano. Intense pleasure burst through her, one spasm after another. And his hand...oh, his hand, so tight against her, such a perfect fit, so exactly where she needed it. She squeezed her eyes shut and rode the wave like a roller coaster, as if there was nothing she could do except surrender and drink in each ecstatic moment.

So maybe surrender wasn't impossible.

Even when the convulsions slowed, he kept her safe in his tight embrace. She hung in his arms, panting, boneless, so limp she imagined collapsing to the floor if he let her go. Her jagged breaths mingled with his low, wordless murmurs. Something about "incredible," and "wow" and something that sounded like "love." But it couldn't be that.

As her awareness returned to normal, she became conscious of the rock-hard erection prodding her lower back. Surely it was his turn. And she wanted to do something for him. Something that might be even half as good as what he'd just given her.

She turned to face him. His eyes were deep and dark, heavy with passion. His nostrils flared as if he was trying to contain himself. But she didn't want him to contain himself. She wanted him to lose his cool the way she just had.

She dropped to her knees, surprising him. Not bothering to be gentle—the man had just made her lose her mind and he looked like he was about to explode—she undid his belt buckle and opened his jeans, yanked them down his legs. The strong curve of his thighs made her mouth water. Between them, his boxer briefs barely held in his swelling flesh.

"You look ridiculously good in your underwear," she murmured as she ran one exploratory hand across that impressive lump, ridges and softness combined. "They should put you on a billboard in your Calvin Kleins."

"Not anymore." He lifted his shirt to flash the red ridges of his scar tissue. "It's right here on my body. Firefighter all the way."

"Hey, I'd still enjoy seeing you on a billboard. But this is even better." She reached in and freed his penis from his underwear. "Up close and personal." She pressed her lips to his hot, velvety erection. She loved his male scent, simultaneously sweet and a little salty. Heat poured off him. Looking up, she saw the rippled muscles of his stomach tighten. "Take your shirt off, fireman. I want to see you."

He hesitated, then pulled it off. She raised herself higher on her knees so she could reach the scars on his abdomen. She kissed her way lightly across them. Scar tissue didn't have the same nerve endings as undamaged skin, so she knew the sensation was probably a little strange. But it was part of him, and it deserved just as much loving attention as the rest.

"This might sound strange, but I find scar tissue amazing," she murmured.

"It's ugly."

"It has a different form, that's all. But your body made this stuff. It patched itself up—along with some help from us medical professionals, of course. And I find that fascinating." Kissing his torso, being so close to those magnificent muscles, was practically decadent. She loved watching his chest rise and fall with the rhythm of his rapid breaths, loved seeing his head tilt down so he could watch her, so intent and predatory. She loved feeling his cock react to her every move with eager pulses.

"I've heard the word 'repulsive' used."

"That's ridiculous, Finn. Objectively speaking, you're the most attractive person I've ever known. A few scars don't change that."

She landed one last kiss on the mass of angry scar tissue, then turned her attention to the thick shaft between his thighs. It throbbed to her touch. She felt tension running through his body. She bent her head and touched her lips to its petal-soft skin. It burned with heat. Such a contradiction—tender skin stretched over tense muscle. Strength wrapped up in restraint, power held back.

Finn practically vibrated under her touch as she slowly swirled her tongue across the head of his cock. Learning, exploring, tasting. She didn't know where this urge came from, this need to feel his strength against her tongue. Never before had she longed to taste a man, or craved the weight of his flesh inside her mouth. The things Finn made her feel...it was insane and totally beyond her experience.

She closed her eyes. The image of Finn's tense expression and flexing muscles fixed in her mind, she abandoned herself to the moment. The slippery sound of her mouth on his cock, the occasional pop as he slid out, the scent of warm skin and sweat, the feel of thick ridges against her lips, her tongue. Every part of her mouth tingled with heat.

She felt his hand tangle in her hair, not pushing her, not guiding her, just wanting contact. It felt good, that light caress. She opened her eyes a crack for another glimpse of his long, naked torso, sweat gleaming on his skin, his head bent, his forehead creased in something like agony.

"Fuck, I'm going to come," he muttered. "That feels so damn good, Lisa. I can't hold back."

She pulled her mouth from his shaft. Her lips felt swollen, her tongue thick. "Don't. I don't want you to hold back. I want you to feel good."

He gave a short, incredulous laugh. "Fuck it," he muttered, and pulled himself from her fist.

"What are you—"

"I want to be inside you." He bent down and scooped her up in his arms.

"But I was—" She ran her tongue over her lips, which still hummed. "I was enjoying that."

"I was enjoying the hell out of that too, but I want you." Two strides and he was at the couch.

"What's wrong with the bed?"

"It's in a different room." He lowered her onto the couch, so she was sprawled half on, half off. Her pants were still undone, so it took only a second for him to get rid of them completely. "Hold on to the arm," he ordered, eyes glittering. "There, above your head. And hang on tight, babe."

She reached overhead and clutched the arm, just as he'd said, while he pulled a condom from his pocket. He rolled it over his bulging erection with shaky hands, then knelt over her, one foot still planted on the floor, one knee jammed against the back of the couch. He hovered over her, devouring her with a fierce gaze, sweat dotting his forehead. One hand landed on the arm next to hers, the other felt between her legs.

She moaned as he traced her sex, still damp and sensitive from her orgasm. He touched her clit and she thought she might come again, right this minute, which didn't actually seem possible based on her experience with her own anatomy. "Finn, that feels so good."

And then he was taking himself into his own hand and guiding his long, thick shaft into her body. She arched and opened for him, using the leverage of her foot on the floor to maneuver more snugly against him.

"Oh man, Lisa. You have no idea what you do to me." He groaned deeply as he slid farther inside her.

He bent her leg against her chest, opening her wider. She thrust her hips up to meet him. Sharp flashes of sensation zipped through her like lightning. Her inner thighs trembled. He eased out, then thrust in again, using her bent knee to give him some control.

Her eyelashes fluttered halfway shut. The visuals were almost too much—the strain on his face, the tension in his jaw, the flexing of his shoulder muscles. They didn't speak anymore, just lost themselves in the slickness and heat and roughness and relentless rhythm. They knew everything from the movements of each other's bodies...

On, on, more, deeper, again, better, higher, that's it, oh my God, that's it, Finn, now, now...

Together, they arched into a blinding, consuming explosion. She heard him shout something. Deep inside, she felt his cock flutter and pulse. He was all around her, hot and strong and beautiful. And nothing else in the world could compare. Nothing.

CHAPTER TWENTY-TWO

The next couple of weeks were the happiest of Lisa's life. Every morning, Finn went to the base to take part in the training drills for the hotshot crew. When he came back, often with a big bouquet of flowers for her, she'd do another therapy session with him. She alternated between working on his scar tissue and massaging his sore muscles.

"This worked out pretty well for you, didn't it?" she teased him as she worked salve into his scars. "A private masseuse available twenty-four seven. Now I know your true motives."

"If you want to know my true motives, all you have to do is ask." And he rolled her under him with a growl.

That was the other thing. Sex. All the time. Amazing sex such as she'd never experienced before.

When they weren't having sex, they talked. About everything. She told him about the crazy quilt of families she bounced between as a child. "Five total, counting my mother's four marriages and my father's two. One to each other, of course."

"I can beat that. I counted up my father's girlfriends once. I got up to fifteen and stopped."

She had to laugh at that. "So why didn't you end up cynical like me?"

"I have no idea. I always believed in love. All variations. Love at first sight. Love in the afternoon. Love between men, women, whatever."

"You're such a sap. It's embarrassing. You should really join Team Cynic. We can make room for you."

"Anything for you, my queen."

She giggled and flicked him on the shoulder. "See, right there's the problem. You wouldn't last a week with that romantic attitude of yours."

"I'll work on it."

"No, don't." She snuggled her nose into the light scattering of fur on his chest. "I like you just as you are."

"What a romantic thing to say," he teased. "I think you're slipping."

He told her about becoming a hotshot. At first, he'd wanted to be a structure firefighter, but then a wildfire had come close enough to LA to bring several crews of hotshots to Southern California. The constant TV coverage of the "elite" crews had fired his imagination. After that, nothing could stop him.

They talked about their first kisses. Lisa had cornered the boy next door because she was curious about what a kiss would feel like. Finn had hand-drawn a Valentine's card for his secret third-grade crush, who surprised him with a kiss.

Lisa explained her "friends with benefits" approach to sex.

"At least it's honest. Do you know how many times I've been asked to show my dad a headshot?"

"What's a headshot?"

"An actor's photo—wait, are you serious?"

"I assumed you weren't talking about a GSW. Gunshot wound," she translated.

He laughed. "A wound to my ego, that's all."

"Poor baby. Don't worry, your nurse is here to make it all better."

At first, she thought she'd be bored, since she wasn't working any shifts at Molly's. But strangely, she was busier than ever.

First Suzanne called and asked if she would please teach the teenagers at the Star Bright Shelter some basic first-aid techniques. That turned out to be tons of fun, their first lesson being how to properly take care of a new tattoo or piercing. She ended up buying a case of Bactine for the shelter.

She got into the habit of meeting Merry at the Venus and Mars Café every morning after Finn had left. She finally broke down and told Merry about Senator Ruiz and everything that had happened. Merry knew her way around Google. She quickly tracked down a story about his divorce from Maria. It mentioned that Maria was now living in Mexico City. Lisa devoured every word of that story, but didn't find anything that explained why someone had set her motorhome on fire.

Merry also found an obscure little news item in one of the Houston papers about a bribery investigation at Houston Memorial.

"Hm, I wonder if that's connected?" Lisa frowned at the laptop. "Should we send that to Deputy Knight?"

"Let him do his own investigation in his own sweet time."

Lisa rolled her eyes. "Merry, be nice to the hot cop."

"Fine. I'll forward it. But he owes me." She spent the next half hour cackling at her laptop, firing emails back and forth with Will.

Lisa sent her own batch of emails to her mother, father, stepmother, her ex-stepfather (her favorite of the bunch), and her stepsisters. All her emails said about the same thing. She was still having fun traveling around and didn't yet know when she'd be back in Houston. She hadn't told any of them the real story, just in case Senator Ruiz decided to question any of her family members.

Her friends in Jupiter Point knew more about her than her actual family did. Interesting.

The big excitement came the day both Lisa's and Merry's phones lit up with texts from Evie at the same moment.

Suzanne had her baby! It's a girl, 8 pounds 2 ounces. Visitors welcome. Josh is a mess.

"Oh my God!" Merry squealed. They both slammed shut their laptops and dashed over to Josh and Suzanne's house, which was filled with well-wishers and casseroles and baby gifts. Suzanne wasn't quite ready to let her baby, Faith, be held by anyone else, but they did get to admire her tiny pink ears and button nose.

"Look at Team Cynic," Suzanne teased the two of them. "You guys are looking a little mushy over there. Is that a tear I spy, Lisa?"

"I'm cynical about relationships, not babies," she responded. Although even that was starting to change, if she were totally honest. Just look at Josh and Suzanne. The baby wasn't even his, but he still teared up whenever he looked at Suzanne and Faith. When Evie said he was a mess, she wasn't exaggerating. He kept giving everyone big sloppy hugs and bursting into happy laughter at random moments.

It was enough to melt the most cynical heart.

About a week after that, she made a fairly shocking discovery.

It happened when she went to the Moon Glow Salon and Spa to apologize about the tabloid she'd "borrowed." It had burned up in the fire. No one had even noticed it was missing, but she felt better having apologized.

When she stepped outside, she found Brianna leaning against her Mercedes, arms folded across her chest, as if she was waiting for her. Brianna's little red Toyota truck was parked right behind her car.

"Hi, Brianna." Lisa gave her a puzzled smile. "Are you looking for me?"

"Yes. I...uh...are you hungry? I could use some breakfast."

"I already ate, thanks."

Brianna didn't move from her position by the Mercedes. "I could really use a hand at the greenhouse. Do you happen to have some free time today?"

Lisa stared at her in confusion. "Greenhouse? I know nothing about plants. I only deal with plastic plants that I can dust, that's my policy."

"Don't worry about it, you'll pick it up in no time." Brianna gave her a sunny smile. "Come on, breakfast is on me. You can call it brunch if you like. Have you tried the banana-walnut pancakes at the Milky Way? To die for. We can take your car if you like."

She opened the passenger door of Lisa's Mercedes and plopped herself onto the seat.

Lisa gaped at her. "What are you doing?"

"Getting into your car. Like we just decided."

"I don't exactly remember deciding anything. What's going on?" Lisa folded her arms across her chest. "No pancakes until you tell me."

Brianna heaved a long sigh, then tapped her forehead against the glove compartment a few times. "I told him this wouldn't work."

"Told who?"

"Finn. He's nervous about you being alone."

Lisa's mouth fell open. "You're kidding, right?"

"No." She screwed up her bright face in apology. "I told him it would be better if he just *told* you."

"Told me what, exactly?" Lisa drilled her with her best Nurse Badass stare. It always worked on obstinate patients. Brianna folded like a cheap suit.

"Have you noticed anything odd over the last couple weeks?"

"Odd?" Lisa shook her head in confusion. "Not especially. I've been at the shelter, and helping Evie mount her new exhibit at the gallery and hanging out with Merry at the café and..." Then it hit her. "Oh my God. Did Finn put you all up to this? He's lining up *babysitters* for me?"

"No, no, no. It's not like that. Okay, it's kind of like that, but we *volunteered*. Babysitters isn't the right word. Friend-sitters is better."

"Friend-sitters," Lisa repeated. "That's not a word. And Finn is a dead man."

Brianna groaned. "Please don't be mad at Finn. He's just worried about you and he's stuck at the base all day. I know the police are on the case, but they can't be with you all the time. So you're stuck with us."

"Us?"

"Me, Rollo, Evie, Merry, Josh when he can tear himself away from the baby. Suzanne can't really do anything right now, but she's put all the resources of Stars in Your Eyes at our disposal. So if you need a water escape, there's a catamaran we can use. If you can ride a horse, there are some lovely trail rides the honeymooners just love. I wish we had air support, but the airstrip isn't quite open for business yet. I did hear that someone's buying it, though. Did you hear about that?"

"Brianna," Lisa interrupted. "I don't need a sitter. I've been taking care of myself for a long time now."

"Maybe not, but do you need breakfast?" Brianna's winning smile could have lit up a city block, and all of a sudden, Lisa wanted to cry again.

What was wrong with her? All these people wanted to help her. They wanted to keep her safe and offer her boats and horses and friendship. And she had to dig in her heels like a stubborn mule? Some things deserved stubbornness—like helping an abused wife escape her husband. But some things didn't.

"Banana pancakes sound pretty good," she said weakly.

Brianna grinned in relief. "Thank God. Finn just texted me and I hate to see His Gorgeousness upset."

"His Gorgeousness? Seriously, that's what you're calling him?"

"Only when I really want to piss him off."

The banana pancakes truly were out of this world. Between them, Lisa and Brianna devoured three orders. "Okay, so how did Finn explain my situation? It's not supposed to be common knowledge."

"He didn't give any details. He said someone has been harassing you. We're supposed to be an extra set of eyes and ears."

"I don't want anyone getting hurt because of me. I couldn't bear that."

"Absolutely not. Finn gave us all strict orders. We're supposed to call Will or nine-one-one if we see anything strange. You're more vulnerable when you're alone, that's all. So you won't be alone. End of story."

"And if I want to be alone?"

"You'll have to suck it up, buttercup." Brianna winked at her. "Once the situation is resolved, you can ditch us all. Until then, you have your very own entourage."

Lisa looked down at her pancakes to hide her emotion. Ditch Jupiter Point? That didn't appeal to her at all. But when—if—the "situation" was resolved, she'd probably go back to Houston. Wouldn't she? Wasn't that where her life was? She'd go back to the nonstop madness of the ER, the humidity, her family's new Porsches, new speedboats, new chemical peels.

She'd say goodbye to this charming little stargazing town. And to Finn.

But not yet. First she had to help Brianna at her greenhouse.

It was a lot more fun than she'd expected. She learned how to repot little seedlings and prune rosebush plants. Brianna told her about Rollo's family and how hard it was getting used to their upper-crust lifestyle.

"You'd fit in a lot better than I do," she told Lisa. "I'm always putting my foot in my mouth."

"If the Warehams don't love you, they're crazy. You're adorable." She said it a little wistfully.

Brianna picked up another plastic pot and filled it with soil. "I'm a gardener with dirt under my fingernails. I'm a peasant in their world. You, on the other hand, are a classic beauty."

Lisa felt the burn of a blush sweeping across her cheeks. Brianna put down the bag of potting soil and stared. "Did I embarrass you? See, I put my foot in my mouth again!"

"No, no. It's not you. I'm just more used to being the kickass night-shift ER nurse, that's all."

Brianna twinkled at her. "You'll just have to be both, that's all. Do you miss the ER?"

"A little," she admitted. "It was my entire life for so many years."

Which was kind of sad, now that she thought about it.

After several hours in the greenhouse, they stopped at Suzanne and Josh's house for a late lunch. Suzanne opened the door with a finger to her lips.

"I finally got her down for a nap," she whispered. They tiptoed inside. Suzanne led them to the back patio, where she'd set out jars of peanut butter and jelly, along with bread and a block of cheese and a motley collection of silverware and plates, everything in a jumble.

"Can you believe I'm the most meticulous party planner in town?" she joked in a slightly louder voice now that they were outside. She set the baby monitor on the table and collapsed into a lawn chair. "This motherhood thing is a whole different deal. Babies don't do what you say, have you noticed that?"

Lisa laughed as she pulled up another chair. "Honestly, this is above and beyond, Suzanne. New moms aren't expected to do anything but sleep and feed the baby. How are you doing?"

"A lot better than I probably look." She grabbed a napkin and dabbed at a spot of drool on her t-shirt. "Sorry, I intended to shower before you guys came over but that never quite happened."

"Where's Josh? Isn't he supposed to be waiting on you hand and foot?" Brianna busied herself making peanut butter sandwiches.

"He's grocery shopping and doing ten million other errands. I thank God for him every day. And every night." She gave a naughty wink. "Back rubs, my friends. That's where it's at these days."

Lisa gazed around the backyard, which was surrounded by a weathered fence and held a kiddie pool, a plastic tricycle and a colorful jungle gym—all too advanced for a newborn.

"Hand-me-downs," Suzanne explained, following her gaze. "Either people around here are very generous or they're anxious to clean out their yards. Maybe a little of both."

A pang of longing twisted Lisa's heart. It all felt so normal and tranquil. Would she ever have anything remotely like this? She'd never wanted it before. She'd been so focused on her nursing work. But the past year had changed her. She didn't know what she wanted anymore. Again, the thought of Finn flashed through her mind, along with a rush of happiness.

She wanted him. God, how she wanted him.

"I spy a blush," Suzanne announced. Lisa put her hands to her treacherous cheeks. "Which leads to my next question. You, Finn, and a cozy little guesthouse. What gives?"

Brianna flicked Suzanne on the arm. "Suzanne, I've just spent the entire day with Lisa and didn't once ask her that. And I'm supposed to be the tactless one!"

"Look, that kid might wake up any second. I have to grab my gossip opportunities while I can."

"You don't have to answer." Brianna turned to Lisa. "She's easy to distract. All I have to do is tell her about the rumor I heard about the airstrip."

Suzanne brightened. "Rumor?"

"See?" Brianna laughed as she distributed the sandwiches she'd made. "Works every time. Yes, rumor. It's a good one, too. I heard two brothers bought the airstrip. I also heard they're very good-looking and very single. Figures."

"What do you mean by that?" Suzanne picked up her sandwich.

"All those years with no hot men in Jupiter Point, and now look at us. We have our hotshots, and now we're getting some flyboys. They're former Air Force, I heard. Or maybe Navy. I don't know. Rescue pilots. Something military and very, very hot, that's all I know."

"Works for me." Suzanne's eyes sparkled. "I see some matchmaking in our future."

As they continued to joke around about the new pilots, Lisa's attention wandered. An odd sound caught her attention. It sounded like a gurgling, with an overlay of static.

She jumped to her feet, nearly knocking over the little glass-topped table. "Where's the baby?" she asked Suzanne urgently.

Suzanne leaped to her feet as well. "In her bassinet...bedroom..." She started toward the house but Lisa ran past her at full speed, through the back door, toward the direction Suzanne had waved.

She burst through the open door and ran to the bassinet. Faith was on her back, spit-up dribbling from her tiny mouth. Choking, her face turning red.

Suzanne ran up behind her. "What's wrong? What's happening?" she cried.

Lisa didn't have time to explain. She threw up her arm to block Suzanne. "Hang on," she barked at her. Reaching into the bassinet, she gently turned the baby on her side and opened her mouth. With a quick swipe of her index finger, she cleared out the spit-up.

Then she waited, holding her breath. Behind her, Suzanne was sobbing softly.

The baby coughed, a strong jolt that shook her whole body. Then came another cough. Lisa reached in and cleared out this new batch of saliva. After a few more strong coughs, the child's color normalized.

"She's okay," she told Suzanne. "A little too much spit-up to handle, but her cough reflex is really strong. She might have been able to clear it all on her own, but sometimes a little help is a good thing."

Lisa gently picked up the still-shaking child and handed her to Suzanne, whose face was wet with tears. She gathered the baby into her arms, hugged her close, cradling her head on her shoulder, soothing her while tears rolled down her own cheeks.

"I've never seen her do that before," she wailed. "Jesus, I nearly had a stroke when I saw you run in here."

"If you want to put your mind totally at ease, you can get her checked out for reflux. All babies spit up, as you know. Some babies have a weak esophagus and the spit-up can get stuck. The best thing is to keep her elevated until her digestive system strengthens. Your pediatrician can check for anything more serious than that."

"What do you mean, elevated?"

"Like so." Lisa inserted an extra pillow under the mattress to lift it up.

"Okay, I'll do that from now on and I'll call the pediatrician right away. I can't believe I was out there gossiping. What if you hadn't been here?" Suzanne showered kisses onto her baby's soft head. "Lisa Peretti, I think you should move in. You can have our bedroom. We'll sleep on the floor."

Lisa laughed. "You'll be fine. *She'll* be fine. She coughs like a champ. She probably would have gotten it all out on her own, but it's the nurse in me. I have to check these things out, I can't help it."

Brianna, who'd been hovering by the door, came to Lisa's side and threw her arms around her in a warm hug. "So we finally got to see Nurse Badass in action. Wait'll I tell the hotshots."

CHAPTER TWENTY-THREE

When she walked into the guesthouse that night, Finn folded her into his arms. "You're a hero," he murmured in her ear. "Anything you want, you got. I have a steak dinner and a bottle of wine waiting for you. How about a bubble bath? A foot massage? A hot fudge sundae? All of the above?"

She sighed against him, melting into the haven of his embrace. Every part of her felt better when it was next to him. "I'm not a hero, silly. That's ridiculous."

"You saved Josh and Suzanne's baby's life. That makes you a hero around here."

"I'm a nurse. I was there at the right moment. That does not make me a hero. And besides," she drew back and swatted him lightly on the chest, "I'm supposed to be mad at you. You've been lining up watchdogs for me behind my back."

He groaned. "Brianna let it slip, didn't she? That girl can't keep a secret to save her life."

"Don't blame Brianna. This is on you. Why didn't you just tell me?"

"You would have said no. Because you pride yourself on your independence and self-reliance and competence and practicality and—"

She reached up to cover his mouth and stop the flow of words.

"Okay, I get it. I get it. It's really sweet of you. And really nice of everyone to go along." She nestled against him and rested her head on his chest. She listened to the reassuring thump of his heartbeat.

"It's no hardship, Lisa. They want to help. They care about you. How long have you been in Jupiter Point, just a couple of months? It already feels like you're part of things here. Everyone knows you because of Molly. And now you're going to be even more of a town hero. No one's going to ever forget today."

Suddenly she was back with the baby, gazing into the bassinet waiting for that first cough. She tilted her face up, resting her chin on his chest. "It felt like I was back in the ER. I miss that. I miss feeling useful."

"Do you?" He traced his fingers along her jawline, making her shiver. "I have an idea about that. But let's eat those steaks first."

Since it was a warm night, they took a blanket out on the lawn. After they'd polished off the steaks he'd grilled, he poured them each a glass of wine. He bent his long legs and settled her against his chest. The scent of wool sweater and shaving cream surrounded her. For a while they sipped red wine in silence as they gazed up at the sparkling panorama overhead.

"I passed my pack test today," Finn told her. "Three miles with a forty-five-pound pack, took me forty-one minutes and ten seconds. That means I'm officially on the crew. I'm a Jupiter Point Hotshot."

"Woohoo!" They clinked their wine glasses in a toast. "I never doubted it for a second—once I started treating you, of course." She winked at him.

"I owe it all to you, naturally." He picked up her free hand and kissed the palm. "I still wish I had something solid on my real family. That's the only piece that worries me. What if there's more inside my head waiting to pop up out of nowhere?"

"All you can do is train, right? Train hard, trust yourself and your crew."

"Right. You're right. I think Sean still has trouble trusting me completely. I don't blame him." He drew circles on her palm with his thumb. Her eyes half-closed from the sweet tingling sensation. "Okay, I lied. Two things make me nervous."

"Let me guess. The fact that you could be inside a wildfire pretty soon?"

He finished his wine, then turned her to face him. "Nope. It's the fact that once the season starts, I'll be gone a lot. And they haven't solved the motorhome fire, so you could still be a target."

"But I have all those friend-sitters," she teased, touched that he would still be worried.

"I have another idea. An even better one. How about a job in which you use your badass nursing skills at a secured location?"

"What, like...a prison?"

He laughed. "No. Well, maybe, depending on how you look at it. It's the *Miracle in Big Canyon* movie. Shooting starts this week at the base and they still need a nurse on call, especially for the fire sequences."

She shook her head "no" before he even finished. "No. No way. My mantra is keep a low profile. A movie is definitely not low profile."

"You'll be strictly behind the scenes. No cameras will be aimed in your direction. They're shooting at the Fire and Rescue compound, which is a former Army base, very intimidating. The hotshots will be coming and going, the Forest Rangers, other first responders. The movie crew will have its own security as well. It'll be the safest place in Jupiter Point."

She fussed with the stem of her wine glass. "What would I be doing? Treating some movie star's sunburn?"

"Unlikely. Annika never leaves the house without SPF fifty."

"*Annika?*"

He shrugged his wide shoulders. "She's starring in the movie. She plays a climate scientist. But she's just one of the people on set. You probably won't have much to do with her. Think about it. You already have the Jupiter Point police and sheriff on alert. You have friends to watch your back. And now you'd have the entire Fire and Rescue compound as a safeguard. What bad guy is going to want to go there? When I'm gone, you can spend the night in our barracks. I can clear that with Sean. And you also have this guesthouse, complete with a built-in body-guard named Rollo. If you want, we can trade Sparky in for a pit bull."

She set her jaw. "We're keeping Sparky." Over the past weeks, she'd grown attached to the little tortoise.

"Is that a yes? I'll call Jill right away if you're willing."

Still, she hesitated. The thought of being around Anni-ka didn't appeal to her one bit. She remembered the first time she'd seen Finn in the street outside the salon, and the way Annika had clung to him so possessively.

"You'd be practicing your profession again. I know you've been missing Nurse Badass. Being Nurse Ass-so-fine-she-makes-a-grown-man-cry isn't enough for you, is it?" He grinned, touching his forehead to hers. Little tremors of delight skipped along her skin, like soap bub-bles from a wand.

"You're such a goofball."

"Goofball. Nice word. It's code for sexy man-candy who makes me laugh, right?"

She laughed. Because he was right. Finn could always make her laugh, and he was always sexy. She didn't know what man-candy was, exactly, but if men were candy, Finn would definitely be her weakness.

"I think you might be my mini Reese's," she murmured as he drifted his lips across the corner of her mouth.

"Your what?

"When I worked at the ER, I used to pop those mini Reese's Peanut Butter Cups like pills. They had the perfect combo of protein, sugar and caffeine, just the boost I needed during a long shift. I used to stock up when they went on sale after Halloween. I was a bit of a junkie when it came to them. I went cold turkey when I left Houston."

His lips paused. "So what are you saying? I'm your mini peanut butter cups?"

"You wanted to be man-candy, right? Would you rather be my Gummi Worms? Those are the ones I always gave to my sister after Halloween."

"No, I don't want to be your Gummi Worms, thank you very much." His dry tone made her laugh. "I'll stick with the mini peanut butter cups. Though I have to object to the 'mini' part on principle. Especially combined with 'cup.'"

She giggled. "Goofball."

His low chuckle sent warm, wine-scented breath past her ear. For one stunning, perfect moment, absolute joy filled her, and she knew she was exactly where she was supposed to be.

*

Finn felt the subtle change in Lisa's body language. A certain softening, a relaxing. Maybe it was the wine, or the full stomach, or all the silly jokes about candy. Maybe it was the currents of warm night air rising up the cliff, bringing the scent of sage and ocean salt. Maybe it was the stars sparkling so joyfully above them. Or maybe it was some magical combination bringing Lisa out of her wary shell.

Whatever it was, he ran out of time to figure it out. A text dinged on his phone. He knew that ringtone. It could mean only one thing.

"Damn, that was fast."

"What happened?"

"First fire call. And it's still April."

He shifted Lisa off his lap so he could pull out his phone.

Brushfire in SoCal. Base in one hour. Driving out tonight.

"Why is it always Southern California?" he muttered as he showed Lisa the text. Her mood instantly shifted into all-business. He could imagine her at the ER, running alongside a gurney taking someone's vitals, issuing commands.

He came to his knees and started gathering up wine glasses. "I'm sorry about our dinner—"

"Don't worry about the cleanup." She took the glasses from his hands. "I'll take care of it. How can I help? What else do you need?"

He should have known that Lisa would respond perfectly to the situation. No complaints, no whining. Shit, what did he need? He hadn't even packed his gear bag yet. He'd barely gotten his official spot on the crew. He had to gather up a spare set of clothes, extra socks, bug spray...

Then it hit him. He was about to take off and leave her unprotected. How was he supposed to concentrate on fighting wildfires when he was worried about her? "I need one thing. That's all. Promise you'll take that medic job on the movie."

"Okay, fine. I'll do it."

Relieved, he pushed himself onto his feet. "Maybe a few other things. When you're here, stay within shouting distance of Rollo. Keep his number on speed dial. Maybe get a concealed-carry license."

Lisa put her hands on his shoulders and turned him toward the house. "Don't you dare worry about me. I promise I'll be careful. I won't go anywhere without an official police escort. I'll watch some self-defense on YouTube."

"This isn't a joke."

"I'm not joking. I mean, a little, but just to make you laugh. Underneath, I'm serious." She marched him across the grass. She was a lot stronger than she looked; she obviously had practice pushing ER patients around.

"I probably won't be gone long. Early-season wildfires tend to be smaller."

"Aren't I supposed to be the one panicking? You're going off to fight a wildfire."

At the door of the guesthouse, he stopped and swept her into his arms. "You don't seem like the panicking type."

"I'm not, generally speaking." She scanned his face, her beautiful dark eyes wide and serious. "Please be careful."

His heart gave a slow somersault. He'd never seen so much tenderness in her face. Was she starting to care for him even a fraction of the way he did for her?

A smile tugged at the corner of her mouth. "You'd better come back soon, because you owe me a bubble bath, a foot rub and an entire case of mini peanut butter cups."

"You'll get it. All of it, and more." He kissed her fiercely, pouring all his passion and protectiveness into the gesture. In the past, he'd always gotten excited about callouts. They felt like a big, wild, intense adventure.

This time, a deep well of emotion ran through the moment. He was leaving, she was staying, and both faced their own kind of danger.

When they ended the kiss, Lisa looked flushed and rumpled. "If I'm going to be working on that movie, I might be at the base when you get back. Will you be flying in on some kind of fancy firefighter airplane?"

He snorted. "Try a weird green van that looks kind of like an ice cream truck. We call it the crew buggy. We practically live in that thing during the fire season."

"Really?" Her forehead crinkled at that image. "That's not what I pictured, to be totally honest. I was thinking helicopters and people jumping out of airplanes."

Another text pinged. Probably Sean making sure everyone was on their way. "Not to worry, sweetheart. We're hotshots. We make it all look good."

With a cocky grin, he brushed one last kiss on her lips, then hurried inside to gather up his personal gear. Lisa leaned against the doorjamb as he threw bug spray and underwear into his duffel. "Want me to drive you to the base?"

"No. I got it. You stay here." He looked up at her, her dark hair loose around her shoulders, her lips raspberry red from his kiss. "I want to picture you just like this while I'm out there cutting line."

She lowered her lashes teasingly. "Really? Just like this? How about like this?"

And she flashed him.

One minute her top was down, the next minute it was up around her chin. Then it was back down again, and he was blinking in astonishment. "Are you trying to torture me before I go? Is that any way to treat a heroic fireman?"

"It's not torture. It's inspiration. Motivation to come back."

She tucked her thumbs in her pockets and cocked her hip, looking like a sassy, sexy dream come true.

"Oh, I'm motivated, all right." He shouldered his duffel and came toward the door. "Motivated to make you pay for that when I get back."

He swatted her on the rear as he passed, making her jump.

"Whatever works," she called after him.

Oh, she was definitely going to pay. But he'd make sure she enjoyed every second.

Setting Off Sparks

No matter how much a person trained, that first sixteen-hour day cutting line was a shock to the system. After three days, Finn's back and shoulders felt like concrete. His eyes stung from the constant smoke. He had to keep chugging water to fend off dehydration. His feet ached in his steel-toed work boots.

Even so, he couldn't stop grinning at random moments. He was back. This was what he'd fought so hard to return to. He loved the intensity of wildfire fighting, the tightness of the crew, the breathtaking surroundings. Battling a wildfire took everything he had, and more. He was constantly testing his limits, working to exhaustion and beyond. The fire didn't stop because they were tired, so neither could the firefighters.

Damn, it was good to be back.

Within a few days, his body got used to the intense pace, and he and the rest of the crew had found the groove. As one of the greenest members, his role was "swamper." He worked as one of a pair of firefighters called a saw team. Their job was to clear away obstructions from the fire line using a chainsaw. The "sawyer"— Tim Peavy—operated the saw while Finn got to clear away any large debris that might be in the sawyer's path.

It was back-straining, muscle-taxing work, and Finn ate it up. He only knew a few of the guys from his days on the Fighting Scorpions—Sean, Baker, Hughie and Josh, who was still on leave with the baby. The rest of the team, he'd gotten to know during training. But nothing bonded a crew like an actual wildfire. By the end of the San Dimas fire, they all felt like brothers.

Which wasn't always a good thing.

"Heard they started filming that movie about us," Baker said as they chowed down on pork and beans near the catering truck at the I.C. "You going to get us tickets to the premiere?"

"Yeah, sure." Finn hunched over his paper plate and forked pork into his mouth. "But you'll have to trim that beard of yours. Take a shower, maybe a walk through the car wash."

The other hotshots at the table laughed. The teasing camaraderie among the brotherhood of firemen was Finn's favorite thing about being a hotshot.

"Anyway, it's not just about Big Canyon anymore. They changed some of the story around, so it's a combo of different fires."

"That's true. I sure don't recall any gorgeous blonds hanging around the Fighting Scorpions. No one who looked like Annika Poole, for sure."

Finn held his tongue, having no interest in discussing Annika.

"I saw something in the tabloids about her," one of the younger guys piped up. "Said she was heartbroken and sobbing her eyes out over the 'one who got away.' They meant you, Finn. You're the one who got away. The beast who broke the beauty's heart."

Finn swallowed a huge mouthful of smoky beans. He recognized the hand of Gemma at work, with that hokey beauty-and-the-beast thing. "Don't read that trash. It's all made up out of nothing. It's for publicity, so people will go see the movie."

"Whatever. I say we all show up at the premiere and parachute down from a chopper."

Finn grinned at that image, which sparked more ridiculous ideas from the crew.

"Let's take the crew buggy down the red carpet."

"We could have, like, a chainsaw quartet."

"Hell, let's book a C-130 to do a fly-by."

They were all laughing when Finn felt a hand on his shoulder. It was Sean, who gestured for him to follow. They walked a few steps away from the others, out of earshot.

Sean scrutinized him with smoke-green eyes in a tired face. "I haven't had a chance to check in with you. How's it going out there, man? Feeling good?"

"Feeling real good. Like I was never gone. I even have a new nickname."

"Yeah?"

"Animal. As in, 'that Finn, he trains like an animal.'"

257

Sean laughed. "I hadn't heard that. Good one. How about the situation with your family? Anything new?"

Finn looked away, scanning the command post, which was a tent city filled with hundreds of people, vehicles, and canvas shelters. In a few days, this spot would be an empty fairgrounds again, home to tumbleweeds and some stray trash. Similar to a movie set, actually, which drew a small army of workers who dispersed when the job was done.

"Nope, nothing new. Just one false lead after another."

"Sorry about that."

Finn shrugged. "Haven't been thinking about it that much lately."

Sean's rugged face creased in a smile. "I know how that goes. Once I started falling for Evie, it got a little hard to focus on anything else."

"Oh, I'm focused," Finn said hastily. "One hundred percent focused, no worries about that." Was that what Sean had pulled him aside to talk about?

"Glad to hear it. Hope this doesn't change that. I just got word from the movie people that your father is on his way to the base."

"Our base? In Jupiter Point?"

"Yeah. He's visiting the set of the movie."

Finn's mouth fell open. "What the fuck? Why? He runs the studio, he doesn't show up at location shoots anywhere outside of Beverly Hills."

"Can't answer that. Maybe he wants to see you."

"He doesn't. He knows I'll be after him with more questions. Besides, I'm not even there."

"Then maybe he wants to see the hot nurse you personally recommended."

Finn laced his hands behind his neck and tilted his head back, feeling the stretch of his sore muscles. "Oh man. I bet you're right. Lisa is going to fucking kill me. Or leave town."

"From what I've seen, Lisa Peretti can handle herself."

*

"I'm going to do bad things to that Finn Abrams," Lisa muttered to herself as she hurried across the Fire and Rescue compound toward the set. Her walkie-talkie was crackling with an urgent command for her presence. She reached down and muted it, since she was already on her way. "Bad, uncomfortable things that he'll never forget."

One of the grips passed her, heading in the opposite direction. "Lisa, you'd better get there in a hurry. We have two hours until we lose the light and Annika won't come out of her trailer."

"I know, I know." she said. "Might be easier for everyone if she stayed in there," she added under her breath.

The grip laughed and headed for the catering table. Movie crews lived well, Lisa had discovered. She didn't ever have to worry about going hungry. She'd been working on the set for a week now, and had eaten more bagels and muffins than she usually ate in a year.

The *Miracle in Big Canyon* production had landed in the Fire and Rescue compound like an Army invasion. Production and crew vehicles packed the parking lot, along with individual trailers for the "talent." Equipment filled every corner of the empty wing—lighting gear, racks of costumes, wooden crates filled with props. Since they were shooting a movie about real firefighters, they were using a lot of the spare gear from the fire cache. Extras dressed in real hotshot gear—"greens and yellows"— wandered around the base.

The sight always made her pulse race because she'd seen Finn wearing his gear and, oh my God, it was sexy beyond belief.

Lisa had even met the actor *playing* Finn. Talk about a mind blower. He was a Spanish actor who had the smoldering romantic look down. All the makeup artists kept gushing over him, but Lisa privately knew that he couldn't hold a candle to the real Finn.

Annika Poole was playing a climatologist who kept warning the U.S. Forest Service, the BLM, and anyone who would listen that wildfires were going to keep getting worse. Apparently, her character was based on a real person—but that person happened to *not* be blond or a dead ringer for Gwyneth.

Lisa's first task as the on-set nurse was helping Annika treat an infected tattoo. She'd found the star in her trailer drinking diet Mountain Dew and moaning from the pain on her hip.

Of course it had to be her hip, a body part Lisa had never expected—or wanted—to see up close and personal.

Annika had recognized her right away.

"You're the girl from the wedding," she said, looking perplexed, as if she were a movie extra who had ended up in the wrong movie. "What are you doing here?"

"Oh, Finn found her, isn't she fabulous?" Jill poked her head into the trailer to deliver Lisa's ID and walkie-talkie.

Annika waved her away. "Go, Jill, Jesus, does the whole crew need to see my infection?"

Jill disappeared, leaving Lisa alone with a cranky movie star. She crouched down next to her, and assessed the red swelling around the new tattoo. "I'm going to clean this a bit, then put some antiseptic on it. It might sting."

"Ugh, whatever. Just bandage it up so I can shoot my fucking scene. Where is Finn, anyway?"

"He's out with the crew."

The perfect skin of Annika's forehead creased in a frown. "The crew?"

"The hotshot crew. You know, fighting a wildfire," Lisa explained.

"You mean a real one?"

Was she speaking a different language here? "Yes. A real one. He got a spot on the Jupiter Point Hotshots. They're down in Southern California right now."

"And you know this because...?"

Oops. Lisa realized her mistake too late. She didn't want to get on Annika's bad side. "It's pretty common knowledge around here. Jupiter Point's a small town."

"Yes, but Jill said Finn got you this job."

"He did." And right now, she was cursing him for that. "He's a nice person."

"Wait, are you boning Finn?"

Lisa didn't answer that, but she didn't have to. The Blush did that for her. An intense wave of heat traveled across her face like some kind of fever. She ducked her head, pretending to devote all her attention to the infected Chinese symbol on Annika's hip.

"What does this tattoo mean?" she asked in a desperate attempt to change the subject.

"It means 'watch your back.'"

Lisa's head shot up. Annika laughed merrily. "You should see your face. Never play poker, Lisa Peretti. I'm just joking. I like you. And Finn—he used to be such a catch. So beautiful. Mmm, mmmm. Those scars are a crime against humanity. But they make for good publicity, so I guess it's not all bad."

Lisa dabbed antiseptic onto Annika's hip, possibly a little more roughly than she ought to. "Sorry, I'll be done in a second here."

Annika nodded, bracing herself against the countertop. "I can't believe Finn's actually firefighting again. I told him, why don't you just *play* a firefighter? I know the executive producer of *Chicago Fire*. They would have cast him in a snap."

"There's a big difference between being a fireman and playing one," Lisa pointed out as she unpeeled a bandage.

"Yeah, playing one pays better."

Lisa carefully placed the bandage over the wound and pressed the sides into place. "There you go. Let me know if you have any pain or tenderness while you're shooting. I'll change the bandage again before I go home."

"Where's home?"

The question caught Lisa by surprise. She looked at the actress blankly.

Annika smiled at her innocently "Maybe we should be friends. Finn and I go way back. I was devastated when he was caught in that fire."

"Yes, I read about that." She'd practically memorized that article in the tabloid she'd taken from the salon. "It was really tough on you, I'm sure. Um, I should get going. There's a, um, possible sprained ankle I should look at. One of the grips."

Annika waved her away, the same gesture she'd used with Jill.

Lisa hurried out of the trailer, deciding to avoid Annika at all costs.

But it wasn't so easy. After that first introduction, Annika acted either very friendly or cold as a glacier. In private, when Lisa was changing her bandage, she was sweet and friendly. She kept asking questions about Lisa's life.

In public, she either ignored her or snapped at her. Lisa had no idea what she was up to, but "watch your back" seemed like wise words.

The most terrifying moment came when Stu Abrams visited the set. That day, the entire crew walked around on tiptoe and performed like a perfectly honed machine. Jill brought him to meet Lisa at her makeshift nurse's station.

Even potbellied and bald as a doorknob, Stu Abrams radiated charisma. He shook Lisa's hand warmly. "Nice of you to join our crew. It's a treat to have a nurse with your qualifications onboard."

"Thank you," she answered in some confusion. Had he actually checked into her background?

"How's that kid of mine? Still playing with matches?"

His dismissive tone rubbed her all wrong. "Finn's at the San Dimas fire. You've probably seen it on the news. The fire came within half a mile of ten thousand residents. They saved an entire ranch town. You must be really proud of him."

Stu's eye twitched. "I must, especially if a pretty girl tells me to."

Lisa's spine stiffened automatically. She despised empty compliments. But before she could answer, he spoke again.

"Tell you what, since you're a friend of Finn's, let's all have dinner. I'll fly you to LA. You and Finn can stay at the beach house in Malibu. A little 'thank you' for patching up this motley crew here."

"Oh, I don't think...Finn and I aren't...it's not like that."
Whatever she and Finn were or weren't, she didn't want
his father in the middle of it.

Satisfaction flashed across his bold features. He gave a
booming laugh that made her jump.

"Glad to hear it. He's meant for better things. Best you
understand that now. Good to meet you, Lisa."

Between that disturbing encounter and Annika's confusing behavior, Lisa found working on the movie almost
as stressful as her nights at the ER.

"Finn Abrams, this is on you," she muttered out loud
as she hurried across the compound. "Damn you."

"Not exactly the greeting I fantasized about."

Finn's voice resonated in her ear, and at first she
thought she'd imagined it. Then she turned around and
there he was. Looking amazing, from the tips of his rugged work boots to the bandanna tied around his head,
holding back his dark curls. With his bronzed skin and
half-inch growth of stubble, he looked like a pirate. A
wide grin split his face, making his white teeth flash.

He looked so good she could barely stand it. She swatted his shoulder, where his hard muscles flexed in response. "Just so you know, I've been waiting days to do
that."

"Oh yeah? I've been waiting days to do this." He swept
her into his strong arms and spun her around. Everything
else—the hotshot crew, the movie crew, anything that
wasn't Finn Abrams—vanished in a rush of giddy delight.

JENNIIFER BERNARD

Held in the wonderful embrace of Finn's arms, tight against his hard chest, Lisa's frustration drained away. She almost forgot what she was mad about.

Almost.

"This is the worst job ever," she mumbled against his collarbone.

He laughed, his chest vibrating under her cheek. Her eyes closed from the sheer bliss of being with him again. "As far as I'm concerned, this is working out great. You're safe and sound, and I get to see you the second I get out of the crew buggy."

She pulled away and looked over his shoulder at the boxy green vehicle parked next to the hotshots' domain. The side doors were wide open and the other hotshots were unloading gear. They were deliberately focusing their attention on their task rather than on Finn and Lisa.

"Shouldn't you be helping them?"

"Nah, they told me to come over and say 'hi.' We noticed that you were talking to yourself. They got a little worried."

"Yeah, well, that's what a week with a movie crew has done to me. Do you know how much I miss my tower right now?"

He tugged her back into his embrace. "I'm sorry about the aggravation. But I'm not sorry about you being here. Have you had any suspicious incidents?"

She shook her head. "No, nothing. No one comes on the lot without being cleared by security, so I do feel safe here. Annoyed, but safe."

"That's all I ask."

Her gaze drifted along his strong neck, to the place where black curls peeked past his collar. Being away from him had almost made her forget how attractive he was. She'd thought of him nonstop, but seeing him in person again took her breath away.

"Is the San Dimas fire out?"

"It's contained. Our part is done. The local people can take it from here." His smile dropped. "We have an off-site training session tomorrow, though. I don't have much time."

Disappointment tightened her stomach. Now that he was here, she realized how much she'd missed him. She wanted to curl up in bed with him and let entire days pass. Entire weeks, maybe. And now he was leaving again.

She didn't let her sadness show, or at least she tried not to. But as always, Finn seemed to have a sixth sense about her feelings. "I'll make it up to you, my queen. When can you knock off here?"

"I don't know. It seems like they go late every single night. They're shooting the big confrontation tonight. Annika gets to yell and throw a laptop across the room.

She's really looking forward to that. The rest of the crew is taking bets on how many prop laptops they have to make."

Finn cocked his head at her. "You're really getting the hang of this movie stuff, aren't you?"

Oh no—she had to set him straight on that one right away. "I would rather work six back-to-back shifts at the ER than change one more bandage for Annika. She's waiting for me right now, actually."

He let go of her hand. "Don't want trouble with the star." He gave her a smoldering look from under that damn bandanna. "But later, you're all mine."

Her throat tightened with desire and heat pooled low in her belly. "Are you sleeping here tonight or at the guesthouse?"

"Babe, I'm sleeping wherever you're sleeping. And honestly, I don't plan to do much sleeping."

She surprised him with a quick kiss on the cheek. "I'm so glad you're back," she whispered.

He put his hand over his heart and smiled at her with so much tenderness her knees weakened. "I'm going to make you even more glad. Swear on my life."

She watched him walk over to rejoin his crew. Her professional eye noticed that he was favoring his injured side. "If you play your cards right, you'll get a massage," she called after him.

Oops. She'd said that a little too loudly.

Baker, the massive black fireman, let loose a long laugh. "Can I play too? I can kick his ass at cards."

She laughed, then hurried away before she said anything else she might regret. Like that she intended to give Finn much, much more than a massage.

*

Post-fire reunions were the best.

Of the sixteen hours before Finn had to report back to the base, he and Lisa spent ten in bed, and most of those *awake* and in bed. Much of that time he was inside her, which was exactly where he wanted to be. The relief of finding her still alive, and still in Jupiter Point, nearly brought him to his knees. All he wanted to do was make love to her, as many times and in as many ways as possible.

He figured he could catch up on his sleep in the crew buggy the next day. Or hell, just quit the crew. Who needed firefighting when he had the hottest, wildest, most fiery woman he'd ever known snuggled into bed with him?

He loved every freewheeling, combustible moment they spent together in bed. He loved it when she straddled him and licked his nipples and worked herself against his cock. He loved flipping her over, dragging her ass into the air and burying himself deep inside her. He loved it when she got so relaxed she sprawled across the bed like a rag doll. She let his lips and hands go wherever they wanted, let him feast on her like a hungry firefighter at a breakfast buffet.

Ordinarily, he would stuff himself after a fire, trying to make up for the calorie deficit after working long days under the hot sun. This time, he resented having to take breaks for food. All he wanted to do was gorge himself on Lisa's sweet curves.

When they were both so spent they were seeing stars, they dozed off together. Her face nestled into the crook of his shoulder, her bent knee propped on his thigh. He didn't want to drift off because it felt so good to hold her. Unconsciousness was the last thing he wanted. But he couldn't fight it forever, and soon he was deeply asleep.

He was awakened by her mouth doing unmentionable things to his cock. Astonishingly, after all the times they'd already made love, he got hard nearly right away. "Jesus, Lisa, I thought I was done for the night."

"I thought I was too," she admitted. Her warm breath heated his flesh, then her mouth slid down his shaft again. He lost himself in the pleasure, the pressure, the joy of that intimate contact. Finally, he couldn't take anymore. He pulled away and shifted position, cupping his body around hers so he could enter her from behind. The plump cheeks of her ass nestled around him. He probed the hot channel waiting for him. It gave way before the hard thrust of his penis. He reached around her front and pressed his palm against her heated, wet nest of curls. She arched against him, and then they were both grinding out a fast, hard, primitive orgasm, like two beasts in the night.

They both collapsed, gasping. "Fuck," he said. Emotion was bursting out of him, pushing at the walls of his heart, impossible to keep inside. "Lisa. Damn it. I have to tell you something. I know you don't want to hear it. But I have to tell you."

"Don't scare me, just tell me." She lay on her side, one arm flung across the sheets, her skin gleaming in the soft moonlight, her dark hair spilling like ink over the pillow.

"I love you."

He held his breath. She went still at his announcement. But she wasn't leaping out of bed, so maybe it would be okay.

"I know you see this as just sex. But it isn't for me. Not since the first moment I saw you. I know I made a joke out of it, with all those cheesy lines. But it was real. I loved you the second you walked into that tower. I looked at you and that was it. Love. Like a...a load of slurry dropped on my head."

"A load of what?"

At least she was speaking. "Slurry. It's the stuff they drop onto wildfires from air tankers. Lands like concrete. Guaranteed to knock you out."

"Finn," she murmured into the moonlight. "What you're describing isn't love. It's infatuation. You're letting your romantic side run away with you."

He wanted to shake her. How could she dismiss his feelings so lightly? Even if they didn't make sense to her.

"No. I might be a romantic, but I've never felt anything like this. Have you?"

He held his breath again. He knew his Lisa. She didn't lie. Her face and its tendency to blush didn't let her.

"No, I haven't," she answered in a low voice. "But that doesn't mean this can go anywhere."

"Why not?"

"Finn. Come on. I've seen your world now, up close and personal. All that Hollywood craziness. I've met your father."

He winced at the reminder. She'd told him about that brief, nasty encounter. "That's not my world and you know it. My world is the crew buggy, chainsaws and slurry. Camping behind the fire lines in the back country, with the sun rising over the mountains turning everything to gold. When you were in that tower, watching for smoke? Staring at the wilderness? That's my world. You said you loved it."

She rolled away from him. "Okay, but that's just part of it. I have a life waiting back in Houston. A job, if I can get it back."

"There are jobs here. Not just on the movie," he said quickly, anticipating her protest. "There's just as much need for badass nurses here as in Houston."

"Why are you trying to ruin this? You're leaving in about an hour. Do you really want to get into a fight now?"

He rolled onto his back and stared up at the ceiling. No, he didn't want to spend his last hour with her fighting. But this battle needed to happen. He knew what he felt. He knew it was powerful and not going anywhere. If she didn't feel the same, he'd have to live with that.

"I love you." He drew in a deep breath. And jumped off the cliff. "I want to marry you."

"Marry me?" She scrambled to her knees. Dawn was creeping in around the curtains, bringing pearlescent light into the room. It made her skin glow. "What are you talking about?"

"Don't worry, you don't have to say 'yes' yet. Or 'no.' Technically, I haven't asked you yet. I just said what I want."

She stared at him. Her eyes sparkled with...something. But not a yes. "Finn, I'm...I'm not the marrying kind. I'm too cynical. I've seen every member of my family get married and divorced. More than once. We don't have a good track record with romance. I just..." She shook her head, gathering the blanket around her like a cocoon. "Let's keep things simple."

He dragged his hand through his hair. "You're not your family, Lisa. You're a compassionate, committed person. We're great together, married or not. So why not married?"

She moved to get out of bed, but he stopped her with a hand on her thigh, her skin silky smooth.

"Maybe you should have more faith in yourself," he said softly. "You have so much love in your heart, you care so much for people. I think you hide behind that cynicism."

"Finn...stop this. I can't—" She broke off, looking so distressed he could have kicked himself. He'd let his impulsive side run away with him.

"Okay, I'm stopping. At least for now. I promise I won't ask again until I'm a hundred percent sure that's what you want."

She pushed the tangled sheets off her body and jumped out of bed. In the dawn light, she was so beautiful, poised for flight. He wanted to grab her hand and tug her back where she belonged. With him.

"All I ask is one thing in exchange."

"What's that?" She picked up a robe and slid into it. He wondered if it was the last time he'd see her naked body.

"I can tell you're kind of freaking out. I get that. Just don't—don't leave without telling me."

She gazed down at him, worrying her lower lip with her teeth. His stomach clenched. She was thinking about leaving. He could read it on her face.

He also recognized the moment when she decided it was a reasonable request. "That's fair." She tightened the knot on her robe. "Okay, Finn Abrams. This is your official notice that I'm leaving the bedroom and heading for the shower."

"That's funny. Really funny."

She disappeared into the shower. He released a long breath.

Had he ruined everything?

CHAPTER TWENTY-SIX

By the grace of God and Abrams Productions, Lisa didn't have to report to the set until late the next afternoon. Finn left in the morning to rejoin the crew. They kept his departure light, with no references to the intense conversation of the night before. The guesthouse felt empty without him. The scent of their lovemaking made her miss him so much that she threw open all the windows to air out the place.

She took Sparky out of his cage and changed his bandage, then let him explore the kitchen floor. She watched him cruise across the linoleum, his bright, curious eyes checking in with her now and then.

Of course, even Sparky made her miss Finn. He'd adopted the darn turtle for her. A *wounded* turtle, no less. Because he knew her heart would go out to an injured creature. It was such a weirdly romantic gesture.

But she was immune to romance! Wasn't she? She was Team Cynic. All the way.

Caring about Finn, missing Finn, loving every moment she spent in bed with Finn—or out of bed—that didn't mean they should get married.

On impulse, she dialed her mother. They hadn't spoken much since she'd left Houston.

"Lisa, sweetie, I have about two minutes before I have to hop in the car for a lunch date. Tell me everything."

"Um..."

"You're in love, aren't you?"

"*What?*" She crawled across the floor to steer Sparky away from a mousetrap. "Why would you say that?"

"A mother always knows."

"That's insane."

"Well, a mother can dream, anyway. It was worth a try. So you're not in love?"

Sparky poked his little head against her knee.

"Why is that the only thing you ever want to talk about? What about my career? What about all the people I've helped? What about how hard I work?"

"Okay, calm down, sweetie. You're right. I know you work very hard. Who have you treated lately? More gunshot wounds? Tell me about your last patient."

"Well, as a matter of fact, it was an infected tattoo on a movie star."

"Ooh, now that's something I want to hear about. Oops, another call's coming in. I'll call you later, my dear. Will you be back for the anniversary party?"

Lisa's heart sank. Her stepsister had sent her an email about the party, which was scheduled for next weekend. But she didn't feel comfortable going back to Houston yet. "We'll see."

"Oh honey. Ten years is something to celebrate. I think this one might actually last!" With a light laugh, her mother hung up the phone.

Lisa looked down at Sparky, who was making his slow way around her foot, poking at every toe.

"So maybe Mom did finally find the right man. What do you think, Sparky?"

He didn't have much of an answer, but then, neither did she. Did her mother's three failed attempts at marriage mean the whole concept was doomed? Or did it simply mean that she refused to give up until she got it right?

Her phone flashed with Merry's number.

"Team Cynic. Thank God," Lisa answered. "I need to hear a voice of reason."

"What jaded and world-weary insight would you like from me today?" Merry's laughing voice lifted her spirits right away.

"Love at first sight isn't a real thing, is it? Definitely not grounds for considering marriage, right?"

"Girl, we obviously have some catching up to do." In the background, Lisa caught the sound of keys clicking on a computer. "Will you be around later today? I'm calling 'cause I came across some interesting information about that hospital where you worked. Do you still have those files you mentioned?"

"Yes, but I won't be here later on. I have to work. You can come by and pick them up if you want."

"They're not your only copies, are they?"

"No, no. I have everything on a thumb drive too."

"Cool. I better go, my editor's on my ass about this feature on the new head of the observatory. But we have some dishing to do, so call me when you're done with work. No matter the hour, hear?"

"Sure."

After she hung up, Lisa took Sparky back to his habitat and gave him some food and water. She wandered to the kitchen window, which was her favorite spot because it offered a glimpse of the sparkling Pacific Ocean. She poured herself a glass of water and finally allowed Finn's passionate words to sink in.

He *loved* her. Wanted to marry her. He knew all about her cynical side, her prickly side, her passion for her work, her crabbiness first thing in the morning, her tendency to keep people at arm's length. He knew all these things, and still loved her.

That was fricking amazing.

Her heart swelled just thinking about him. With her eyes closed, she could still feel his kisses all over her body, the warmth and magic of his presence.

Maybe she should try something new. Give this romance thing a chance.

*

When Lisa got to the set later that afternoon, she knew right away that something had happened. The first crew member she passed—a grip—smirked at her. At the catering table, everyone scattered as soon as she appeared. She piled fresh honeydew melon and a bagel onto a plate and made her way to the nurse's station.

She found a piece of paper on the desk they'd set up for her. It was a blurry printout from a website. The gossip site TMZ, she noted, before scanning the headline and photo. The headline read "ANNIKA BURNED BY LOVE TRIANGLE." Then came a collage of three photos. One must have been taken yesterday when Finn had returned to the base. It showed Finn swinging her around. He was grinning, Lisa was laughing, and they both looked completely caught up in each other. The other photo was an aerial shot of the guesthouse, with a red circle around it and the words "Secret Love Nest." In the third photo, Annika, dressed in her "climate scientist" costume, held her hip as she blotted a tear from her beautiful face. The caption of that one read, "BRAVE ANNIKA SAYS SHOW MUST GO ON."

Pure horror shot through her. Jesus, she was in a *tabloid*. Just months ago, she'd been reading a tabloid, now she was *in* one. After all this time trying to keep a low profile, she was featured in a gossip photo spread. Her face was clearly visible in the shot of her and Finn.

Oh my God. Did the article identify her?

Quickly she scanned the text. "Production staff refused to identify the mystery woman, but sources tell us she's the on-set nurse. Sexual healing, anyone?"

How long would it take before her name was all over the place?

She crumpled up the printout and threw it across the room, where it bounced against a water cooler. So much for *safety*. She wanted to scream; she wanted to quit on the spot.

Jill, the production coordinator, skidded to a halt in the doorway. "You're mad."

"Mad?" Was mad the right word? Furious. Frightened. Invaded. "Annika must be freaking out."

Jill gave her an odd look. "She's a pro. Don't worry about her."

"I should explain about me and Finn. It's not how they're making it seem." She started for the door, but Jill blocked her path.

"Really. Don't worry about Annika. Her publicist, Gemma, is one of the best in the business. We work with her a lot."

Lisa stared at her as the truth slowly sank in. "This was deliberate. A publicity stunt. Someone planted this story. Annika? The studio? Who?"

Jill gently pushed her back toward her chair. "Look, how about you sit down and I'll get you something? Any pills handy for a moment like this?"

"*Pills?*"

"Anxiety, relaxation, Wellbutrin, Xanax, you must have something in your bag of tricks? Just so you know, I had nothing to do with it. Publicity is not my scene, I just keep the trains running. Come on, sit down."

"Stu Abrams. He did this."

"Do you need to go home? I can have someone drive you, not a problem."

Lisa pushed her away, which wasn't as easy as it should have been. The woman was wiry but strong. "I need to get out of here."

She flung herself out the door and fled from the office area. She threaded her way past extras and grips and the security guard who stood watch at the entrance. Which one of these crew members had sold her out by snapping that photo?

In the fresh air of the parking lot, she stopped to catch her breath.

Options. She needed options. And she needed privacy to figure them out.

She looked for her Mercedes and found it blocked in by a delivery van. Besides, she was much too shaken up to drive.

The wing where the hotshots were located caught her eye. The crew had left earlier today, so she'd have the place to herself. That was all she wanted. A place to clear her head and come up with a plan.

She slipped into the reception area, a sprawling space bounded by concrete walls and furnished with a big metal desk, two well-used couches and a big television. It screamed male hangout, but right now, that worked for her.

She flopped down on one of the couches and drew in a deep breath.

The place smelled like Finn. Like smoke and chainsaw oil and soap. Crap. A wave of missing him swept over her. She could practically feel the charm of his smile, the warmth of his gaze.

This was all Finn Abrams's fault. She should have known to stay far away from him and his fucked-up Hollywood world.

A tear trickled to the corner of her eye. Annika and the studio had used her like a prop. And she'd walked right into it like a lamb to the slaughter. Maybe spending time in Jupiter Point had made her forget how horrible people could be. All that kindness and concern had thrown her off her game. She needed to get back to "Nurse Badass," the queen of the ER, the woman who stared down gang-bangers and stood up to abusive husbands.

Most of all, she needed to leave town. As quickly as possible. The movie set was no longer safe. If someone was still looking for her, their job had just gotten a lot easier.

Decision made, she jumped when her cell phone beeped. Checking the number, she saw it was Merry.

"Hey girl," the reporter said cheerfully. "I'm walking up to your place right now. I forgot to ask where you stashed the key."

"It's under a rock by the koi pond. I didn't want it any-where near the guesthouse, obviously. There's a rock shaped like a beehive, do you see it?"

"I do. Hey, are you all right? You sound funny." Lisa heard the sound of feet moving quickly across grass. Mer-ry always tilted forward as she walked, as if getting from point A to B was something to be endured and made as efficient as possible.

"I'm fine. I just—" She couldn't deal with any questions right now, especially since she was going to be leaving, with no idea when or if she'd be back. "No comment."

Merry sighed. "Okay, now you're just reminding me of Will Knight. I swear I think he uses that for everything. 'Did you make an arrest? No comment. What planet is Jupiter Point named after? No comment.'"

Lisa laughed, her heart squeezing. She was going to miss the friends she'd made here in Jupiter Point. Across the room, a bulletin board caught her eye. She got to her feet and wandered in that direction. It was covered with printed notices—schedules, communications about man-datory trainings, a few photos. A snapshot of Finn drew her like a magnet. He was bare-chested, caught in mid knuckle push-up, muscles flexing, sweat dripping into his eyes. His face was set in gritty lines of determination. His scarred side was facing the camera, and every ridge and distortion of the scar tissue was visible.

It didn't detract from his appeal one bit.

She craved him in that moment. With every cell in her body, she wanted him next to her. Skin to skin. Or clothes to clothes. Any way she could get him.

"Lisa, are you there? Something's not right here."

She snapped back to attention. "What do you mean?"

"Looks like the door's unlocked. Think maybe you left it that way?"

"No, absolutely not. Rollo has a key too, maybe he..." With a flash of horror, she remembered the other shot in the newspaper. The Google Earth shot of the guesthouse. "Merry, get out of there. Now."

"What? Oh my God, I think someone's been in here. It's a big mess, looks like someone ransacked the place—"

"Merry!" Lisa cried urgently. "Just get out!"

She heard a sharp cry. A crash. Then nothing.

CHAPTER TWENTY-SEVEN

"Merry? Merry?"

No answer from her friend. She could still hear sounds on the other end of the line, but they were all muffled, as if Merry had dropped the phone in the dirt and forgotten about it. But it sounded like footsteps...Rollo? Brianna?

"Hello? Hello? Merry?"

She looked around wildly. Hanging up the phone didn't seem like the best thing to do. What if Merry came back on the line? She ran to the old metal desk, which held a phone, a police scanner, a desktop computer and a clipboard with a sign-in sheet. Grabbing the phone, she hesitated.

If she called nine-one-one, what would she say, exactly? "I was on the phone with my friend when I heard weird noises and she stopped talking to me?"

Instead she put her phone on speaker and pulled up the contacts list, then dialed Will Knight's number. He answered right away.

"It's Lisa Peretti. I think something happened to Merry out at Rollo's guesthouse. We were on the phone and she said it looked like someone had broken in, then I heard a crash and she stopped talking. I didn't know if I should call nine-one-one or—"

"I'll take it from here. I'm glad you called me. Where are you?"

Just the sound of his confident—Merry might say arrogant—voice made her feel less anxious. "I'm at the base."

"Stay there. I'll call you with an update as soon as I have one."

After she hung up, a violent fit of shivers took hold of her. She needed to be with Merry. If she'd gotten hurt because of her, *instead* of her...*again*...she'd never forgive herself.

Don't jump to conclusions, she told herself. Maybe nothing happened. Will Knight would figure it out.

The door creaked open. She leaped to her feet in a panic, as if whoever had broken into the guesthouse had found her here too.

"Lisa? Are you in here? Someone said they saw you head this way?" Jill peered around the edge of the door.

"I'm here. Need a little space, please."

"Absolutely. Just wanted you to know that I got ahold of Finn."

"He's training today. Off-site somewhere."

"Yes. No cell service, but I got him on the dispatch channel."

"I'm sorry, why would you do that?" Even though part of her longed to talk to Finn about this, she didn't want to add fuel to what the tabloids were saying.

"Finn wanted to know if anything unusual happened. I'm under strict instructions. This isn't exactly unusual, in our world? But I can see it is for you." Jill's walkie-talkie crackled, but she turned it down. "Anyway, he gave you a message. He said do not, under any circumstances, return to the guesthouse tonight."

A sharp pang of guilt shot through her. Why hadn't she told Merry to leave the second she'd called? It hadn't occurred to her that someone might show up at the guesthouse that quickly.

"He told me to book a hotel room for you and keep it top secret. Except from him."

Lisa pulled her lower lip between her teeth. Did she trust Jill to keep anything top secret? Hell no. She was done with being naive and allowing herself to be a pawn in someone's game. "Thank you, that sounds great."

Jill nodded and pulled out her smartphone, tapping at it so rapidly Lisa could barely see her fingers. "Done. Must be nice, having a man like Finn watching out for you. He's a good one, always has been. Known him since he was a kid. I texted you the reservation."

"Thank you." Just then her cell phone crackled back into action. "I have to take this, Jill."

"Are you coming back to the set?" Under Lisa's incredulous stare, she backed down. "Just a love scene shooting tonight. We should be fine."

As soon as Jill was gone, Lisa clapped the phone to her ear. "Hello? Merry?"

"No, this is Will. Merry's...uh...well, she's asleep."

"Asleep?"

"Yup. Best guess is, someone shot her with a tranquil-izer dart, got a closer look and realized they hit the wrong woman again, then took off."

"Oh my God. I can't believe it. But Merry's okay?"

"She's okay. She's in the backseat of my Chevy. She probably won't be too happy when she wakes up."

"Because of what they did?" A series of awful scenarios flipped through her mind.

"Because she'll be at my house. She's not injured enough for Urgent Care. And I can't get into her place. So she'll be sleeping it off at Chez Knight."

Lisa released a long breath of relief and rolled her shoulders.

"Obviously this means someone still wants to find you, Lisa."

"I know. I have a plan. Will, there's a...um...a turtle there, in a cage. Did you happen to notice if he's okay?"

A long pause, followed by his amused answer. "Turtle looked just fine. Deputy Knight, reporting in."

"Thank you, Will. Call me when Merry wakes, up, will you? After she finishes yelling at you?"

"Will do."

Lisa grinned as she ended the call. What she wouldn't give to see the sparks that would erupt when Merry woke up in Will's company.

She checked the time. It was close to evening. Finn would be back at the hotshot base soon. All her stuff was still in Finn's guesthouse though it didn't amount to much. A bag of Suzanne's clothes. Her portable safe. She'd drive back and pick up the essentials, say goodbye to Sparky, then hit the road before she ran into Finn.

She couldn't see Finn. If she did, it might be too hard to leave. But she had to. There really was no other option. Neither the base nor the guesthouse was safe anymore, and she definitely didn't trust Jill's hotel offer. She could just picture the headline. *Nurse's No-Tell Hotel Nookie.*

Just get out of town. Right now, before Finn gets back.

Decision made, she ran into the parking lot and found her Mercedes. Her last remaining possession, really. She drove out of the Fire and Rescue compound without so much as a glance back. It never paid to look backwards when you couldn't go that way. The best thing to do was move on.

She drove away from the base toward the highway. The sun was setting beyond the hills, the pine trees along the road casting long shadows. They made her think of the vast forests she used to watch from her tower, day after day, looking for smoke.

She'd just spotted smoke—metaphorically speaking. And she wasn't going to hang around waiting to get burned.

*

You could cut the tension in the crew buggy with a butter knife. The crew was exhausted from their training in the hills. Baker was snoring in the far backseat—a deep, rattling, snorting sound that kept everyone else awake.

Not that Finn could have slept anyway. He'd called Lisa as soon as they'd gotten within cell phone range but gotten no answer. From Jill, he learned that Lisa had never checked into the hotel. He tried texting and calling Lisa several more times, but she never picked up.

He had no idea where she was. And a constant knot in his stomach made him want to rip someone's face off.

Possibly his father's. Or Annika's. Definitely Gemma's. How could they pull a stunt like this?

It was nearly nine by the time they reached the base. Finn worked his way past the other hotshots, who were waking and stretching and groaning from the road trip. He jumped to the ground and hurried to open the side door, where the gear was stored. He was probably sorer than anyone else, but he was also the least likely to complain. He didn't want Sean booting his ass off the crew.

He flung open the door and grabbed a duffel in one hand, a gas can in the other. The quicker he could get this damn buggy unloaded, the quicker he could track down Lisa.

His phone rang. Will Knight, calling him back. He held the phone between his ear and his shoulder while he continued to unload the truck.

"Any news?"

"Got a lead on a suspect. Mrs. Murphy at the bookstore noticed a strange car idling on Constellation Way earlier."

"Mrs. Murphy is your best lead?"

"She actually wrote down the license plate number on the book she was ringing up. I have someone tracking down that purchase now."

Finn snorted. "You've got to be kidding me."

"We'll get him. This shit is getting on my nerves."

Finn was way past nerves and onto "tearing shit apart."

"How do you know it's just one guy? What if there are more?"

"We haven't noticed any other suspicious strangers in town. And by 'we' I do mean Mrs. Murphy."

"Goddamn it, Knight." He tossed an empty gas can into the storage area with a clang. "Why not fire the entire police department and hire Mrs. Murphy?"

"Why would we do that when she gives us tips for free?"

"I'm not laughing. And Lisa isn't answering her phone. Have you heard from her?"

"Not since I picked up Merry. But Mitch at the Arco station spotted an early-model Mercedes heading north."

"Keep me posted." Teeth clenched, Finn hung up and slammed his fist into the side of the crew buggy.

He should have locked Lisa inside somewhere until he got back.

When he turned around, Sean was glaring at him, arms folded across his chest. "You just punched the buggy. Get out of here."

"I'm sorry, man. I'm worried about Lisa, she's—"

"I said get out of here." Sean's rugged face softened. "We got this. Go do what you need to do. We got a couple days' downtime. Just keep your phone on."

He pressed the heel of his hand into his forehead. The scars on his face throbbed, which meant he was tired. "Okay. Thanks man."

"Call us if you need anything."

After managing a sort-of smile, he practically ran for his car.

On the windshield, he saw a note from Annika. "Call me. It's F-ing urgent. A."

She'd also left messages on his phone, but if she was actually going old school and leaving a note, she really wanted to talk to him.

He got in his Tahoe and plugged his phone into the car's sound system. "Did you do this, Annika?" he asked as soon as she picked up.

"You owe me. We had an arrangement and you messed it up. I had to get creative."

Only in Annika-world did that make any sense at all. Finn rubbed his forehead, where a headache was forming with little midget hammer blows.

"It's going great, Finn." Her glee resonated across the phone line. "We're one of the most searched on Google.

Gemma's dying, she's so excited. I have some more ideas about how this can go. Can you come by my hotel?"

"You've gone too fucking far this time."

"What are you talking about? It's publicity. I'm sure that nurse understands. It's for the good of the movie."

He reached the end of the road that fed into the highway and jerked to a halt. "Just tell me this. Did my dad have a hand in this?"

"Why are you being so mean to me?"

"Do you know where Lisa went?"

"Oh, is she missing? That's a great twist for the blogs."

With a growl, Finn hung up on Annika and prepared to turn left, toward Jupiter Point. Then he hesitated, drumming his fingers on the steering wheel. Lisa wasn't there. He knew it. She'd probably decided that she was a danger to her friends, and that they couldn't keep her safe anyway. She was probably back on the run. Going north.

But she had an old Mercedes, and he had a new Tahoe. And he was so jacked up on rage against everything connected to Hollywood that he could drive until dawn if he had to.

CHAPTER TWENTY-EIGHT

He finally spotted Lisa's Mercedes at a gas station two hours out of town. She'd parked in the shadows and was inside paying for her gas. Even with her long hair tucked under a beanie, wearing a loose sweater that disguised the shape of her body, he recognized her. He waited until she emerged from the door, then stepped in front of her.

The shock on her face made him smile grimly.

"Surprised to see me? Have you forgotten your promise not to leave without telling me?" He took her arm and guided her to his car.

"I was going to tell you. I *am* going to tell you. I was just waiting until I got some distance between us."

At least she was honest about it.

She didn't resist as he opened the car door and ushered her in. Actually, she looked relieved, and let her head sink back against the headrest. "You know something? Maybe it's because I'm essentially made of Red Bull by now, but I'm not even surprised to see you. You never give up, do you?"

"Do you want me to?" He slid the key into the ignition and started up the car. "Honestly?"

She rested a hand across her eyes. She looked almost as exhausted as he was—maybe even more. "I don't know.

It all seemed pretty clear when I left the base. Hit the road and don't think twice."

His jaw flexed with the need to tell her wrong she was. "Buckle up, babe."

As they pulled away from the gas station, she craned her neck to look back at her Mercedes. "Wait. I can't just leave my car here."

"Your car is very recognizable. It's not safe for you to drive it around."

"Fine." She gave in and buckled her seat belt. "I know that, by the way. I was going to find a different car as soon as I got a chance."

"I'm sure your plan was completely foolproof." He slid a wry glance her way and was satisfied to see her smile.

"Hey, it was the best I could come up with at such short notice."

He picked up speed on the highway. The power poles slid past like a flip book, faster and faster. The rhythm was hypnotic, as was the scent of Lisa's hair drifting from the passenger seat.

"In case you have any doubt in your mind, I knew nothing about this stunt. When Jill told me, I was fucking furious. I guarantee she's never heard me rage like that."

She let out a long sigh. "I didn't think that, Finn. Even I'm not that cynical. But I'm totally out of my realm here." Lisa dropped her head against the back rest and groaned. "It's like something out of a soap opera. 'Naughty Nurse Lures Hero Fireman Away from Tearful Annika.'"

"Naughty nurse, huh? I like the sound of that one." He attempted a smile, but she didn't answer in kind. Instead, she turned her head and glared in his direction.

"She was crying over her new tattoo. Her *tattoo*. Not her broken heart. And I'm not cut out for this."

"Not cut out for what?"

She clutched her head with both hands. "All this *drama*. I'm a simple person. I want to practice my profession, help people who need it, and go home to peace and quiet at the end of the day. Maybe take a few minutes to pet the turtle."

"I know. I know, sweets." He wanted to laugh about her mention of the turtle, but managed not to.

"Finn, listen to me. I've been thinking about this ever since I saw that headline."

He knew what was coming. He knew she was about to say that his life would never work for her. That they couldn't be together because of his Hollywood ties and the drama and whatever else she might come up with.

"Don't say it, Lisa. I'm not that person. You know I'm not."

"Do I? Do I really know you? Ever since I met you, there's been one crazy thing after another."

Now that pissed him off. "And all those things are my doing? The fire at your motorhome? The goddamn tranquilizer gun? Seems to me you have your own drama following you around."

"Yes, and I've been trying to deal with that, but you keep interfering. Now I'm trying to leave town, which is what I should have done to begin with, and once again *you're interfering!*" Her voice rose on those last words. In her voice, he heard all the exhaustion and frustration she must have been feeling since Merry's attack.

He felt the same goddamn way—even more so, maybe. Because all he wanted to do was *help* her. *Be there* for her. And all she wanted was to push him away. "Okay."

"Okay?"

"Okay. You win. I'll stop interfering. After tonight."

She gave a shaky, confused laugh. "After tonight? Why tonight?"

"Because we both need sleep, and you shouldn't be making any big decisions when you've just been Annika-fied. And I have a plan for a safe place to sleep tonight."

"Not that hotel. Sorry. I'd bet my last remaining possession that photographers are staking that place out."

"Not the hotel. I think you'll like this. If you don't, I'll drive you back to your car and you can go wherever you want."

He took his eyes off the road to glance at her briefly. Lines of fatigue were etched across her lovely face. Even though he knew she was trying to kick him to the curb, his heart ached with love for her.

"Go ahead and close your eyes," he told her softly. "I got this. I'll wake you up when we get there."

"Okay. But after that, we have to talk, Finn. I'm serious. My mind isn't going to change because of a nap."

"We'll talk. I promise."

Her eyelids flickered, as if she was struggling to stay awake. But the hypnotic movement of the car was irresistible, and within a couple of minutes she was asleep.

*

Lisa was so exhausted, she slept through the entire road trip. She was only vaguely aware when the car stopped. Strong arms wrapped around her and carried her like a child. She snuggled against the body holding her. She knew she should wake up. She told herself to. But it felt so good to be nestled right where she was. And she trusted those secure arms around her. So her eyes stayed closed and a delicious sense of safety stole over her.

Then she was being gently lowered into a comfortable bed whose familiar scent felt like a homecoming.

She dropped into a profound sleep.

She dreamed of stars and moons and flying. She dreamed she was flying from night to day, floating through high mountain air in her own private bubble, like the Good Witch of the East. Someone was with her, someone whose love surrounded her with golden light. She couldn't see him, couldn't hear him. But he was there, warm and constant.

She opened her eyes slowly, as if they were coated in honey. It took a moment for her to understand where she was. As soon as she did, joy lifted her heart. This bubble filled with golden morning light—that was the Breton lookout tower. She was curled up on the cot where she'd spent so many peaceful nights last summer.

Finn stretched out on a blanket on the floor. He was still asleep, his mouth open slightly, black stubble darkening his jaw. He lay on his back, his arms folded across his chest. She had the feeling that he was on guard and would wake up at the slightest sound.

She allowed herself a moment to trace the shape of his mouth, the swell of his biceps under his t-shirt, the strong line of his neck. From this angle, she couldn't see his scars. He was all splendor and perfection. Pure male beauty.

But neither side—the scarred one or the dazzling one—told the whole story of Finn and his heart. Every time she tried to put him in a box, he burst out of it and swept her off her feet again. Flirtatious player—no. Just sex—no. Short-term fling—no. Even wounded, hurting, and lost, as he'd been the first time she'd met him at this very tower, he'd tugged at her heart. Now, every corner of her being was filled with him. His thoughtfulness, his generosity, his protectiveness, his vulnerability, his wit, his charm, his grit, his strength, his...

Oh Lord. She loved him. Her entire heart and soul belonged to him.

No. No no no. She wasn't the kind of person who fell in love. She was too practical. "Love" never worked out, she knew that firsthand. She'd just have to get over this "love" thing. Like some kind of virus.

She made herself stop staring at Finn and sat up to survey the beloved interior of the tower room. Talk about peace and quiet—the space hummed with it. Rays of golden sunlight shone through the plate glass like silent songs of joy. Birds flitted past, riding the air currents to their first snack of the morning. They were probably singing to the morning sun, although she couldn't hear them through the thick glass.

She quietly got out of bed and tiptoed past Finn's sleeping body into the main room.

It was still too early in the season for anyone to be stationed here, and a light layer of dust covered the atmospheric measuring instruments she'd worked with last summer. Every hour, she'd tested temperature, humidity and barometric pressure, then marked down the readings in a ledger. The routine had kept her busy and fended off her worry about Maria. At night, she'd tracked the movements of the constellations and the planets with the help of a stargazing app.

Even now, a sense of deep peace came over her as she settled into the window seat and surveyed the wilderness that reached in all directions as far as she could see. An ocean of forest spread before her. She recognized each slope and ridge and valley. Last summer she'd become intimately familiar with every aspect of the topography here. Out of habit, she swept her gaze across the expanse of pine and birch trees. No sign of smoke anywhere, just fresh morning light captured between arching branches and sturdy trunks.

She sighed and let all the last traces of stress drain out of her body. How long had that stress been haunting her?

Ever since she'd seen Maria's desperate expression when she'd pushed open the door to Exam Room 4 at Houston Memorial.

In a flash, the scene came back to her with complete clarity.

CHAPTER TWENTY-NINE

"You'll still help me, won't you?" Maria whispered as Lisa locked the exam room door. "The way we talked about?"

"Are you sure? There's no going back. I have to break some rules to do this."

"I don't want you to get into trouble for me."

"Don't worry about me. I'm going to switch your identity with someone else's, just temporarily. I have another patient who just got released. For the next hour, your name is Margaret Whipple and you had a bad reaction to plastic surgery."

Lisa grabbed a wheelchair from the hallway and settled Maria into it. She spent a heart-thumping few minutes bandaging her head with layers of gauze. They didn't want any of the other hospital personnel to recognize her.

She took Mrs. Whipple's clipboard and hid Maria's behind a sharps disposal container.

"Don't look up," she warned Maria. "Look like you're out of it from the meds. Kind of slump over and stare at your lap." She draped an extra blanket over her and wheeled her out of the room.

They took a circuitous back route, passing an orderly, a janitor, and two family members who had gotten lost. Lisa ignored them all, not wanting to interact with anyone who might remember her. Then, about a hundred yards from the red exit sign, she spotted a familiar looking figure. Senator Ruiz.

Maria drew in a sharp breath and flinched backwards. "He's not supposed to be here. He said he had business."

"Shh. Head down," Lisa hissed.

When she was sure that Maria had a grip on herself, Lisa rolled the wheelchair forward. She schooled her expression into that of bored nurse who couldn't wait for her shift to end. Senator Ruiz carried a rolled-up newspaper in one hand as he walked briskly down the aisle. He didn't give them a second glance. In fact, he seemed more focused on someone behind them.

One of the hospital administrators passed her from behind, veering around her as if she were nothing but a roadblock. She wanted to protest, but bit her tongue instead so she didn't draw attention to herself.

The administrator kept going. She recognized him as Dan Block, the one she and the other nurses called "Blockhead."

"Excuse me," Block muttered as he passed Senator Ruiz.

The senator grunted but gave no other response.

What a couple of jackasses, thought Lisa. But she kept her gaze fixed ahead of her, toward the door that led to the back exit.

Dan Block hurried around the corner out of sight. What the heck was he doing back here? And why did he too have a rolled-up newspaper in one hand?

Oh my God.

In the tower, Lisa jumped up so suddenly that the rolling chair went flying.

Senator Ruiz had passed something to Dan Block inside the newspaper.

Money? A bribe? She remembered the way all her notes about Maria's case were ignored. What if the senator had been bribing someone at the hospital to erase any record of Maria's injuries? What if he'd been bribing Dan Block?

She remembered Will Knight's Google search at the cafe. The new hospital wing sponsored by Senator Ruiz. Was that part of the payoff? And hadn't Merry found a news article about suspicions of bribery at the hospital?

She paced back and forth in the morning sunlight, all the puzzle pieces colliding in her head. Maria had made her peace with Ruiz. They'd divorced, she was living in Mexico, he was sponsoring the domestic violence bill. He was funding a new hospital wing.

So what did Ruiz want with Lisa? He didn't know who she was. He hadn't even noticed her that day. She was sure of it.

Then a puzzle piece fell into place as adrenaline flooded her system like rocket fuel.

Dan Block knew her. He probably hadn't thought twice about passing her in that hallway—until he'd realized that she was gone, along with Maria Ruiz.

Ruiz wasn't after her. Blockhead was.

It explained so much. It would probably be pretty easy for Block to find out where she was. The hospital had all her contact information, work history, social security number. She was no expert when it came to staying off the radar.

She summoned up what she knew about Dan Block. Married...four kids...two in college...that was about it. No master criminal, but definitely someone who might be susceptible to bribery.

Strangely enough, a sense of relief came over her. A bumbling hospital manager was behind all of this, not a well-connected vengeful ex-husband. She could solve this. Put an end to it once and for all.

"Hey, sunshine." Finn's voice resonated in her ear.

She spun around and flung her arms around him. His solid body felt so perfect against hers.

"Hi Finn." She beamed up at him, feeling light and bright and happy.

"Wow, hi to you too."

"Are you a parking ticket?" she asked him.

He cocked his head. Even his frown made her weak in the knees.

She winked at him. "You have fine written all over you."

After one stunned moment, he burst out laughing. "I see what you're up to. You're turning the tables on the master. Trying to out-pick-up the pick-up king."

"Worked, didn't it? Here you are. Right where I want you." She breathed deep, filling her lungs with the scent of him. Still warm from sleep, a little sweaty from the crazy night they'd had, even so, he smelled wonderful to her. "Thank you for bringing me here. It was exactly what I needed."

"I know." His tender smile felt like everything she'd ever want or need. "You're easy to please. No trips to Paris, no diamond earrings. Just a night in a lookout tower and you're happy."

For a moment, she basked in it—the tranquility of the tower, the presence of Finn. Utter perfection.

He brushed a thumb across her cheek. "Why were you dancing around just now?"

"I remembered something. Something that explains what's been going on here." She filled him in on the details of her discovery.

"You know what this means, right? I'm not being chased by Senator Ruiz. It's just a guy at the hospital we know as Blockhead. I refuse to run and hide from that idiot. All I have to do is tell the police what I saw, and he'll have no more reason to go after me. I can put all this craziness behind me."

He listened closely, but instead of the relief she'd expected to see, a worried frown creased his forehead. "But you didn't really see anything. Just a newspaper changing hands."

"True. But I have some files I took from the hospital. They prove that records in the computer system were being altered." With a jolt, she remembered the guesthouse break-in. "They might be gone. But I have a backup. Two backups, actually. I always keep one on me, one in my car, and then I always kept the files in my safe in the motorhome."

Finn was looking more and more worried. "Maybe they were looking for those files."

"Maybe. I need to call Will right away." She pulled out her cell phone, ready to dial. Then her stomach plummeted. She knew what she had to do, and it wasn't report her vague suspicions to Will Knight.

"What's wrong?"

"I have to go back to Houston."

He stared at her, a muscle ticking in his jaw, emotions clashing in a silent war. She could imagine the forces tugging in opposite directions. He knew that she was right. On the other hand, watching her go would be hard for him.

"I'll come with you," he said eventually. "I'll be your bodyguard while you bust a senator and a hospital bigwig for bribery."

"No." She put a hand on his bare chest. "Absolutely not. You have a job here, a job you fought for. You're staying here, Finn. I'll go straight to the Houston DA that Will knows. He's already looking into shenanigans at the hospital. I won't be in any danger."

He turned away, sliding away from the touch of her hand. She ached to put her arms around him, tell him that she loved him, that she wasn't going away for good—but was that true? Once she got back to Houston, maybe all this would seem like a dream. An enchanted dream.

"This thing with us, Finn..."

"Yeah?" His voice held a wary edge as he turned back to face her. She couldn't read his expression. Was he angry? Resigned?

"It's been amazing. Like something out of a fantasy."

He laughed abruptly, and again she couldn't read the emotion behind that laugh. "You have interesting fantasies. A fire, a shooting, a publicity-mad actress...none of those things would show up in any of my fantasies."

"You know what I mean. It's not real life. It's this strange, out-of-the-ordinary thing. Like," she glanced around the airy space, "like this room. Above the trees, away from regular life completely."

He stepped closer, eyes darkening. "What exactly are you trying to say? Spit it out, Lisa. I'm a grown man, I can take it."

Oh God—he thought she was dumping him. Was she? No—yes—no—she didn't know what she was doing. "This is all new to me, Finn," she burst out. "I don't know what's going to happen. I feel things for you that I've never— But I don't know what it means."

He caught her hands in his. "Do you have to know? Can't it just be?"

"I'm afraid. Afraid of what will happen once I go back to Houston. Gravity will take over. I'll definitely have to stay for my mother's anniversary party, there's no getting out of that. All of this might feel like a weird, amazing dream."

He ran his hands down her back. Her spine arched under his touch. She always responded to him, no matter when or where or what else was going on. He smoothed his hands down her hips, touching his fingertips to the skin on the back of her legs. It was the most sensitive spot on her body, which he knew perfectly well. "If you're afraid you'll forget about me, don't you worry. I'll remember for both of us."

Her breath caught and tears filled her eyes. "Oh, Finn..."

"Besides, there's an article in the tabloids with photographic evidence and many inaccurate details. Those tabloids last forever, you know, like cockroaches. You'll be in some dentist's office and pick one up and it will all come back to you."

A spurt of laughter escaped her. Did he know about the tabloid she'd filched from the Moon Glow? She'd never tell.

Finn continued. "This is a good thing, Lisa. You can finally put an end to this craziness. And I don't think you're going to forget. I think you'll remember Finn Abrams the

Animal, that annoying-yet-charming guy who just wouldn't leave you alone."

She gave a shaky laugh. The slow circles he traced on the backs of her legs felt like sweet fire. "I'm glad you didn't leave me alone. I'm just starting to get used to you."

He tilted her head and claimed her mouth in a fierce, demanding kiss that shook her down to her toes. "Good. I want you to be used to me. I want you to go back to Houston and tell your story to the DA. Then tell your family that you love them, but you don't belong there anymore. Then I want you to swing by your apartment and pack up all the possessions you've been missing. Then I want you to hop on the next plane back and text me the flight number so I can meet you at the airport." He hauled her into his arms and swung her onto the counter that occupied the middle of the room. "But that's just me. What do you want, my queen?"

"You." She gazed into the fiery warmth of his dark gaze and felt she could do exactly that forever. "I want you. Right here, right now."

"No one can look in, right?"

"Just the birds and the bees."

"Not worried about them." He slid his hands under her t-shirt.

"Maybe the bird-watchers, too."

"They're scientists, right? They're familiar with mating rituals."

She laughed breathlessly as he parted her legs and ran his hands up her sensitive inner thighs. They started to tremble right away. The sensation was so exquisite her eyes half closed. He made an appreciative sound—a growl really—deep in his chest. "Make love to me, you sexy beast," she murmured. "That's what I want.

He was already doing just that, with his hands, his tongue, and his incredibly talented instincts.

CHAPTER THIRTY

The next day, Finn drove Lisa to the regional airport, which was about forty-five minutes outside of Jupiter Point. The drive seemed to go absurdly fast. Watching her go back to Houston felt like ripping his heart out. But she was doing what she had to do. He couldn't keep her, all he could do was support her. So he kept the tone light, teasing her about all the things she was leaving behind by returning to Houston.

"Are you sure you have no last-minute messages for Annika? Want me to get her autograph for you? She'd probably sign a copy of that article for you."

"Ooh, something for my scrapbook." She rolled her eyes. "Tell her that working with her was the greatest privilege of my professional life. And also, tell her to watch her back."

"Say what?"

"Inside joke. She'll get it."

Finn shook his head at the thought of Lisa sharing an inside joke with Annika. After he put Lisa on the plane, he had some pissed-off phone calls to make.

In a crisp white blouse and black pants, with a red leather tote bag, Lisa looked more stylish than he'd ever seen her. She'd twisted her hair into an easy knot at the base of her neck. This was a side of Lisa Peretti he hadn't seen before, a side she hadn't shown to Jupiter Point. As if she was already disappearing into her old life.

But she had to go back. And he refused to make it harder for her. So he kept the jokes coming.

"I don't know how Mrs. Murphy is going to handle the lack of excitement. I heard she has Knight on speed dial now. He's talking about going into witness protection."

"I know a witness he'd like to protect. I called Merry this morning and she sounded kind of...funny. Has either of them said anything about the night of the break-in?"

"Not a word. At least not to me."

"This might call for margaritas at the Orbit. That's when all the secrets come out."

His heart lifted. That was the first time she'd actually said something concrete about coming back. He turned onto the road that led to the airport. A small plane was just taking off, retracting its wheels as it rode the air currents. "By the way, did you hear that Sean's old airstrip will be open for business soon? Knight and Day Flight Tours. As in Will Knight."

"The sheriff's deputy?"

"Yup. The new owners are his two brothers. I guess he convinced them to leave the military and come start a business in Jupiter Point. The hotshots are pretty excited about it, actually. We could potentially get a little more air support."

"Wow, I can't believe I'm going to miss something so exciting for the single women of Jupiter Point."

And—there went his heart sinking like a stone. That sounded like she wasn't going to come back.

As he followed the signs directing him toward the departure level, she turned to him. "Please just drop me off at the curb. I can't stand extended goodbyes."

"Are you sure? You don't need help with your bags?"

"No, I got it. You saw my suitcase, it's half-empty. I guess I should thank Blockhead for making me travel light."

He pulled up at the curb and stopped the car. A sense of panic filtered through him. An airport security guard patrolled the walkway—they wouldn't have much time here.

He got out of the car and went to the trunk to retrieve her one and only suitcase. She propped it up and took the handle, then rested her tote bag on top of it. Suddenly everything felt very formal and awkward.

He cleared his throat. "You have someone meeting you at the other end, right? You won't be alone?"

"Will's old law school buddy is actually picking me up. I'm going to make my statement right away."

"He's picking you up? Tell him to knock it off if he tries any of my pick-up lines."

Lisa gave that joke what it deserved—about half of a smile. "Finn, I want you to know something."

He braced himself for something he didn't want to hear. A brush-off, a backhanded compliment, a dagger in the heart disguised as affection.

"You are so much more than you think. More than your charm, your name, your firefighting skills."

Just as he'd expected. He didn't want flattery or kind words from Lisa. He wanted her heart. He tried for that light tone again, pointing at his scarred side. "Not just a pretty face, am I right?"

She shook her head, smiling, a tender gesture this time. "You're a gem." She rose up on tiptoes and pecked him on his unmarred cheek, then the scarred one. "And I—we'll talk soon. I'll text you as soon as I land."

Stunned, he could barely watch as she pulled her suitcase behind her onto the curb.

What the hell. Could the woman be any more frustrating? He dragged a hand through his hair. "Is that it, then?"

She turned back in surprise. "Oh, right. Thanks for the ride to the airport. And thanks for letting me leave the Mercedes at your place. Take good care of Sparky. Stay safe out on the fire lines. And...take care of yourself. Don't forget to keep that scar tissue stretched out. I left some salve for you at the guesthouse."

"Very thoughtful. Thank you. I'll do that." Finn stalked back around to the driver's side of the Tahoe and slid inside. He turned the key in the ignition and gunned the engine. "Safe travels, Lisa."

He gave her a thumbs up. She gazed after him as he pulled away from the curb, the look in her eyes one of pure confusion.

Seriously? Did she seriously not understand why he might be annoyed? After everything they'd gone through, after he'd laid his heart before her on a silver platter, all she could say was "you're a gem?"

*

"I mean, she didn't even say what *kind* of gem she was talking about," Finn told Rollo and Josh later that week, over his fourth ale at Barstow's Brews. "A gem could be a diamond, or it could be a cubic zirconium or whatever. A *gem*. For fuck's sake. Has any woman ever called you a gem?"

"It's definitely the kiss of death," said Josh. He was busy texting shots of his beer to Suzanne. They'd agreed to take turns going out at least one night a month. To Finn, it seemed that Josh was having more fun taunting his wife with his stupid beer selfies than he was actually drinking the stuff. "If any girl told me I was a gem, I'd have to have a serious talk with her."

"You guys are nuts." Rollo rested his muscled forearms on the table. "Gems are jewelry. Plenty of women like jewelry. Not Brianna, but every single one of my mother's friends. Why would 'gem' be some kind of insult?"

Finn couldn't quite put his finger on it, or maybe he was too hammered. He just knew it didn't sound right.

"Some woman called you a gem?" Will Knight dropped into the chair next to Rollo. He sat on it backwards, resting his forearms on the back. "Them's fighting words."

"See?" Finn shot a pointed look at Rollo. "These guys don't believe me. Tell 'em, Knight."

"Oh yeah. That's what MaryBeth called me in junior high after I helped her pass calculus. Right before she told me she couldn't go to prom with me. If a girl calls you a gem, it's time to pack up and go home." He tilted his bottle to his lips.

"Right. Time to pack up and go home." Finn drank from his glass tankard and gloomily watched the game of darts underway across the room. Lisa would never go to prom with him. Or the adult equivalent. She would sleep with him, she would laugh with him and snuggle with him, she would fight with him and scold him for being overprotective—but she didn't love him. She'd never even hinted at such a thing.

The sound of Lisa's name caught his attention. "I heard from my buddy in the Houston DA's office," Knight was saying. "Peretti really came through with her statement. It looks like her theory is right about the hospital accepting bribes to alter their records. We're going to circle back to the man who attacked you guys on the hiking trail now that we have a name. It'll be good to close up so many loose ends all at once."

"Right on, brother." Rollo clinked his glass against Knight's beer bottle.

The deputy took a swig and smacked his lips together.

"Yup, great day for the boys in blue. I'm thinking that puts us one up on the firefighters, right?"

Finn, Josh and Rollo all jeered at him. "Three against one, dude. Three against one," Finn pointed out with a wave of his tankard.

"Might have to argue with your math." Knight jerked his head toward the bar. Finn squinted at two men in leather jackets who resembled the deputy. One of them, probably the older one, had a shaved head and a stern look, and was even taller than Will. The other leaned one elbow on the bar as he flirted with the waitress.

"Those the flyboys all the girls are talking about?"

Knight grinned. "Day one and the word is spreading, is it? That's what I like to hear. If anyone asks for specifics, make sure to mention they're both single. And that they both love brownies and casseroles."

"Casseroles?" Josh screwed up his face dubiously. Finn had to agree that they didn't look like the casserole type.

"Yup. Also, they're crashing at my place while they get the business up and running. Oh—and anything but green beans. Can't stand green bean casserole."

"You mean, *they* can't stand it," corrected Finn.

"Right. That's what I meant." Knight smirked and polished off his beer. "But you know what they aren't? Not even a little bit?"

They all took in his cocky grin. "What?"

"Gems."

Finn flipped him off. "Fuck you. I'd rather be called a gem than some of the things Merry Warren has called *you*."

Josh backed him up with a "mmmm-hmm," but Rollo shot him a warning look. Finn ignored it.

"Did you ever catch the guy who shot her with a freaking tranquilizer dart?"

Knight's face lost all its good humor. "We're pursuing several leads. I'm keeping Merry in the loop."

"In the loop? Where is this loop? Her place or yours?"

The deputy pushed off from his chair and rose to his feet. "If you want to get into a fight, sober up and come find me. I don't fight drunk guys sobbing into their beer because their girl left town."

Finn got halfway to his feet before Josh yanked him back down again. "Take it easy, Finn."

"He can't talk to me like that."

"Dude. You *were* sobbing into your beer. You're drunk. Obviously. And you're sad because Lisa took off. Right after calling you a gem. So do us a favor and don't attack a sheriff's deputy in our favorite bar, from which we would probably get banned. Okay?"

Finn allowed Josh to shove him back into his chair. Rollo relaxed too, though he kept a wary eye on everyone. Of all of them, Rollo was the most fearsome with his fists. But he hated to fight and avoided it at all costs.

"Everything okay here?" Sean Marcus. Great. Just what he needed, for his boss to show up. Evie was with him, holding his hand and looking blissful. They both looked disgustingly happy. Finn ground his teeth.

"Yeah, we're good. Just discussing the meaning of life. Not sure what it is yet, but I'm pretty sure it has something to do with women." Knight tilted his bottle at them and ambled toward the bar to join his brothers.

Finn looked up at his boss. "What's up?"

"You look like shit."

"Really?" Actually, that thought pleased him. He felt like shit. Might as well look the part. "Cool."

Evie glanced at Sean and shook her head slightly. Some kind of silent communication passed between them.

"What? What are you guys psychically discussing through your telepathic love link?"

Rollo and Josh both cracked up at that phrasing.

Evie lifted her eyebrows. "That's very descriptive, Finn. It sounds like you know what you're talking about. Got a little 'love link' of your own going on?"

"Don't poke the bear," Josh warned her. "He's had about enough for one night."

"Sorry. Here's the thing, Finn. My mother has a doctor's appointment tomorrow, and I need someone to drive her. The Dean's sick, Sean has a meeting with some people coming in from Boise and I have an exhibit opening. Normally I'd ask Lisa, but..." She shrugged. "Anyway, I asked Mom who she'd like to take her to the doctor, and she chose you."

Finn noticed that she sounded a little surprised by that. "Molly and I have a little thing going on. You didn't know?"

She unleashed the radiant smile that had made so many Jupiter Point men pine after her, until Sean had claimed her heart. "I guess I didn't know how serious it was. So can you do it?"

"Unless we get a call, of course."

"Good man." Sean squeezed his shoulder, then gave him a hard shake. "Now stop drinking and go home so you're nice and sober when you transport my mother-in-law."

"Yes, sir."

CHAPTER THIRTY-ONE

The next morning came much too soon. Finn woke up with a pounding headache. A text from Annika made it even worse.

Paparazzi alert.

He groaned and rolled out of bed. Almost landed on the floor, but caught himself just in time. He straightened up and snagged his phone from under the sheets.

What r u talking about?

Gemma doing her thing. Just play along.

Oh, sweet Jesus, this couldn't possibly be good. Why did Annika and Gemma think they could play games with other people's lives like this?

With what? He texted back.

Proposal rumors. The nurse is gone and I'm prepared to forgive you. That's her script. Genius, right?

"Motherfu—" He broke off with a glance at Sparky's cage, as if the turtle could possibly care what kind of language he used. What was Annika's real game here? Sure, publicity. But was she trying to maneuver him into an *actual* proposal?

He dialed her directly. She answered with a sigh. "Don't get all grouchy-bear about this. You take things so seriously, Finn."

"What are you up to? Be real for one minute."

"Don't be mad at me. Talk to your father."

"What?"

Oh, now he was definitely wide awake. He headed for the kitchen, the nearest source of water. "What did Stu have to do with this?"

"Would you stop stressing? It'll be fine. Maybe it's a sign that it's meant to be. Maybe we should stop fighting destiny."

He remembered the last time he'd talked about destiny. He'd been looking at Lisa at the time, and feeling like suddenly life made sense.

But ever since that first text to let him know she'd landed in Houston, Lisa hadn't called, texted, Skyped, Facebooked, or anything. She'd disappeared in a poof of airplane exhaust.

Maybe this "destiny" idea was pure crap. Along with "love at first sight" and romance in general. Maybe Team Cynic had it right.

Right then, he felt more depressed than he ever had in his life. He hung over the kitchen sink, scooping water into his mouth to get rid of the sour taste of—everything.

"What did my dad have to do with this?" he asked again. "Is this some kind of setup?"

"Like I've been saying *forever*, you really need to make up with him. And that's all I'm saying. I just wanted to warn you about the paparazzi. Don't I deserve some props for that? Gemma thought it should be a surprise. So where's my thanks, huh?"

Finn hung up the phone because he couldn't handle another moment.

This was why he'd chosen wildfire fighting. Fire, dirt, oxygen, trees, sweat, blood, tears, a mission, a purpose. Distance from crap like this.

Finn dragged a hand through his hair, then hauled himself upright and staggered toward the bathroom. He had some aspirin somewhere. He ran the faucet, splashed water on his face, then popped an aspirin and washed it down.

After a long, steaming shower, his headache subsided. He downed more water and took inventory of his current state. Sober, for sure. Cold, clear and sober. Maybe painfully so.

He grabbed his phone again and called his father. For maybe the first time ever, Stu answered right away. Usually his calls got picked up by his assistant.

"Whatever you're up to, knock it off. Annika and me are never going to happen."

"She's going to be a big star, Finn." The sound of father's staccato, rasping voice brought back so many memories. He was always busy, always talking, making deals, moving and grooving, too fast to stop and talk to his lonely son.

"Good for her. But I bet she can make it on her own. How about that? Why does she need all this bullshit?"

"That's the way it works."

Finn paused. His father sounded more tired than usual. "Are you okay?"

A brief silence made him tense up. Was something wrong with Stu? Why the hesitation?

"What do you want, Finn? What will it take to make you come back to LA?"

Finn frowned at the phone. Yup, something was definitely off here. "The season's just starting. I'm going to be busy all summer, probably until October. I can visit after that."

Yeah, that might work. They could talk. Patch things up. Improve their relationship.

"I'm not talking about a visit. I'm talking about moving back."

Or not.

"Not in the cards, Stu." Checking the time, he realized he needed to get a move on or he'd be late to pick up Molly. With paparazzi around, he'd have to allow extra time.

He put the phone on speaker so he could dress as he talked. "I like it here. I like being a hotshot, I like my crew."

He pulled on a black hoodie and work boots—a generic outfit that stood a good chance of fooling the paparazzi—then went to the kitchen to get some coffee started.

The morning light made him think of Lisa and the day after the motorhome fire.

She'd stood right there at the sink with her hair falling down her back. A sharp ache tugged at his heart. When would he ever stop thinking about her?

Outside on the lawn, a crane glided through the air and tilted to a stop next to the koi pond.

"What about your..." Stu practically growled the next words. "Your so-called birth parents? You want to know who they are, don't you? Will that make you come back?"

The entire world came to a dead stop. Finn froze. He could barely make his mouth form his next words. "Where the fuck are you going with this?"

"You want it. The name. That's what you want most. You're willing to bankrupt yourself for it. All that money you spent, but I'll always have more. You can't win."

The truth coalesced in a crystal moment of shock. "Are you saying you know who my parents are? You said you didn't."

"I didn't. But I do now. Just come back and I'll tell you what you want to know."

He laughed, because it was so surreal. "Stu, that's nuts. If you can find out, so can I. It's just a matter of time."

"Not time. Money."

Holy shit. All those false leads Ericsson kept sending him. Was that Stu's doing? "Have you been paying Ericsson behind my back?"

Stu's silence said it all.

Numbly, Finn watched the crane step into the pond. The water was so still that he could see a perfect reflection of the bird—a dark crane-shaped shadow extending underwater.

"Why? Why would you do that?"

"I have my reasons," Stu said gruffly. "Come back and I'll tell you."

"So you know. You know who I am."

"I know. But you gotta come back, Finn."

"Come back," Finn repeated. He felt numb to the tips of his toes. The need to know his true background had consumed him for the past year and a half. His quest had gotten him nowhere. Thousands of dollars down the drain, and he still knew nothing about his real origins.

But he could know...if he did what Stu wanted.

"Quit firefighting," his father was saying. "Come back to LA. Be the Finn Abrams everyone knows and loves. Dump Annika if you want. She's irrelevant. Find someone else. Find a hundred someone elses. I want you back."

A hundred someone elses.

Thoughts swirled through his brain, a whirlwind of anger and need and confusion. But that one sentence—*a hundred someone elses*—offered a spark of light for Finn to cling to. There weren't a hundred someone elses for him. There was only one.

The thought grounded him like an anchor tossed into a seabed. Yes, he wanted to know his true parentage. But was that the most important thing?

At the far end of the lawn, Rollo and Brianna crept across the grass on tiptoe, clearly trying not to disturb the crane. Bri knelt on the wet grass and aimed a camera at the graceful bird, while Rollo kept a steadying hand on her shoulder.

His friends. The people who always had his back. His true family.

"No, Stu. I'm not quitting the fire service. I'm not moving back."

"Then you'll never know who you really are."

"Wrong," Finn answered sharply. "*You'll* never know who I really am. You never have. I'm like a prop to you."

"Bullshit."

"Park me with a babysitter, pull me out when you need a family photo op. That's what it was like. I was there, Stu. I remember."

"Son—"

"Why is it so important to you that I come back to LA? What difference does it make in your life? Just tell me that."

Stu muttered a string of curse words and ended the call.

Typical—he always hated being put on the spot. Finn could never nail him down on anything.

"Jesus!" Finn exploded in frustration. What fucked-up game was this? The more he thought back on that insane conversation, the more he felt sure something was wrong with Stu. Aside from the dick move of paying off his detective—by the way, he wanted his money back--his father didn't have his usual blowtorch energy. But if something was wrong, the stubborn man would never tell him. No, he'd rather dick around with his life and bribe and manipulate him.

Shit. He paced across the living room trying to calm himself. If only Lisa was here. She'd have some kind of logical, down-to-earth take on this. Maybe she'd make one of her wry comments that always made him laugh. Or maybe she'd just sit in his lap and run her hands down his chest and make everything else fade away with her touch.

Or maybe she'd forgotten all about him.

CHAPTER THIRTY-TWO

After pulling himself together—it took about a gallon of coffee—Finn pulled on a baseball cap and a pair of sunglasses and made his way across Rollo's lawn to his car. If paparazzi were waiting for him, they couldn't legally come onto Rollo's property. They'd probably be on the street, at the base of the long, winding driveway that led to the cliff-top house.

At his Tahoe, he hesitated. They probably knew what he drove—they had ways of knowing such things. But they might not recognize Lisa's Mercedes, and besides, her car had that special seat for Molly.

Decision made, he selected the Mercedes key from the ring and slid into the driver's seat. Lisa's scent enveloped him, making his gut go tight. Not only did it smell like her, but she'd left little traces of herself everywhere—a gas receipt on the console, an earring buried in the seat cushions.

He drove down the hill and, sure enough, there they were. Three unfamiliar vehicles were parked on either side of the driveway and four photographers lounged against them, their cameras dangling from their necks.

His trick with the Mercedes didn't work. As soon as he drove past them, someone shouted, "it's him!" and everyone raised their cameras and clicked. Then they rushed to jump into their cars and follow him.

What did they think, that he was off to propose to Annika in a baseball cap and a borrowed Mercedes? He couldn't understand how these photographers thought. It made no sense.

While the paparazzi scrambled to give chase, he stomped on the accelerator and zipped down the road that led into town. He had to lose them before he got to Molly's. If he couldn't shake them, he'd call Evie and tell her someone else should step in. It might agitate Molly to see a horde of photographers on their tail.

Luckily, by the time he reached the town limits, he saw no sign of the paparazzi's vehicles. He stayed off the main streets as he wound his way to the McGraws'. When he reached their house, he parked in the garage, well out of sight. Then he changed from a baseball cap to a knitted beanie. Sometimes a little thing like that could throw off the photogs. Satisfied that the coast was clear, he knocked on the McGraws' door.

Twenty minutes later, he buckled Molly into the passenger seat of the Mercedes. She gazed around the interior fondly. "I m-miss Lisa."

"Yeah, I do too."

"Her m-mother's anniversary party is today."

"Really? I bet she's excited about that." He started up the car and backed out of the garage. How did Molly know about Lisa's mother's party? Maybe she was calling Molly while blowing him off.

Molly chuckled. "They say s-scratch a cynic and you f-find a romantic."

"Yeah, well, they also say scratch a rash and it'll get even worse." His gloomy response made her laugh even more.

"She c-cares for you, Finn."

"Yes, she does, and that's because I'm a gem. Ask anyone." He flashed her a smile, even though his reference obviously confused her. He turned back to look at the road ahead and slammed on the brakes. He flung an arm across her to keep her in place. "Oh shit."

The paparazzi vehicles were back, illegally driving two abreast, blocking the street so he'd have to slow down.

He pulled over and parked the Mercedes. The paparazzi stopped too.

"Who-who are those people?" She peered at the two vehicles, which were backing toward them.

"Paparazzi. It's a long story and completely not worth telling."

Before they could get a shot of him and Molly, he ripped off his sweater and draped it over her head. She watched him curiously as he adjusted it to make sure she could breathe.

"I don't want those vultures getting a shot of you. I'm sorry, Molly. I have to deal with this. It'll just take a few minutes. I'll be right outside the car. And you might want to cover your ears because there will be profanity."

She giggled, her white, fluffy halo of hair bobbing up and down. "So ex-exciting!"

"Yeah, that's one way to look at it. Be right back." He swung out of the car and stalked toward the photographers. Camera lenses poked through the windows as he approached.

"Listen, guys, you're obstructing traffic and there's nothing to see. I have no comment on anything. Can you let us pass now?"

"What about Annika? Are you going to propose?" one of the cameramen shouted from inside the Escalade.

"I said no comment." A flat 'no' might spark more questions and rumors. In his experience, sticking to 'no comment' was always the best policy.

Another photographer was aiming his camera at the Mercedes and the shrouded Molly. "Who's in the car? Is that the nurse?"

"No comment. Take your pictures and be done. Let me pass, I'm late for a medical appointment."

"Medical? Is it about your father? What's his prognosis?"

"What?"

"Your dad's illness, any comment on that?"

The cameras clicked and clicked. He struggled to school his expression to reveal nothing, so they'd have nothing to print. Was Stu really sick? Did they know something real or was it just a ploy to get a reaction from him?

He fought to show no reaction, but it was pointless. Fuck, he was no actor. He spun away from the Escalade and loped back to the Mercedes. He threw the car in reverse and backed all the way to the next street, where he made a screeching three-point turn and then jammed down on the accelerator to get them the hell out of there.

As they drove, he tugged his sweater away from Molly's face.

"They're behind us now," he said, trying to keep his voice even. "Sorry about that."

"Starly s—sometimes has p-paparazzi following her," Molly said. "It's quite thrilling. Especially in our little town."

"Thrilling is not the word I'd use. If I want thrills, I'll go to Magic Mountain. We don't need this kind of crap in Jupiter Point. It's supposed to be quiet and serene here. What happened to all our peace and quiet?"

"The hotshots c-came."

He laughed at that response. True, the arrival of his crew had definitely shaken things up here. "On behalf of the Jupiter Point Hotshots, I apologize. All we want to do is put out fires and keep people safe. We didn't intend to make this kind of trouble."

"You're a sweet boy." She smiled over at him. "A very good boy."

A loud pop sounded from behind him.

"*Shit.*" Finn stared at the rearview mirror. The paparazzi's Escalade must have blown a tire. It was swerving all over the street, black smoke pouring from one of the tires. The Camry was trying to avoid it, but couldn't. The two vehicles slammed into each other with a horrible crunch and spun to a stop in the middle of the street.

Oh hell. Much as he'd like to leave the pesky paparazzi to deal with their own idiocy, he couldn't. He wouldn't be able to live with himself. He pulled over to the side of the road again and grabbed his phone.

"Sorry, Molly. I have to make sure they're okay."

"Yes, you g-go. I'm fine here."

As he ran toward the crash, he dialed nine-one-one and filled in the dispatcher. When he got close enough to the two cars, he did a quick scan and sniff for gasoline.

Since he didn't see any danger signs, he jogged to the driver's side of the Escalade. The photographer had a gash on his forehead and was testing his shoulder gingerly. "What the fuck happened?" he asked when Finn appeared.

"Looked like a blowout."

"Damn." He groaned and groped for his glasses, which had gotten knocked onto the dashboard. Finn reached through the half-open window and grabbed them for him.

"Paramedics are on their way," he said. "I just wanted to check on you."

"Thanks. And sorry about before. We're just doing our job." He put on his glasses and squinted. "Hey, is someone stealing your car?"

Finn swung around to look at the Mercedes.

A man in a backpack and a deer hunter cap was running across the street toward the driver's side door. He had a gun in one hand.

Dear God. *Molly.*

"Call the police," he ordered the photographer, and hurtled back down the street toward the Mercedes.

"Hey!" he yelled as he ran. "Police are on their way. Don't be stupid!"

The man ignored him and flung open the door of the Mercedes. Then he jerked in surprise. He hadn't expected Molly, Finn realized.

When Finn was only a few steps away, the gunman swung around and aimed his weapon at Finn. "Stop where you are. Where's the nurse?"

"She's not here. She's back in Houston. You're too late, she already made a statement. Whoever hired you, they're probably already in custody."

The man, who had a sandy crew cut and a nervous manner, kept the gun on Finn. "This is her car, right?"

So he wanted the Mercedes? Jesus. "Take the car. Let me get the woman out of it. She has Parkinson's and I'm taking her to the doctor. You don't need her. And you'd better let me take her quick, because the cops are coming."

The gunman gave a brusque nod and gave him a go-ahead gesture. Finn ran to the passenger side and flung open the door.

Molly fixed wide eyes on him. "W-what's happening?"

"He wants the car and we're going to give it to him." He bent down to unfasten her seat belt.

"Don't touch anything else," the man said sharply.

"Anything else? Like what? There's nothing in here." He put one arm under Molly's knees and the other around her back. As he maneuvered her out of the car, he wondered if that was correct. Maybe Lisa had left something important in the car. Her backup file, maybe. Though why that would matter at this point, he had no idea.

Not important. All the mattered right now was getting Molly to safety. He settled her trembling body into his arms. "I'm so sorry about this, Molly. Bet you're regretting picking me as your transport, huh?"

She shook her head. "I'm g-glad you're here." She pulled his head farther down to whisper in his ear, "He has a l-lighter. I smelled gas. I think he wants to burn the c-car."

Finn gave a quick glance at the man, who was impatiently scanning the street ahead. "We'll get out of your way now," he said, hiding the panic roiling inside him. He took a casual step toward the sidewalk. He had to get Molly out of here without causing the man to panic or change his mind or decide to take a hostage or...

Stop it. Just get out of here.

The man ignored them and turned his attention to the Mercedes. Finn kept going toward the sidewalk, relieved when his foot hit the curb. This area of Jupiter Point was known as the Flats; it held metal shops, furniture warehouses, that sort of thing. The closest building was a commercial bakery that supplied packaged bread to stores along the central coast.

If he could just get inside, they'd be safe.

Even though Molly couldn't weigh more than a hundred and twenty pounds, she made an awkward bundle. He hunched his torso around her as a kind of shield and headed for the bakery. But when he reached the front door, he saw no signs of activity, no lights. Damn it—closed.

He couldn't go back, so he kept going. The next building on the street was a sprawling warehouse, its front door another half-block away. But between the two ran a side street—more like an alley. Maybe he could find a side door into the warehouse, and in the meantime stay out of the gunman's sight.

He veered onto the side street and instantly felt safer. Even though the man wanted the car, not them, the further away they got, the better.

Yeah, it would suck to tell Lisa that her car was stolen. But that was nothing compared to protecting Molly.

"F-Finn," Molly cried. "He's c-coming!"

He swung around.

Molly was wrong—the man wasn't coming. But the Mercedes was. It rolled slowly down the alley with no one at the wheel. Trailing liquid behind it. He sniffed. Gasoline. He must have steered it into the alley on purpose. So it didn't blow up in the main street?

Blow up. Holy mother of God—it could explode at any moment. There was no way he could reach the end of the alley in time, not while carrying Molly.

Finn scanned the alley for a way out and spotted a Dumpster about fifty yards away.

He ran for it. It was like running a sprint while carrying a hundred pounds of cement. He made a mental note to thank the entire Jupiter Point Hotshot crew for making him train so hard. Even so, his thighs burned by the time he reached the Dumpster.

He propped open the lid. The Dumpster was filled with packaged loaves of bread that must have recently expired. Instead of garbage and rotting produce, all he smelled was the comforting, yeasty scent of wheat rolls.

"We got lucky, Molly. It's like a nest in there. The best-smelling Dumpster on the planet."

She clutched at his shoulders. "Why...what's happening?"

"We're getting in," he told her. "Ever heard of Dumpster diving?"

Her white hair bobbed as she nodded. He swung her over the edge of the Dumpster and half-tossed, half-guided her onto the pile of plastic-wrapped bread. "You okay? How you doing?"

She glanced around the big metal container. "Hungry."

He laughed. "You're a wonder, Molly. You're not panicking at all, are you?"

Looking into the tight space, he hesitated. A shudder of fear passed through him. Whatever was coming their way, getting into the Dumpster seemed even more terrifying. He'd be shut up, closed in, helpless...

But one look at her terrified face decided him. He couldn't leave her alone here. No way. This was their best chance if that car did blow up.

He hauled himself over the edge of the Dumpster and tumbled in, doing his best not to land on her.

Slip-sliding on the plastic bread bags, he maneuvered her so she lay behind him. That way he would take the brunt of whatever danger came at them.

"Seen any peanut butter and jelly in here?"

She laughed softly, a shaky sound that clutched at his heart. With one last look at the oncoming Mercedes, he reached for the Dumpster's top and pulled it down. It didn't fit perfectly, so he could see an uneven strip of light between the lid and the edge.

"Thank you, Finn," Molly whispered from behind him, patting his back. Her hand trembled against his shirt.

He drew in a long breath of yeasty air. The walls of the Dumpster seemed to close in around him. The last time he was crammed into a tiny space with danger threatening outside—oh God. The trunk. The same feeling rushed back—claustrophobic fear. Dark confusion. Terror. And—a memory.

A name.

And then a blast shook the Dumpster. The world rang like a bell, then turned bright as a supernova.

Then black as smoke.

CHAPTER THIRTY-THREE

Lisa collapsed onto the white leather love seat in the sunken den of her mother and third stepfather's house in River Oaks. The hum of chattering guests and ice clinking in glasses drifted from the rest of the house. With the anniversary cocktail party still in full swing, Lisa needed a break from all the hot gossip.

Especially since she was Topic Number One.

After she'd made her statement about what she'd witnessed at the hospital, an investigation had been launched. Senator Ruiz and Dan Block had both been questioned and the hospital's computerized records seized. Unfortunately, she no longer had the original files since they'd been stolen from Finn's guesthouse. But she'd handed over her flash drive. A forensic accountant and a computer expert were examining everything now. The truth would come out.

In the meantime, her role in the drama was done.

Almost.

She opened the binder she'd stashed in the den when she'd first arrived at the party. All week, she'd been carrying it around with her, trying to make up her mind. It held an offer from the hospital. Kind of a put-up-or-shut-up offer.

Her mother danced into the room, champagne cocktail in hand. With the classic Texas-blond blowout and more gold jewelry than a treasure chest, she gleamed under the overhead chandelier. "Are you pooping out already? Boo on you."

"Taking a break, Mom. We're not all party animals like you."

"I shouldn't complain. I never expected you'd be here at all."

"Am I such a crappy daughter as that?"

Sue Ellen let loose a husky laugh. "Oh sweetie, that ain't it. I know how you feel about anniversaries and all that silly stuff we get up to." She swayed next to the love seat.

Lisa steadied her with a hand. "It's not silly. Ten years is quite an accomplishment. I'm happy for you both."

"Well?" Her mother waved at the binder. "Did you decide?"

"I did. You can be my witness."

She opened the folder, grabbed the pen she'd clipped to the document and flipped to the final page. She signed her name with a flourish, then added the date.

Sue Ellen winked at her. "I see what you just did there. You chose the man. You and me aren't so different, are we?"

Lisa made a face at her. "I didn't sign this because of a man."

The document was a small settlement from Houston Memorial. They'd also offered to hire her back if she preferred, along with a huge raise and a management position.

"Oh? Why, then?"

"The air is so clean and clear in Jupiter Point. Did you know that there are *stars* up there and you can actually see them? And the scenery is just breathtaking."

Her mother laughed and laughed. "It's that fireman, isn't it? I know that look." She circled her index finger in front of Lisa's face. "Seen it on my own face enough times. It's called love, sweetie. L.O.V.E. Loooooove."

"Oh Jesus, here we go." But a smile quivered at the corners of her mouth.

She wouldn't admit it to her mother, but she missed Finn like crazy. She missed him so much she couldn't even call him. She was afraid any contact would make her lose it, and she had to take care of business here.

It kind of shocked her, actually. In all her practical, hard-working life, she'd never been this moonstruck.

But that wasn't why was going back to Jupiter Point. Of *course* it wasn't. No, she wasn't going to be the kind of woman who made decisions based on a man. It just made more sense to accept the settlement. And her Mercedes was still in Jupiter Point, so she had to back. And then there was Sparky...

Her phone rang, the McGraw name flashing on the screen.

"Hello?"

"Lisa? It's Evie."

The serious tone of Evie's voice made her straighten. *Molly.* Something must have happened to Molly. "What's the matter? Is your mother okay?"

"She's fine, thanks to Finn. But he's still unconscious. There was an explosion and—"

"*What?*" Half-blind with panic, she launched to her feet, then spun around every which way. "Where is he? Oh my God. Oh my God. *Where is he, Evie?*"

"He's at the regional hospital near the airport. They think he'll be fine. They ran a CAT scan and saw no swelling. But I thought you might want to know."

"I'm coming. First flight." Lisa picked up her tote bag, grabbed the binder and thrust it at her mother. "Mom, will you..." She couldn't remember what was supposed to happen to the document and she didn't care.

"Sure, sweetie. I'll take care of this here. You go. And hurry, you don't want to miss any of that fine stargazing."

Lisa barely noticed her mother's teasing wink as she ran out of the door. "Thank you. Love you."

She pressed her phone to her ear. Evie was still talking. "There's more, Lisa. I have bad news about your car."

"What?"

*

Finn drifted back to consciousness to the memory of baking bread. A beeping sound nagged at him. A warm hand held his. It almost felt like...

"Finn?"

Lisa. His eyes flew the rest of the way open. She wore a pink cardigan over a soft white t-shirt and looked like an angel to him. He feasted on the sight of her. But her dark eyes were so wide and worried, skin pale in the fluorescent light of wherever he was.

Hospital, he realized.

He sat bolt upright. "Molly! Where is she?"

"She's fine. She's already back home. Not a scratch on her. Last I heard, she was telling the entire tale to Mrs. Murphy."

He lay back on the hospital bed. His head throbbed like a mother—

Mother.

"I remembered, Lisa. I remembered my family. Their name is DeLuca. I was Elias DeLuca. My mother's name was Brandi, my father was Ryan. I think they partied a lot. She was probably smoking downstairs and passed out."

It all came back like shattered glass flying in reverse, reforming a broken window. The paparazzi, the Mercedes, the Dumpster. Molly. His heart started to race and the monitor beeped faster.

"Hey, hey." Lisa squeezed his hand. "It's okay. Everything's okay."

"There was a man with a gun, he wanted your Mercedes."

"Actually, he was looking for any other files I might have hidden in the car. Dan Block knew I had some, but he didn't know which ones or how many. He hired someone to destroy whatever evidence I had. That's why the motorhome got torched—apparently he didn't know we were in it, he was just trying to get rid of potential evidence."

"But our cars were right there."

"He came in from the woods so no one would see him, and I guess we were pretty quiet. We were kissing at the time, as I recall."

As did he. He remembered every second of every kiss with Lisa.

"So then with the Mercedes, he didn't have time to thoroughly search it, so he just blew it up. My last remaining possession." She made a wry face. "Pretty rude, if you ask me."

"I'm sorry. I should have done something but I had to get Molly out of there."

She fixed him with a fierce look. "You did *exactly* the right thing. The car means nothing. And Blockhead's going to pay, especially now that they've arrested this jerk. He's going to sing like a bird. The other one, from Breton, probably will too, now that Block's going down."

Finn nodded, his energy flagging. "I might have to sleep now. You won't leave..." He swallowed the words before he sounded like he was begging.

"Finn Abrams-Elias DeLuca, you should know that I am never leaving again." She lifted his hand to her cheek, her long hair sifting softly across his skin. "When I heard you were hurt..." She broke off, biting her lip. Something gleamed on the upper curve of her cheekbone.

"Is that a tear?" he asked softly.

"It might be." She wiped it away with her thumb. "Finn, I love you so much. I think I loved you since that first ridiculous pick-up line. You're the only person I could ever be with, even though I have no idea why you stuck with me when I kept pushing you away. When I thought something had happened to you, I died inside, a hundred thousand times."

In wonder, he took in the worry and love splashed across her face in shimmering tears. "You love me?"

"I love you so much."

"A hundred percent?" He was really fading now, fatigue wrapping his head in a thick fog. But he had to get something straight before he went under again.

"Excuse me?" She wiped away another tear.

"A hundred percent sure. I can ask you to marry me again."

She blinked at him as a wave of crimson flooded her face. "Finn, you have a concussion. This isn't the right moment for this. Be practical."

"No. *You* be romantic." Sleepy-eyed, he interlaced their fingers together.

"You should sleep now. You need rest. I promise I'll be romantic when you wake up."

"Really, you promise?"

Bending over, she dropped a kiss on his scarred side, the one closest to her. "You'll see. I can be romantic if I need to. Just promise to rest. I love you."

He sank back into sleep on a cloud of bliss.

When he woke up again, the room was filled with people who weren't Lisa. Sean and Evie, Josh, Rollo, Brianna, Merry, Will Knight...and his father.

His gaze flew right to Stu. There was something about Stu, about being sick...

Stu held up his hand in a "we'll talk later" gesture as Sean stepped forward.

"You still with us?"

Finn did a quick internal survey of his head and body and realized he felt a lot better. Maybe even a hundred percent better. "Can't get rid of me that easy. I'm an animal, you know."

"Yeah, you are." Sean reached his fist out for a bump, then gave up on that and turned it into a fierce arm grip. "You saved Molly's life, man. Jesus. I'll never forget that."

God, were those *tears* in his boss's eyes? Was everyone going to cry when they came in here?

Evie came next to Sean and kneeled by the bed. "Mom said you were a hero." Her soft voice shook. "I am so grateful to you, Finn." Her silvery eyes shone with a sheen of moisture.

Okay, now all the tears were making him nervous. "Evie, it wasn't like that. I kind of got her into the situation to begin with. Those paparazzi, the carjacker—"

"Nope, none of that was you," said Sean. "The paparazzi had a crash, you did the right thing by helping. How were you supposed to know a carjacker was following? Apparently he thought Lisa was in the car with you."

Finn scowled in confusion. "He didn't know she was back in Houston?"

Will Knight stepped forward. "Communication breakdown. Once the police got involved, Dan Block was afraid to contact his hired thug and call him off. Overall, not the brightest criminal mind on the block. So to speak."

Merry grinned, then wiped the smile from her face as if she didn't want to give Will the satisfaction. "He's the same guy who ransacked your guesthouse, Finn. I snapped a partial picture on my phone before he zapped me."

Finn's head throbbed, not because of the concussion anymore, but because of Lisa's absence. She'd promised not to leave, but she was nowhere to be seen. A whole hospital room full of people, none of them the one he wanted the most. "Where's Lisa?"

"Oh, she said to tell you she'll be right back," Brianna sang from the back of the room. "She went to—" She ended in a squeak as Rollo clapped a hand over her mouth.

"It's a surprise," Rollo explained. "A concept Brianna still has trouble with now and then." He grinned as his fiancée jabbed an elbow into his ribs.

"I'll need to take a statement when you're up to it," said Will Knight. "And I'm sure it's going to be a doozie."

Finn nodded wearily. "No problem. So..." He looked around at all the hotshots and friends gathered around. "I love you guys. I don't really know you, Will, I'm talking more to my crew now."

"Gotcha." Will laughed.

"I love you all. I'm really happy you came here. I don't want to chase you out, but could I have a moment alone with my dad?"

In less than a minute, the room was cleared of everyone except Finn and Stu. His father came close to the bed, more hangdog than Finn had ever seen him. "You fucking scared the living shit out of me, Finn."

Finn gave a bittersweet laugh. "How about me? I had to hear from the paparazzi that you're sick? Damn, Stu. Why didn't you tell me? What's going on?"

"Eh, just some surgery coming up. Some chemo. Fuck the paparazzi, it's none of their business."

Finn stared at the man who'd raised him, more or less. A parade of babysitters and hot girlfriends had helped, but the center had always been held by Stu. No recovered memory was going to change that. "It's my business, though, isn't it?"

"You were so hot to learn about your birth parents." Stu's bushy black eyebrows pulled together in a frown. "The cancer news put me into a tailspin. You're my only family left, but I'm such a lousy father. I was afraid if you found your real family, that would be it."

"But...they're dead. My parents."

"Yeah, and even so they're better fucking parents than I was. I'm sorry, Finn. I acted like a movie mogul trying to control everything, instead of a human being." He rubbed a hand across his heart as if it pained him. "I should have told you I was sick. I should have told you what the detective found."

"I remembered on my own."

"Yeah?"

"But that doesn't mean I don't..." He hesitated. Stu didn't use words like "love" except to refer to a great marketing campaign or a new chef at Spago. "I still love you."

Stu's mouth twisted. He started to say something, but it ended in a grunt.

Whatever. It didn't matter what Stu said.

A feeling of peace settled over Finn. The kind of peace that came when all the questions didn't matter anymore. He knew who he was inside. The rest was just noise.

"But Dad, you gotta knock off the manipulation crap. No more tabloid stunts. No more publicity bullshit."

Stu spread his arms wide. "You got it, son. You live your own life, the way you want to. I just hope I'm part of it."

Finn flashed him a thumbs up, because he couldn't really form the right words.

"Well, maybe *one* more tabloid stunt," Stu added. "Just one more."

"No." Finn raised himself more upright. "Call it off, Dad. I'm serious."

"Can't. It's already on." He gestured toward the doorway, where two people had just appeared.

The first was Lisa, whose face was lit up with the glee of a kid at Christmas. The other was the photographer from the Escalade. A bandage covered his forehead, but he was grinning too.

Stu stepped away from the hospital bed. "I can't say no to a pretty girl, Finn. You know that." He winked and made way for Lisa.

She floated toward him. He couldn't drag his eyes away from her glowing face. "What are you doing?"

"Posing for the tabloids." She set one hip on the bed and nestled against him, curling her body romantically against his. "They wanted a proposal, remember?"

His jaw dropped. "But I don't have a ri—"

Stu cleared his throat. "Yeah you do." He tossed something in Finn's direction. It glittered as it caught the light. "Ellie's," he added. "Yours now."

Finn caught it in his fist.

"Wait wait wait," Lisa said in a rush, pushing Finn's hand away. "This is *my* romantic gesture, proof that I don't care about any of the Hollywood stuff, the cameras, the tabloids, none of it matters. I just want you. That's why I invited them in and—"

But Finn was not about to miss this chance. "Sorry, babe. I've been thinking about this moment for too long. Lisa Peretti, love of my life, most beautiful badass nurse of all time, would you—"

Lisa clapped a hand over his mouth. "Finn Abrams, kindest, most compassionate, most wonderful firefighter of all time, the only man I've ever loved, would *you*—"

"Marry—" he spoke through her fingers.

She adjusted her hand. "Marry me and make me—"

"The happiest man—" he blurted.

"Happiest *woman*—"

"On earth?"

"In the universe?"

They both burst into laughter. Finn could swear that sparks were literally dancing around them. Lisa kissed him with passionate abandon, as if the whole world could be watching and she wouldn't mind. Which it might be, since the photographer was taking shot after shot.

Finally, she drew away. She was blushing so hard her face looked like a strawberry. "Did you get enough, do you think?" she asked the photographer.

He lowered his camera. "Sure. Didn't hear a yes from either one of you, though."

Lisa turned back to Finn and touched her forehead to his. In the private, intimate space between their faces, she whispered the sweetest word in the world at the same moment he whispered the same thing.

Yes.

CHAPTER THIRTY-FOUR

In the cozy bed in the guesthouse, Lisa wrapped Finn's body around her like a blanket. She inhaled the warm, woodsy scent of his almost-sleeping body. This—this was the best kind of luxury. To be loved by someone you loved in return—it was practically decadent. Especially when you'd spent most of the past week in bed.

The dreamy hours between bouts of lovemaking had given them a chance to catch up on everything they'd gone through while they were apart.

"As soon as I got to Houston, I wanted to come back," she told him.

"I thought you were done with me. Done with our little 'sex-capade.'"

"I'll never get enough of your sex-capades." They snuggled for a while after that. "You know, when I went back to the hospital to meet with the management, so many emotions came over me. All the stress, all the suffering I saw there. I remembered what you said about running into the crisis. I did that, yes. But I was running *away* from my heart. I didn't stop running away until I found you, Finn. Until I fell head over heels for you."

His breath caught. "Such a romantic." Even though he was obviously teasing her, he couldn't mask how her words moved him.

She lifted herself on one elbow. "Are you blushing?"

"What? No. Big strong firemen do not blush. If you see any red at all, it's an inflammation of my scar."

"Pfft. I know a blush when I see one." She peppered his scarred side with kisses. "That's okay, I won't tell anyone you're a total sap. Everyone already knows anyway."

"Yeah, I guess they do. Tabloids don't lie. Oy, that picture of us in the hospital. The hotshots will never let that one go. Ever."

She laughed. Jeez, would she ever stop laughing around Finn?

"And Stu told me Annika blew a fuse over that story. She fired Gemma. Or vice versa, hardly matters. Stu's staying out of it."

"I've been thinking..." She hesitated. The idea had popped into her head in his hospital room, but she still didn't know how he would react. "As you know, I'm a medical professional currently between jobs. What would you think about inviting your father here to Jupiter Point to recuperate from his surgery? I'll take care of him, and you can spend time with him when you're not on a fire."

After a long, stunned silence, he flipped her over onto her back. "You would do that? You would really take care of my asshole father?"

"I'm not afraid of assholes as long as they're not setting my motorhome on fire or attacking my friends."

"You are incredible. How'd I get so fucking unbelievably lucky?"

She grinned up at him. "That's not one of your cheesy pick-up lines, is it?"

Before he could answer, the phone rang. She snatched it up and found Merry on the line.

"*That man.* Gah. He owes you a favor, doesn't he? Can you call it in for me?"

"Who does? Who could possibly make you this mad?" she asked innocently, even though she knew perfectly well who Merry was talking about. Only one man got under her friend's skin like this.

"*Don't* make me say his name."

"If you're talking about *Will*, Will doesn't owe me any favors. He was the one who rescued Finn from the Dumpster, so I owe him." She winked at Finn, who still cringed at any mention of that Dumpster. "I'm sure you guys can work it out. You're both grown-ups."

"You're being a bad friend," Merry hissed, sounding nothing like a grown-up.

On Finn's side of the bed, another phone rang. Finn picked it up with one lazy move of his muscled arm. "Finn here."

A deep voice carried into the room. "You're a writer, Finn, right? Used to be? I need a translator. Someone who understands what's going on in that woman's brain."

"What woman?" Finn winked at Lisa, who smothered a giggle. He stroked a finger up and down her upper arm. "Who are you talking about?"

"No comment."

"I heard that 'no comment'!" Merry yelled from Lisa's phone. "I hear those words in my nightmares!"

"Is that Merry? Let me guess, she's pestering you guys for a story. She never stops, does she?"

Finn and Lisa looked at each other and shrugged. As one, they laid their phones side by side on the nightstand. Will and Merry kept talking, phone to phone.

"You're going to have 'no comment' written on your tombstone, aren't you?" asked Merry.

"You sound a little too eager to witness that."

"Oh, I'm sure you'll take your time getting to the Promised Land, just like you do everything else."

"Funny, I don't usually get complaints from women about that."

"You just haaaad to go there."

Lisa looked around for something to muffle the phones. All she could find was the star-and-moon fabric from her motorhome, which lay on top of a pile of stuff she still had to unpack. She reached for it, the movement giving Finn the opportunity to stroke her naked side.

Shivering with pleasure, she folded the indigo fabric and tucked it around the two phones. There. Will and Merry's sparring was now just a buzz.

She snuggled back into the warm circle of Finn's arms. "Sounds like things are going well with those two."

"Maybe I should lend Sparky to Will. Romantic Gestures 101—buy a turtle."

She laughed and nibbled on his firm chin. She brushed her cheek against the rough grain of his stubble. "He doesn't stand a chance. Merry's the last remaining member of Team Cynic. She'll hold the line. It's her civic duty."

He pulled her on top of him and stroked the curves of her ass, making her melt and squirm. "You badass cynics sure know how to make a man work for it."

She licked his neck, savoring the intoxicating flavor that was just Finn. Only Finn. "It just takes the right person, that's all. Someone who can see past our beastly exteriors to the sappy souls inside."

"Did you just call yourself beastly?" He swatted her butt lightly.

"Yeah. What are you going to do about it?" She loved it when he got all commanding—and he knew it.

"I'm going to make mad, incessant love to you." He moved her up and down on his swelling shaft. "I'm going to keep you naked in bed until you forget the meaning of the word 'beastly.' I'm going to make you so happy, even your smile will set off sparks. Any more questions?"

"No questions." Hot joy swamped her as she gazed into his loving eyes. "Okay, maybe one."

"What?"

"Should we hang up our phones first?"

He burst out laughing and rolled her under him, bracing his strong, scarred, powerful body atop hers. Deep in a place beyond logic, she knew that days just like this—

filled with heart and laughter—lay ahead as far as the eye could see.

And she gave silent thanks to the stars and their mysterious ways.

ABOUT THE AUTHOR

Jennifer Bernard is a *USA Today* bestselling author of contemporary romance. Her books have been called "an irresistible reading experience" full of "quick wit and sizzling love scenes." A graduate of Harvard and former news promo producer, she left big city life in Los Angeles for true love in Alaska, where she now lives with her husband and stepdaughters. She still hasn't adjusted to the cold, so most often she can be found cuddling with her laptop and a cup of tea.

ALSO BY JENNIFER BERNARD

Jupiter Point

Set the Night on Fire (Book 1)
Burn So Bright (Book 2)
Into the Flames (Book 3)
Seeing Stars (Prequel)

The Bachelor Firemen of San Gabriel

The Fireman Who Loved Me
Hot for Fireman
Sex and the Single Fireman
How to Tame a Wild Fireman
Four Weddings and a Fireman
The Night Belongs to Fireman

One Fine Fireman
Desperately Seeking Fireman
It's a Wonderful Fireman

Love Between the Bases

All of Me
Caught By You
Getting Wound Up
Drive You Wild
Crushing It